"Adventure ensues when f  ed West, risking all to keep of danger, a chivalrous mountain man, and a compelling mystery to unravel, and you have the recipe for an engaging historical novel."

—Lori Benton, author of *Mountain Laurel*

"Misty M. Beller is a master at bringing bygone eras to life, and *Rocky Mountain Rendezvous* is no exception to that. Brimming with vivid imagery, historical details, and a compelling storyline, it is a book her readers will absolutely adore."

—Jen Turano, *USA Today* bestselling author

"What an adventure! *Rocky Mountain Rendezvous* brought the wilds of the Wyoming area and Juniper's unique story to life. Misty Beller has a new fan!"

—Kimberley Woodhouse, Carol Award–winning and bestselling author of the SECRETS OF THE CANYON series

"I've long been a Misty Beller fan and her book *Hope's Highest Mountain* didn't disappoint. Misty tells a wonderful tale of adventure and romance as her characters face challenges from the past and present that threaten their ability to deal with the future. My only negative thought is that I'll have to wait much too long for her next book."

—Tracie Peterson, bestselling author on *Hope's Highest Mountain*

"In *A Warrior's Heart*, Misty created a world I hoped was a real place with characters I wanted to live near and become friends with. Her heroine, Brielle, could be every girl's hero. Looking forward to the next book in the series."

—Lauraine Snelling, author of THE RED RIVER OF THE NORTH series on *A Warrior's Heart*

"This is a treasured story surely to be remembered. I know I will."

—Jane Kirkpatrick, bestselling author of *Beneath the Bending Skies* on *A Warrior's Heart*

"Fans of the series will love this romantic mountain saga."

—*Publishers Weekly* on *Faith's Mountain Home*

ROCKY
MOUNTAIN
RENDEZVOUS

Books by Misty Beller

Hearts of Montana

Hope's Highest Mountain

Love's Mountain Quest

Faith's Mountain Home

Brides of Laurent

A Warrior's Heart

A Healer's Promise

A Daughter's Courage

Sisters of the Rockies

Rocky Mountain Rendezvous

ROCKY MOUNTAIN RENDEZVOUS

MISTY M. BELLER

BETHANYHOUSE

a division of Baker Publishing Group
Minneapolis, Minnesota

Published by Bethany House Publishers
Minneapolis, Minnesota
www.bethanyhouse.com

Bethany House Publishers is a division of
Baker Publishing Group, Grand Rapids, Michigan

Printed in the United States of America

Library of Congress Cataloging-in-Publication Data
Names: Beller, Misty M., author.
Title: Rocky mountain rendezvous / Misty M. Beller.
Description: Minneapolis, Minnesota : Bethany House Publishers, a division of Baker
    Publishing Group, [2023] | Series: Sisters of the Rockies ; 1
Identifiers: LCCN 2022053717 | ISBN 9780764241536 (paperback) | ISBN
    9780764241864 (casebound) | ISBN 9781493442171 (ebook)
Classification: LCC PS3602.E45755 R63 2023 | DDC 813/.6—dc23
LC record available at https://lccn.loc.gov/2022053717

Scripture quotations are from the King James Version of the Bible.

Scripture quotations labeled NIV are from the Holy Bible, New International Version®.
NIV®. Copyright © 1973, 1978, 1984, 2011 by Biblica, Inc.™ Used by permission of
Zondervan. All rights reserved worldwide. www.zondervan.com

Cover design by Dan Thornberg, Design Source Creative Services
Cover model photography by Magdalena Russocka / Trevillion Images

Author is represented by Books & Such Literary Agency.

Baker Publishing Group publications use paper produced from sustainable forestry
practices and post-consumer waste whenever possible.

23 24 25 26 27 28 29   7 6 5 4 3 2 1

To my sweet daughter, Haven, my inspiration for Juniper.
I'm so proud of what a kind, smart, caring
young lady you're becoming!

ONE

JULY 1837
GREEN RIVER VALLEY (FUTURE WYOMING)

Ants. The men looked like an army of ants crawling around in the valley below.

Juniper Collins studied the chaotic sight from atop her horse far above on the mountain pass. Her mount shifted beneath her, the mare's movement uneasy. The action seemed to set off the same agitation in her sisters' horses on either side of her. The four of them had come hundreds of miles and traveled nearly two months on this mission, but they hadn't expected the trapper rendezvous to look like this.

Mayhap *horde* would be the better word for the mass spreading before her. A horde of men and horses and lodges and . . . Air congealed in her lungs. How would they ever find someone in this madness who knew the Peigan Blackfoot woman named Steps Right?

"Oh my." Rosemary, the oldest of the four sisters, spoke just as the first shouts echoed across the open land.

"Wagon ho!" a man's gruff voice yelled.

"It's here!" The fellows nearest them waved hats.

"Let's go, boys!"

And just like that, the horde stampeded up the slope toward them. The whoops and yells charged ahead of the men, all racing toward the wagons right beside Juniper and her sisters.

"Run!" As usual, Rosemary took charge. She spun her horse away from the wagons, right into the flank of Juniper's mare. Rosemary waved her hand to shoo them all ahead of her. "Quick! Behind those rocks."

The horses scrambled to obey as all four of them aimed toward a cluster of boulders that would be large enough to hide them.

Juniper reined in behind her sisters to make sure no one dropped back, and the first men reached the wagons just as she tucked her mare behind the rocks. Some of these swarming trappers must have seen them dodge this direction, but the wagons looked to be the biggest draw. The crazed men probably hadn't even realized women had arrived with the supplies they'd been waiting all year to trade for.

"Ho up! Ho there, I say!" Mr. Provost waved his hat and spun his horse, his shout barely rising above the clamor.

A gunshot ripped through the air, its boom finally lowering the volume of the trappers a small bit.

"Quiet!" Again Mr. Provost bellowed above the commotion.

The trappers ignored him as they surged around the wagons.

Two more rifles fired, puffs of gunsmoke clouding around the drivers of two of the middle wagons.

At last, the mountain men stopped pressing forward, and an unsteady quiet settled over the group.

Mr. Provost's voice sounded once more, this time not as frantic. "Settle down, the lot of ya. No trading until morning, an hour after sunup. Any man who touches these wagons before then will be shot."

A grumble spread through the crowd, but the mass of men eased away from the rigs. Mr. Provost turned his mount toward the first wagon and moved in front of the lead mules. "Make a road, men. Make a road."

The sea parted before him as the grumble turned to the rising tone of conversation. A few trappers yelled out as the group passed.

"You came just in the nick o' time, Provost."

"Hope at least two of those wagons are full o' whiskey."

"Got a white beaver skin yur gonna love. Save me a barrel of the good stuff."

Mr. Provost tipped his hat at a few of the voices as he rode past them. The men in the crowd seemed remarkably restrained now compared to their stampede moments before.

How would Juniper and her sisters ever find someone among all these people who could direct them to the Blackfoot woman their father had known twenty years ago? Should they start by asking among the white men or the natives?

For that matter, telling the difference may not be as easy as they'd expected. Though she'd not looked hard at faces, more than one fellow possessed skin dark enough that she couldn't be sure if they were half-Indian or simply spent too much time in the sun.

A tiny squeal sounded from behind her, and she spun

to see Lorelei, the next sister down from herself in age, struggling to hold onto the newest pet she'd picked up on the trail—a coyote pup. A tiny thing, only a few weeks old, with barely enough teeth to gnaw the scraps of meat Lorelei shredded into tiny pieces for him.

At the moment, the little fellow was no longer content to ride on her lap, instead clawing and howling to escape her arms. Lorelei scrambled for a better grip of the animal as she cried out, "No!"

But the tiny creature slipped from her arms, leaping from the saddle to the ground. In a flash of fur, it darted toward the two tallest boulders.

"Boots, come back!" Lorelei leapt from her horse and scrambled toward the rocks. The fluff of a coyote tail slipped behind them.

Juniper's belly clenched. That pup had already caused enough trouble. Running loose among all this chaos was dangerous, though, especially if Lorelei chased after him.

She slipped from her own mount and grabbed the reins her sister had left hanging. Maybe Lorelei would finally let the animal go if she didn't find it right away. That didn't seem likely, for the girl possessed a heart too sensitive toward animals, and the pup was too young to survive on its own. She'd discovered the animal curled in its den, orphaned by the shot of one of the supply train hunters. She'd managed to keep it alive for a week now and was determined to nurture the pup until it was old enough to hunt on its own.

But if she truly couldn't find the animal this time, perhaps she would have no choice but to let it go.

As Lorelei disappeared around the same boulder the coyote had, Juniper glanced at her other sisters. Rosemary's expression had turned worried, her body tensed like she might leap from her saddle any minute. "Lor, come back."

"I'll help her." Faith, the baby in the family at sixteen, released a sigh as she dismounted and handed her reins to Rosemary.

"Here, boy. Come, Boots." Lorelei's gentle murmur drifted from the rocks, though they still couldn't see her.

Faith slipped out of sight the way Lorelei had gone, and moments later, a strange sound made Juniper tense. Something like a squeal and shout combined. What had her sisters stumbled upon back there?

"Lor? What's happening?" Rosemary leaned forward to slide from her mount but paused when Lorelei and Faith stepped from behind the boulders.

Both possessed empty hands, and Lorelei's face held a bit of thunder. Had she lost the pup?

A third person followed them—a man. Apprehension pressed in Juniper's chest, and from the corner of her eye, Rosemary straightened and reached for her rifle.

The stranger held Boots in the crook of his arm. She couldn't decipher the man's expression. Almost amused, yet his brows lowered in something like a scowl.

When all three had stepped from the rocks, Lorelei spun and reached for the pup. "I'll take him now."

"Who is *that*, Lor?" Rosemary had her rifle aimed now, her tone one of a protective elder sister.

The man glanced at the animal lying quietly against his chest, then to Lorelei, his expression shifting in a way that showed his hesitation. "Ma'am, this is a coyote pup, not a pet. Wherever his mama is, she'll not take kindly to human scent on him."

Lorelei straightened. "I've become his mama, ever since the real one was shot by a wagon driver. I've been feeding him, and he's happy to ride on the saddle with me. I'm in no danger, sir, except maybe from the likes of you. Hand over my coyote, if you please."

The man's brows shot up, and his gaze shifted from Lorelei to sweep over all four of them. Then he shrugged and held out the pup. "Be careful. The Almighty made his kind to bite the hand that feeds it."

Perhaps so. But this man hadn't met Lorelei Collins yet. No animal would think of biting her sister. In addition to her tender heart, she also possessed an uncanny way of winning the affections of wild creatures with merely a word and an outstretched hand.

Juniper should probably hold her tongue, but something in the man's demeanor, the way he acted like Lorelei hadn't the sense of a schoolgirl, pushed the words out. "My sister knows how to handle him, sir, far better than you, I'd say. That pup would have died a week ago without her."

As Lorelei removed the coyote from his arms, the man's focus lifted to Juniper. Something too much like a grin played at the corners of his mouth. "That's good to hear." Then he moved back to take in all four of them again. "Welcome to the rendezvous, ladies. I'm Riley Turner. A pleasure to make your acquaintance."

Then, without giving them a chance to respond, he turned and walked back through the boulders, disappearing as mysteriously as he'd arrived.

Riley Turner paused partway down the slope and glanced back, but he could only see the cluster of rocks now.

Women.

He'd met so few females these past years, and none from back East. The sight of them had nearly addled his brain. Why would white women come to this place, where rivers of whiskey flowed and a host of otherwise smart men took leave of their senses?

The supply wagons often brought an extra visitor or two, men who wanted to experience the happenings of the trapper rendezvous—an event that had become infamous among Easterners. He'd even heard an artist might have come along this year to capture the scenes for others.

But no word of women coming had reached his ears.

He'd not planned to be part of the welcoming party—too many others would swarm the rigs—but when he spotted the four riders split off toward the rocks, he'd not been able to help himself.

And a coyote pup? Only Easterners would think it a good idea to try to tame a wild animal. If the mother truly had died, there might not be danger right away. But going against the natural order of things almost always ended badly. He'd learned that fact while growing up in the Illinois wilderness and during those two years in the cavalry, but now he understood it far better after living in this unsettled country.

Every man who lasted in this territory discovered quickly enough how to find his place in the rhythm of the land and animals. Those who didn't learn but managed to stay alive headed back East, back to civilization.

A place Riley would be happy never to see again.

He turned and continued his trek to the lodge he shared

with three others. Dragoon and Jeremiah had both trotted off to meet the wagons, and a glance ahead showed Ol' Henry still sat by the fire, stirring the pot of stew hanging from the tripod. A lifetime in this wilderness had taught him better than to jump up just because a few supplies rolled into camp. The man had seen more rendezvous than any other fellow Riley knew. He'd trapped all the way down into the Mexican territories and even up north into British-owned lands. Ol' Henry never ran short of tales that could shock even the most experienced trapper.

As Riley approached their campfire, the man nodded a greeting. "What bit of excitement did the wagons bring this time?" His leathery skin was dark from years in the sun, but it also had an almost-bluish tint. Like he'd sat in a haze of gunpowder too long.

Riley eased down to sit in his usual spot. "Women. Four of them, definitely from back East. Sisters, I think."

Even Ol' Henry's eyes grew wide. "You tellin' a tale?"

Riley bit back a chuckle. Though Henry knew how to keep a straight face, he also possessed a flair for the dramatic that brought his storytelling to life.

He shook his head. "It's true. Don't know why they're here, but I can't think this is a safe place for them."

Ol' Henry looked toward the pass the wagons had come through, but his eyes seemed to see much farther. A low whistle slipped through his lips. "Don't doubt it. They must not know what they've bit into, coming into this rendezvous with so many men soon to be full o' the drink those wagons brought." Then the man shifted his focus to Riley, his gaze sharpening in a way that pierced. "Reckon they need someone who knows how to look out for them."

Riley raised his brows. "Maybe." Perhaps Ol' Henry hadn't meant *him* exactly, but the words matched the niggle that had pulsed through him the moment he first laid eyes on the ladies.

The last thing he needed was to take on the task of watching over a group of Easterners. And women were the very worst sort.

TWO

"These accommodations should do well for you." Mr. Provost pulled aside the door flap of an Indian teepee, of all things, and waited as though he expected them to enter first.

Juniper couldn't bring herself to step forward. Apparently, neither could her sisters, for they stood in a cluster, taking in the sight. Perhaps it wasn't an Indian teepee, for hundreds of similar tents dotted the valley, and she'd seen bushy-bearded white men moving in and out of the dwellings. But they matched the way Papa had described the Indians' homes when he'd come to this place two decades ago.

She'd never imagined the smell would be so . . . robust. A combination of animals and sweat. It reminded her a little of being in the barn back when they still lived on the horse ranch, without the rich scent of hay.

Faith stepped forward first, always the daring one, though she was the youngest. Her action seemed to propel Rosemary, whose protectiveness had grown even stronger on this journey. Their oldest sister shot Mr. Provost a look just shy of a glare as she stepped past him through the doorway.

Juniper nudged Lorelei. Though she couldn't deny curiosity about what the place looked like inside, she wouldn't leave her sister out here alone. Though only three years separated the two of them, Lorelei was only eighteen, still so young and innocent. Finally, Lor stepped forward, and after taking in one last breath of outside air, Juniper followed her sisters through the opening.

Inside wasn't as bad as she'd anticipated. Light from the doorway and the hole at the top where the poles met gave the place an airy feel. The animal skins that formed the walls had been stretched so tightly that a bit of sunshine filtered through them. They likely wouldn't even smell the odor soon.

A throat cleared behind them, and they all turned to Mr. Provost. "I have to get back to the wagons and help set things up. You ladies are welcome to eat around our campfire again tonight if you'd like." He cleared his throat again, this time a hint of nervousness in the gesture. "You need to . . . er . . . I mean . . . our agreement was for the journey out. You'll need to get your own food and supplies after tonight. The boys who cleared out of this lodge said you're welcome to stay in it as long as you're at the rendezvous."

For the second time in a mere five minutes, Juniper could only stare as her mind sorted through the implications of his words. Had their agreement truly only been for the time spent traveling? She looked over at Rosemary, who was eyeing Provost with a hard, calculating look. Juniper and Rosemary had met together with the clerk at the supply company to coordinate the details, but she couldn't remember any part of the conversation that covered food while they were here at the rendezvous. Perhaps that had been the lapse—failure to raise the topic.

From the hard line of Rosemary's jaw, she would quickly set the matter to rights. "Fitzpatrick made no mention that we would be stranded without food when we reached this valley. We gave you more than sufficient coin, and now you expect even more to feed us while we're here?" She folded her arms across her chest in a stance that had made more than one man back down.

He did drop his gaze, and his boot scuffed the flattened grass. "I'm afraid not, ma'am. We're here to trade for furs, not coin. Unless you have beaver or wolf pelts to exchange, I'm not able to give you anything. I wish I could, but it's out of my hands. I've strict guidelines I'm required to adhere to."

Juniper's jaw dropped. "Nothing? We'll have no food at all? You'd stand by and watch us starve?"

He finally lifted his focus to her. "You won't starve, Miss Juniper. The men around here won't let you." His gaze flicked between her and Rosemary. "There might be some of them who would trade meat they hunted for coin. For that matter, I suspect you'd be welcome at every stewpot around. No need for payment."

Rosemary straightened, her shoulders growing even more rigid. "We'll pay our own way."

That was a condition they'd all agreed to before coming west. They couldn't allow any man to think they were in his debt.

Mr. Provost backed into the doorway. "All right, then. It was sure a pleasure having you ladies ride with us." His nervousness slipped into a look so grandfatherly it was impossible to be too upset with him. He wasn't the one who'd made the unfair agreement, after all. Only the man required to enforce it.

Faith spoke up before Juniper had a chance. "Thank you, sir. We do truly appreciate your kindness and protection."

But after he disappeared through the opening, another glance around the empty lodge placed reality in clear focus. Lorelei managed to put to voice the words swirling in Juniper's mind. "What now?"

ᑐᕫᕬ

Riley stared across the camp in the morning light at the men gathered outside the sisters' lodge. They weren't meeting or discussing anything, from what he could tell. Just waiting.

Several large frames with hides stretched on them obscured his view of the lodge the Martelli brothers had vacated to give the Collins sisters a furnished home, but that must be what these men were clustered around. Every half minute or so, a new fellow would approach, swap words with someone already waiting there, then settle in with an expectant gaze turned the same direction as the others.

A knot clenched in his middle. Even having native women at the rendezvous made the trappers extra feisty. But white women among men who likely hadn't seen that commodity since the missionaries' wives two years before, well . . .

These four would be trouble. He couldn't imagine a scenario where that wouldn't be true.

Did they plan to stay on here, or was this merely an adventure to see the rendezvous, and they'd be returning East with the supply wagons in a few days? If the former, best they marry up posthaste. Next week, if they knew what was good for them. They needed protection from the rougher portion of this bunch.

But he was not just thinking for the women's sake, though that was definitely a good reason. Their presence would set off so many skirmishes among the men, people were bound to be hurt. Especially once the whiskey flowed, now that this morning's trading had commenced. He couldn't stand the stuff himself, the way it took away a person's good sense. That was part of the reason he'd joined with Ol' Henry, Dragoon, and Jeremiah. None of them were given to drunkenness, not even during the rendezvous.

Speaking of, why weren't all these men lined up at the trade wagons to swap their goods? Maybe that would be a way to run them off so the women could at least poke their heads out of their lodge without being gawked at. Or worse, accosted.

"What you figure they're doing here?" Dragoon stepped from the lodge behind Riley and crouched by the fire. He speared his knife into a chunk of meat sizzling on the rock they used for cooking. The rest of them had eaten an hour or so earlier, but Dragoon never liked to beat the sun up in the mornings.

"I'd like to know that myself." Ol' Henry sat on Riley's other side, with a cup of dark brew cradled in both hands. The stuff was probably weak enough to taste like sour water, but Ol' Henry loved his coffee. He rationed his supply more than he rationed his gunpowder all year long. It was said he once sliced off a fellow's fingers when the man reached for the tin where Henry kept the beans. Legend had it that Ol' Henry had been returning to the camp when he saw the man with the curious hands. He'd whipped out his knife and flung it across a distance of a dozen strides.

That fellow was lucky it was only two fingers he lost, not

his life from blood poisoning. With no doctors anywhere in these parts, the closest thing to a healer was one of the native shamans. And their ways weren't very close to what was taught in medical schools in the States.

Dragoon turned to Riley. "Why don't you mosey over and join that group of fellers waiting for them to peek out? Maybe you can overhear why the women came. 'Sides, you're of an age to go a'courting. Maybe one of them will take a shine to you."

Riley snorted. The last thing he needed was a female to keep up with in this wilderness. Especially not a dainty lady, fresh from her fancy parlor. Those four sisters had no business venturing out here without a man—or a whole army—for protection.

Any man who did marry one of these sisters would have to take her back East where she belonged. And a journey like that didn't figure into any of Riley's plans. North to Rupert's Land, sure. Maybe even west of the mountains to see the Pacific Ocean. And one day he might finally manage to trek the backbone up the Rockies like he'd been imagining. But not east. He could breathe far better in this rugged land.

He shook his head. "You won't find me joining those uncouth skinners. I'll happily run them all off, but that's the best I can offer."

A spark lit Dragoon's eyes, and the corners of his beard lifted. "Now that might be fun. We could create a diversion. It's not hard to find something interesting enough to draw the attention of these fellows."

Wariness prickled Riley's chest. "I thought you were going to trade your pelts this morning so you could get prime pickings of the supplies."

Dragoon raised a shoulder, his nonchalance clearly feigned. "You might've struck on something when you said to wait a bit until the line dies down. Besides, what I'm thinking won't take more than a few minutes."

Riley studied his lodgemate. Dragoon was the rowdiest of the four of them who'd trapped together this spring, though usually that meant he was simply more outspoken during the stories told around the campfire. He wasn't one of the true disorderlies, like the ones who filled up with whiskey and rode through camp howling and shooting off enough rounds for an entire month's hunting.

Dragoon had been known to play a prank or two on the rest of them, but it was always innocent fun. Surely that's all he meant now. Still, better to make sure.

He eyed the man. "You're not planning to do something that'll make the situation worse for those women, are you?"

Dragoon's brows lifted. "'Course not." His voice held a tone of contempt, either for the men parked in front of their lodge or toward Riley for thinking such a thing of him. He spit a chunk of meat into the fire, and Riley couldn't help watching the fat sizzle among the leaping flames. He returned his focus to Dragoon.

The man flashed a stained smile. "I'm trying to help them. You can come, too, if you want. Both of you." With a groan, he pushed up to standing and wiped the grease from his fingers on his buckskin leggings. "Time to get busy." Then he turned and strode from camp toward the river—the direction opposite the women's lodge.

Should Riley call after him and find out exactly what Dragoon planned? He slid a look at the wisest man in their little group. "You think he's about to cause trouble?"

24

In addition to more stories than a man could hear in a lifetime of evenings around the campfire, Ol' Henry had also developed an uncanny ability to read people. He'd experienced enough of these mountain men's shenanigans to know beforehand if something was about to go sideways. Usually.

The lines across Ol' Henry's leathery face deepened, though it was hard to tell if the expression was a smile or a grimace. "I don't reckon he'll set out to cause trouble. Might better be on hand in case, just in case. If you need help, send up a shout."

Better be on hand in case of what? Riley had heard stories of bored trappers tying torches to the tails of foxes or rabbits and setting them loose among the lodges to stir up excitement, but Dragoon wouldn't do anything like that. He had plenty of respect for life and for the belongings that were hard enough to come by in this treacherous land.

In a country where the misstep of a pack mule on a mountain slope could destroy a faithful companion and helpmate—not to mention half a year's hard work in beaver skins—any mountain man worth his salt knew better than to allow a prank to go too far.

Yet many did, especially when filled with strong drink.

Riley pushed up to his feet. "Guess I'll go watch in case he brings half the camp down on himself." In truth, Dragoon could hold his own amongst the rabble, but someone needed to be near in case the women got caught in the fray.

He'd barely rounded the stretched hides when a volley of shots echoed from somewhere to the left. They couldn't be more than a quarter mile away, though the rock cliffs on either side of the valley made the sounds bounce in every direction.

That had to be Dragoon's distraction, though the explosions rang like a whole platoon of guns were being shot. He must have gathered a few other fellows to have fun, and the echo of their weapons amplified the noise. A piercing screech sounded amidst the melee—a combination of a wildcat and an Indian war cry, and maybe a wolf's howl thrown in the mix. A shiver plunged down Riley's spine as the scream rose higher, wailing like a dying beast.

The men loitering around the Collins sisters' lodge had taken note too—Lazarus buried in his tomb couldn't have missed the ruckus—and they moved toward the source. Some sprinted, while others jogged behind them. The gray-haired in the bunch only managed a quick hobble. They were out for entertainment, not trying to outrun a grizzly.

As the last men filed away, Riley took a step toward the lodge. The women would have the opening sewed shut if they knew what was good for them, but he should at least make sure they had food and clean water.

Before he could take a second step, a figure from the meadow's edge bent low and sprinted toward the lodge's opening. He tensed to charge forward and stop the fellow before he could invade the women's privacy, but then a flash of the face appeared under the hat brim.

A woman. The oldest of the sisters, if he recognized her correctly. Was her name Rose?

She rounded the front of her lodge and paused at the flap long enough to speak to those inside. Though she wore pants and a man's baggy shirt, he should've realized straightaway she wasn't one of the trappers. Hers were store-bought fabric, not the buckskin leggings and tunics most of the mountain men wore in the summer.

Riley had been trapping in this mountain wilderness for three years now, and it'd been longer than that since he'd seen a real lady strolling the streets of St. Louis, but even *he* knew the clothes she wore would be scandalous back East. They made sense for function here, though they certainly showed off curves these men didn't need to see. What had she been doing away from her sisters and the protection of their lodge? Perhaps seeking a quiet place for personal matters, though she'd been playing with fire to leave in the first place. At least she'd made it back safely.

She disappeared inside the lodge, and all was quiet around it, thanks to Dragoon. The sisters likely wouldn't appreciate Riley's breaking the peace. They probably would think he was just another lovesick ruffian. But he couldn't walk away without making sure they had what they needed so they wouldn't have to venture out in this crowd again. Etienne Provost would have seen to that last night, but just in case . . .

He pushed himself into a casual stride as he meandered toward their lodging. When he was a step away from their door, voices inside gave him pause. Women speaking, a sound he'd rarely heard these past few years. He'd spent a fair amount of time in one native camp or another, trading goods, swapping news, or just sharing a meal and some conversation. The braves in this land were just as good company as any trapper. But the native women didn't often speak when there were outsiders around.

He let himself listen for a moment, soaking in the melodic cadence the fairer sex managed so well.

"The only thing he'll take is furs? Still?" That sounded like the voice of the one who'd harangued him about that troublesome coyote. The prettiest one. Juniper.

"The man's daft. And heartless. Or maybe he's afraid of whoever hired him to bring the supplies out. It didn't matter what I offered—and I really laid it on thick—he repeated those exact words like his tutor didn't teach him to say anything else. 'I can only trade for furs, Miss Collins. I'm afraid you'll have to find food elsewhere.'" Her voice took on a decidedly sarcastic tone. "I thanked him for his advice and told him I'd simply stroll down to the mercantile."

Riley's mind tugged back to the words *"didn't matter what I offered."* Bile churned in his belly. *"I really laid it on thick."* The words brought to mind the women from the saloons in the towns the cavalry would camp near. Some of them would go to great lengths to convince a man to sample their wares.

These sisters hadn't looked like *those* kind of women, but who else would traipse out here to a land where decent women didn't dare step foot? Why hadn't he considered that before? They'd get more business than they wanted out here. The thought made the sour taste rise up to his throat.

Yet regardless of their level of virtue, they still had to eat. And it sounded like they were in need.

THREE

Though Riley still stood rooted outside the women's lodge, he'd stopped listening to their conversation as his thoughts whirled. In truth, he'd learned far more than he wanted to.

He tapped on the thick leather. "It's Riley Turner, the one who helped catch that coyote pup yesterday."

All sound within ceased. Maybe he'd better state his business.

"Just came to check and see what you might need. My friend set off a distraction upriver, so your spectators are gone for a few minutes. Now is the time I can bring you food or water or such."

The door covering wiggled, then fingers gripped its edge and created an opening just wide enough to reveal a set of eyes, a lightly freckled nose, and a refined chin.

Those striking blue eyes assessed his face, then skimmed down the length of him. They cut to the side, taking in the surroundings behind him. Then the flap closed over the opening again.

Juniper. Something about the name fit her, though he'd

never considered juniper trees to be pretty. They had a wholesome quality. Not dainty, but not large and grandiose. Miss Juniper couldn't be wholesome though if she was *that* kind of woman. It must be her pretty face and air of innocence that drew her customers.

Her muffled voice sounded through the leather. "It *is* him. And there's no one else out there."

A surge of something like pleasure whipped through him. These women knew him as more than simply one of the crowd. But considering their profession, maybe that wasn't something he should rejoice in.

Through a crack in the opening, his gaze caught on a figure several steps back. Or, more accurately, his focus caught on the rifle she held.

Pointed at him.

His mouth went dry at the dark circle of the barrel. He fought the urge to edge sideways. It was good they had protection. As long as they knew how to shoot that thing. And when to keep their finger off the trigger.

Better he hurry this conversation along. "Just tell me what all you need and I'll bring it."

The door flap opened again, this time wide enough to reveal Miss Juniper's entire face. "We'd like to buy food. And we have questions for you. Do you have provisions we can pay for with coin?"

He shook his head. Coin wasn't often seen in these parts, and for good reason. You couldn't eat it, and the supply wagons wouldn't accept it in trade. "Keep your money. We only have meat left, but there's plenty of that. Do you need water too? And firewood?"

She glanced sideways again, as though looking to someone else for the answer. But she spoke to him as she did so. "We can get those things ourselves. But we have questions. I'm sure we'll need to ask them to a bunch of people."

The flap pulled wider, revealing the older sister standing beside Miss Juniper. "Can we come with you to get the meat? That way we can ask as many men as possible along the way. And we'll pay for the food."

He glanced around behind him. A few men had been walking one lodge over, but now paused to stare. A native woman was among them, probably the wife of one of the men.

Others would come back soon too. As soon as they realized the ruckus was only a few fool-headed men raising a stir.

He turned to the women again. "What kind of questions? I'll answer you now. I'm sure I can speak for the rest." That last bit may not be true, but he could bluff as well as the next man. At least enough to satisfy the curiosity of these females. He'd heard enough tall tales from mountain men to be able to manufacture one or two of his own.

The oldest sister—Miss Rose, or was it Rosemary?— eyed him. "We've come looking for someone. I suspect we'll need to ask a number of people before we find someone who knows her."

"Her?" He shook his head. "There aren't any other white women west of the great falls. Except the wives of two missionaries last year, you four are the first who ever ventured this far. It wasn't a wise choice either. Especially not alone. Some of these men are just curious, but there's plenty who will imbibe far too much drink and not think twice about . . ." He couldn't bring himself to say anything more than that. Even now, his cheeks burned, and not from the sun already starting to heat the air around them.

Miss Juniper's face looked a bit rosy too, but her elder sister only straightened. "We're not looking for a white woman. Her name is Steps Right. She's from the Peigan Blackfoot tribe. We're not certain of her age but at least forty years."

He'd not expected these women to even know the tribe names, much less be searching for a specific woman. "How do you know her?" How could these four have crossed paths with a native, unless maybe on the journey out?

Miss Rose's scrutiny intensified. "Does that mean you know her?" She seemed to be watching for some deeper reaction from him.

She wouldn't find duplicity here, at least not on this count. He shook his head. "Never heard of her. There's a Peigan band camped downriver a ways. The only woman I've met at the rendezvous is the wife of Lone Rider." Meeting her had been a courtesy to Lone Rider, and he'd not asked for an introduction to any others.

Three more men had stopped to watch as he stood here talking. They had no more time.

He backed away a step. "I'll go get some meat and water. And I'll ask the fellows I'm rooming with whether they know Steps Right from the Peigan tribe."

"We'll come with you." The fourth sister, who'd been tucked behind these two, now moved into view. What was her name? She had a touch of red in her hair, just enough to distinguish her from her sisters, but not enough to make her stand out in a crowd. She nudged Miss Juniper, or rather, grabbed her arm and tugged her forward.

Riley shook his head once more. These women might

be accustomed to dealing with men back East, but they'd taken leave of their senses if they thought he'd allow them to stroll with him openly through the camp. "Stay here. I'll bring what you need and ask your questions. These mountain men haven't seen a white woman in who knows how long. Even the ones with decent manners will give you more attention than you're looking for."

The youngest sister stepped forward, dragging Miss Juniper along. "We'll not stay holed up in this leather hut all day, if that's what you're thinking. You can escort us as we ask around, or we'll do it on our own."

He backed up another step as she barged out of the lodge, the other three close behind her. They all seemed to be in accord with her words. The sister who'd been holding a gun on him a heartbeat before reached down and picked up that troublesome coyote pup before following the others through the door opening.

He pressed his lips together. That frustrating animal was the least of his worries now. These four would be as tempting as a buffalo carcass to a pack of hungry wolves when they strolled through camp. Especially if they didn't mind trading favors for information.

Maybe he and the other three at his lodge could help protect them a little. Ol' Henry was there, of course, and Jeremiah would be back from trading soon enough. He had no way of knowing how long Dragoon would amuse himself with his distraction, but he'd surely enjoy a bit more fun protecting these four.

He finally nodded. "Come with me, then." He eyed the oldest sister in her men's trousers. It was hard to say which would inspire a greater reaction from the men—her shape in those pants, or a bit of ruffle on a dress. Likely either would stir up these women-starved men.

As he turned and started toward his own fire, he couldn't help shaking his head. He may have just walked himself into more trouble than if he'd tossed a rock at a hungry grizzly.

Juniper's throat closed so tightly it was hard to get a breath in and out as she gripped Faith's arm and followed Mr. Turner. The fellow seemed to think they'd taken leave of their senses coming all this way without a chaperone. And as so many hungry eyes turned their way, she was more and more inclined to agree with him.

That horde outside their lodge all morning had been bad enough. At least Rosemary had been able to secure the flimsy leather door flap to shut out their prying looks. And Lorelei had parked herself in the center of the hut, with her rifle aimed at the opening. But out here, there was no barrier against all the ravenous looks.

They edged around several scaffolds that had hides stretched across them. She moved closer to them to pull Faith away from the two men they were passing. Both wore the thick bushy beards, deeply tanned skin, and shoulder-length hair that seemed to be standard issue for these mountain men, but the thick creases marking the exposed skin around the eyes of the one on the left proclaimed him to be at least twenty years older than the fellow on the right.

She accidentally caught the eye of the younger man, and his dark brown beard split to reveal teeth only a few shades lighter as he stepped toward her, anticipation brightening his eyes.

She jerked her attention forward again and tugged Faith faster, nearly trotting on Mr. Turner's heels. He slowed as they approached a lodge with a campfire in front, where a man sat alone, both hands cradling a tin cup.

Mr. Turner looked at the fire and motioned to the logs placed around it. "Have a seat." He sent another look around them, as though he expected an army of . . . what? Buffalo? Indians? Mountain men foaming at the mouth?

Juniper moved in first and settled on a stump. Lorelei sank down beside her, cradling little Boots, then Faith and Rosemary. She turned her attention to the man whose quiet repose they'd interrupted and offered him a smile of apology. "Hello. Sorry to barge in."

Though his skin looked even more weathered and leathery than many others she'd seen here, his beard wasn't nearly as slick and long. His pallor had almost a bluish tinge. He didn't look sickly, but she couldn't imagine what else would give that coloring. As he studied her, his eyes softened, and his mouth curved into a pleasant smile. Nothing suggestive in his expression at all. "It's a pleasure for you ladies to visit. The fellows call me Ol' Henry."

Before she could introduce herself, Faith jumped in. "We're the Misses Collins. That's Juniper, Lorelei, Rosemary, and I'm Faith. That in Lorelei's arms is Boots, the baby coyote she's raising."

A frown plunged across Mr. Turner's brow as he leaned over the fire and laid out four hunks of meat on a rock near the flame.

Henry—should that be Mr. Ol' Henry? Or simply Mr. Henry?—was nodding, his smile spreading to reveal a flash of grayish teeth. "I'm glad Riley brought you over. We were worried about those men lining up twenty thick outside your lodge."

Mr. Turner—Riley—straightened from the meat and stood, then reached for one of the thicker logs from a pile of firewood and moved it closer to Ol' Henry before he perched on its end. "Tell us more about this Peigan woman you're looking for. Ol' Henry here has been trapping for at least twenty winters. There's a good chance he's sat at the fire of every Peigan chief on either side of the Rockies."

She sent another look to Ol' Henry. Twenty years seemed impressive, though his appearance looked like he might have been at the work for fifty. If the tales the wagon drivers told of wild animals and wilder men were true, surviving twenty years in this land must be quite a feat.

Both men were looking at her and her sisters, waiting for more details. Juniper glanced at Rosie, the same way Faith and Lorelei did. She was usually the spokeswoman among them.

Rosie didn't hesitate. "Our father knew her when he traveled through the land between the Missouri River and the mountains, about twenty years ago. He was injured in a buffalo hunt on the plains, near a giant boulder shaped like a windmill, and this Peigan woman named Steps Right found him and sent for help. We're not certain of her age, but she would be at least forty years old. We have something to give to her, and we want to make sure she received the horses our father sent her." Rosemary pressed her mouth closed, as that was all they'd agreed they would tell.

In truth, Papa's final request had left so many questions. Why now, after all these years, was it so important to find this native woman who may or may not still be alive? If it was so important to return the blue bead necklace back to her and make sure she received the gift of two horses he'd sent after his return east, why hadn't he done it while he lived?

When she and her sisters had gathered around his bed after that awful carriage accident, he'd been so pale, every word requiring painful effort. Tears had clouded Juniper's vision, and she'd only wanted him to stop talking, to save his strength so he could recover, despite the surgeon's prognosis. Of course they'd agreed to find this woman named Steps Right. Anything to calm his urgency.

Now, Ol' Henry's brows lifted. "That's all you know of her? A Peigan woman more than forty years old? Your father couldn't remember anything more?"

Rosie leaned forward to brace her arms on her legs. "Mr. Turner said there's a Peigan band here at the rendezvous." Avoiding the question. Good. "We're planning to find them and ask if a woman named Steps Right lives among them. Do you know if any of them speak English, or will we need to hire an interpreter?"

The two men exchanged glances, and it was hard to tell exactly what that look said. Then Ol' Henry turned to Rosie. "There are a few men in that band who speak passable English, and one of them a bit of French. I suspect they'll be struck dumb seeing you ladies. You're not a common sight in these parts."

Heat flushed up Juniper's neck. She had to stop growing embarrassed about their gender. It just wasn't a thing spoken of so freely—or so often—back in Virginia.

Of course, they'd expected things to be different out here. They'd discussed at length how careful they would need to be in this rough camp, how they should never wander around alone. How important it was for them all to carry a gun everywhere they went. And they'd spent long hours learning to use the rifles and boot pistols. But knowing and planning hadn't quite prepared her for actually experiencing this place.

All these men.

"I'll go for you." Mr. Turner spoke up for the first time since he'd brought them to this fire. His gaze hovered on Rosemary, then slipped to Juniper for a single heartbeat. He really was a handsome man, especially when those pale green eyes landed on a girl. They had the power to make her pulse rush.

But that was the last thing she could allow. She and her sisters had discussed this too. None of them could fall for any of the men out here. There were plenty of decent fellows back home, and allowing some mountain man to sweep a girl off her feet could put all of them in danger. At the very least, it would get in the way of their mission.

They'd come to find Steps Right. Nothing else. At least nothing that concerned the male of the species.

Mr. Turner's attention flicked back to Rosemary, freeing Juniper from the draw of his eyes. Though she couldn't help a little jealousy toward her older sister. Rosie always got the attention. She was the oldest, after all. The one people looked to when speaking to any of them.

Juniper turned her own focus to Rosie as her sister shook her head. "We'll make the inquiries. It might be wise for us to take along an interpreter, though." She looked between the two men. "Do either of you speak their language?"

"It's not safe for you all to go." Mr. Turner's voice came a little louder than before, evidence of his frustration. "I can be your spokesman. Tell me everything you want to ask, and I'll state it word for word."

He was wasting his breath, for Rosie wouldn't be swayed. This was another thing they'd agreed on. Because they knew no one here at the rendezvous, they wouldn't trust their message to anyone except an interpreter, and only then when they were present with him. There was so much they didn't know about this woman they sought. She might well have a jealous husband who would thwart their efforts to find her.

Rosemary held herself calmly. "Is it that you fear for our safety among the tribes? If they're dangerous, why would they be allowed here at the rendezvous?" Papa hadn't talked of the Indians very often when he told stories of his travels. Mostly he described the land and the animals. But when he had mentioned the natives, he usually spoke of them as friendly, or at least curious. Juniper wasn't naïve enough to believe all were like that. Just like all white men weren't harmless. Every man had the power to choose his path for himself.

Mr. Turner shook his head, and even through his beard she could see the tightening of his jaw. "The Peigan are the most peaceable band of Blackfoot. They're not a danger exactly, not to the men here. But for white women . . ." His voice trailed off as though they should know exactly what danger there would be for white women.

She could imagine several different possibilities. She fought her flush, and this time she was fairly sure she won.

Rosemary turned to Ol' Henry. "Sir, do you speak the language of the Peigan? Might you be willing to accompany us as interpreter? We'll pay for the service."

Juniper had to bite her lip to keep her smile tucked away. Rosie had more pluck than a scrappy rooster.

"I'll be your interpreter." Mr. Turner nearly grunted the words, clearly against his will.

Rosie shifted back to him. "And you are fluent in their language?"

"I speak the hand talk fine. That's the sign language all the tribes in these parts use."

Rosie studied him for a long moment, and Juniper had to bite down harder to keep in her grin. Her sister knew how to make men sweat. She'd honed her bartering skills after Mama passed and had plenty of opportunities to sharpen them more since they'd decided to take this journey together.

She would make Mr. Turner think thrice before he did something she didn't approve of.

At last, she gave a single tip of her chin. "Can you take us now?"

It almost looked like the edges of his mouth twitched. Like maybe he was fighting a grin too. "You ladies eat while I go trade my furs before all the good supplies are gone. Then we'll set out."

FOUR

Riley needed more men. Fellows he could trust. The entire time he was trading his furs—when he should have been focused on bartering and all the nuances of word and expression that went along with that exchange—his mind worked through how he could keep those Collins women safe.

If he could get enough friends to form a wall around them as they moved through camp, the women should be protected from the trappers, especially as the men began to imbibe the drink they'd been trading for all morning.

But in the Peigan camp . . . A half-dozen trappers with rifles wouldn't be able to hold their own against the fifty or so warriors gathered there. But he had no reason to think there would be a need for bullets.

As long as no one touched the women. Surely the braves wouldn't try it. Or was he fooling himself?

He'd not been around at the rendezvous two years ago when the missionary wives came through. But he'd heard stories of how fascinated the natives were with the women's hair. Not so much the dark brown of Mrs. Spalding, but they'd thought Mrs. Whitman's blond curls came straight from the sun god.

Thankfully, all four Collins sisters had darker hair, though Miss Juniper's was lighter than the others. And her sky-blue eyes . . . How had she obtained that captivating color when her sisters' were all brown?

His belly clenched. He'd need a whole army to protect Juniper. And if any man, Peigan or trapper or member of the British Parliament, touched her . . .

Yep. He needed to find lots of men he trusted.

Leading his pack mule loaded down with the supplies he'd just purchased, he stopped by the lodges of a few men he'd trapped with these past years. Neither Scruggs nor Watson were at home. At the next lodge, though, he learned Barnaby had gone to ready his horse for a race that would take place in an hour or so.

A horse race. That was one of the rendezvous pastimes the men loved most, and nearly everyone participated. Some ran their fastest horses, but most simply cheered them on and bet on the winners.

An event like that was sure to distract the trappers from the women. If they timed things right, most of the fellows would be out on the straightaway behind the lodges when he and the sisters rode down to the Peigan camp.

And the Peigan warriors would likely be up here participating in the festivities too. If he took the Collins sisters down to where that band had set up lodges, the only people they were likely to find would be the women, enjoying a few hours of leisure without warriors underfoot.

Would that be a good thing? If the women would speak

with them, they were just as likely to know if Steps Right lived among them. Native women probably enjoyed a bit of gossip just as much as ladies from the States. Peigan women wouldn't be eager to answer questions from white men they didn't know, but maybe with the Collins sisters along with him, they would be more willing.

For the first time since the campfire, this coming mission didn't make dread crawl through his chest. This wasn't hope, exactly, but . . . perhaps they could find a lead. He wasn't so foolish as to think they'd find Steps Right in the first camp they visited.

As his own campfire came into view, the sight of feminine figures around it made his step catch.

He'd escorted the women back to their quarters and told them to stay there until he returned for them. He'd even offered to saddle their horses and bring them to the lodge opening, for the Peigan camp was a good three miles south and they would need to ride. But the women had insisted they needed to retrieve their animals themselves, so he'd told them he would come to take them out to the herd when he was ready.

Why were they now sitting around his cookfire, settled in and looking very much like they belonged there? Miss Lorelei even had that wild animal curled in her lap. At least Ol' Henry sat with them, and Dragoon stood at the edge of the group too. The two could provide some protection. The former was speaking, a grin marking his features, and the rest watched him with full attention.

Riley couldn't hear what Ol' Henry said, but he'd stake half the supplies on Scarecrow's pack saddle that the man was spinning a yarn. The tale might very well be true, but

Ol' Henry had a way of dramatizing each part that kept the listener hanging on every word.

Riley slowed the mule so the sounds of his approach wouldn't break the spell of Henry's story.

"You see, ol' Meeks had met up with that same bear before, and neither one of 'em walked away without a scratch the first time. Just one whiff of Meeks's scent and the whole memory played clear as a hot day in the grizzly's mind."

Ol' Henry leaned forward, a sign the tale was getting good. "There Meeks was, clinging to the tree, as high as a second-story window. The bear stood stock-still on the ground below, nose sniffin' the air. Then he stood up on his back paws and lifted his eyes up into the tree branches. Meeks said he'd rather face a hundred poison arrows than the steely glare of that grizzly staring into his soul."

A grin flashed in Ol' Henry's eyes. "The beast let out a roar to wake Father Abraham himself, then planted both front paws on the tree trunk and pushed. Meeks clung to the upper part as it swayed, back and forth. He'd kept hold of his rifle while he climbed, and now hugged it between him and the tree. It seemed likely the pine wouldn't be upright much longer with the bear pushing so hard. The only way he'd survive this meeting was if he could hold on an' get a shot too."

Ol' Henry paused his story to lift his cup to his mouth. His movements were painfully slow as he sipped from the drink, then let out a long, satisfied sigh.

The women all leaned in, but from his angle, Riley could only see the expressions on Juniper's and Rosemary's faces. The eldest sister frowned like she might want to snatch the cup from Ol' Henry's hands if he didn't get on with his tale. Miss Juniper looked so hopeful. She was actually sitting on her fingertips, as though that helped her be patient. She sure was a pretty thing, the way the summer sun brightened her face and glimmered off her hair.

At last, Ol' Henry returned the cup to his lap. "So ol' Joe Meeks was up there, swayin' in the treetop, and the bear didn't give any sign he planned to stop pushing on the trunk. Like any good mountain man, Meeks kept his Hawkins loaded, so all he had to do was point the rifle, aim, and fire. Just like shootin' a rabbit from a bucking horse."

Henry paused again and lifted the cup to his lips. Miss Rosemary leaned forward. Maybe she really was going to snatch the drink this time.

Riley took a step. He'd heard this story before, and it might be better if he finished it off before blood was shed. Every now and then Ol' Henry drew out the suspense a little too far. "Joe Meeks managed to get the rifle to his shoulder but didn't aim so well."

All eyes turned to him as he reached the circle around the fire. "The first shot hit the bear's front leg. At least that stopped the swaying of the tree, but it made the grizzly even angrier. Meeks loaded again while the bear roared, then it rose up against the trunk once more. Meeks aimed and fired just half a heartbeat before the bear could start the swaying. This shot struck its neck, but still didn't do the beast in. It took two more bullets before the grizzly dropped to a limp heap on the ground."

The women's eyes were all rounded, but Ol' Henry looked like he was holding in laughter. Almost as if he'd been trying to get a rise out of someone, and Riley's stepping in suited him just fine.

A hush had fallen on the group, and everyone was still staring at him. His neck itched beneath his collar. "There's a race beginning in less than an hour. That would be a good time for us to ride down to the Peigan camp. I'll unpack my supplies, then we can go catch our horses."

He turned and began unstrapping his goods. Dragoon moved to the other side of the mule to help, which gave Riley a good chance to enlist his aid for the journey. He kept his voice low and his back to the women as he relayed the details. Dragoon's brows raised, though his fingers never stopped working the ties.

When Riley finished, Dragoon hoisted a barrel of gunpowder onto his shoulder. He kept his voice low and turned his back to the women. "You think they're telling the truth that they don't know anything more about her? They've come all this way with only those few facts?"

Riley shrugged as he hauled a barrel of salt off the saddle. "Not sure. That might be why they insist on going themselves. For now, my only job is to keep them safe. When I get a better feel for the situation, I'll worry about the rest."

He followed Dragoon into the lodge and set his barrel beside the one Dragoon carried in. The man had hit on what was really bothering Riley about this situation.

He knew they hadn't given him all the information. They said they had, but they were holding back. They had to be.

He shouldn't blame them. After all, they'd only met him the day before. They had no idea if he could be trusted with their secrets. Maybe they'd figure that he could be soon enough, and then he could better help them find the woman.

Until then, he'd consider his only job to be keeping them alive.

FIVE

Getting to the horses proved harder than Juniper expected, especially with the circuitous route Riley led them to avoid the crowd gathering along the raceway.

He'd said the Lord must have planned the horse race just for them, to give them a chance to leave camp while the men were distracted. God had occupied so few of her thoughts these last months since Papa's death, or maybe even the past few years. It seemed strange to attribute something like a horse race to His planning.

She'd once believed He oversaw their daily lives, that He worked things out for their good. But she'd never been able to see the good in Mama's death, nor in the way her grieving father had sold off their horse farm and moved them to the city. Richmond had been a dark, depressing, smelly place compared to the open air and sunshine of the ranch.

A few voices rang across the distance, pulling her from the memories.

"You gals planning to race?" a grizzly-looking man yelled.

"I'll put my money on any one of you." This one she

couldn't see, but his voice slurred like he'd spent the morning in a rum house.

"Will you come be my lucky lady?" A tall stranger waved his hat from the middle of the crowd.

But the men were far enough away to be ignored, especially when Riley moved his horse to shield them from the onlookers. His gaze shifted back and forth, his stance uneasy. He didn't speak, but his eyes urged them to hurry. He didn't need to say it aloud.

Dragoon also eyed the men gathering for the race, but the strain didn't tighten into new lines on his face the way it did with Riley.

Juniper's hands trembled as she tied the saddle straps. What had they been thinking not to bring a guardian when they came west? Riley seemed to have taken that task on himself, and he appeared trustworthy enough. At least he hadn't done anything to make her think otherwise. He was a bit overbearing, but that wouldn't endanger them.

She pulled the cinch tight, then patted her mare on the shoulder. Her finger traced out the figure eight pattern of the brand her father used to apply on the shoulders of all the ranch horses. These were the few riding animals he'd kept when they sold the land and moved to Richmond after Mama's passing. This brand held so many happy memories. Even now, seeing the symbol steadied her.

Once they'd all saddled and began riding southward, the horses fell into an easy stride. As the flat land they rode on widened, she and Rosie rode beside Riley, with Faith, Lorelei, and Mr. Dragoon bringing up the rear.

As the sounds of the horse race faded behind them, she heard Mr. Dragoon speak. "I must say, I'm surprised to see you ladies riding astride. Figured gals from a fancy city would ride sidesaddle."

Juniper glanced at Rosie. Mr. Dragoon would have been a great deal more surprised if he'd seen her in trousers that morning. Riley hadn't even mentioned that detail. Normally, Faith would be the sister most likely to shed her skirts for men's pants, but Rosie had thought she'd be less conspicuous as she searched out Mr. Provost.

"We all grew up on horses." Faith piped up in answer to Mr. Dragoon. "Papa raised champions that people traveled for hundreds of miles to purchase."

Riley's gaze shot to Juniper, but she didn't meet the questions she could feel in his look. "Do you still . . . ?"

She shook her head but kept her focus forward as she fought the burn assaulting her eyes. Papa's death made all the losses feel so fresh. She managed to swallow enough of the knot in her throat to keep her voice from wobbling. "Our father sold the ranch three years ago, before we moved to Richmond." After Mama died.

He'd never been vocal about his love for Mama, but there had always seemed to be respect and affection between them. Juniper had never realized the extent of it until he uprooted all of their lives so dramatically and sank into his shell of grief in that dark townhouse.

It had taken a full two years for her and her sisters to draw him back into something of a normal life. Then they'd only had a few more months with him before . . .

Silence threatened to sink over them again, and she didn't have the strength to break it, not with the memories weighing on her.

"Oh!" Lorelei's squeal jerked Juniper upright, and she

spun in her saddle. Her sister clutched the coyote pup tight to her chest. "You're not running away again. Do you hear me, Boots? Settle down."

The animal seemed to understand the words, for it ceased squirming and seemed to sigh with relief, tucked there against its mistress.

Juniper turned to face forward again and caught Riley's dubious look over his shoulder as he muttered, "Not sure we should have brought him."

She almost smiled. He didn't sound frustrated about the animal anymore, just grumpy. "There's no place to lock him up in our lodge. He would get past the door flap too easily."

His expression turned dry. "That's because he's a wild animal. Wild animals are supposed to run free."

She widened her eyes in the sweet look she'd always charmed Pa with. "Lorelei will set him free as soon as he's old enough to find food on his own."

Riley only shook his head. He might not have made peace with her sister's unusual pet, but at least he realized how futile it was to try to convince her to let him go.

Lor had never been able to look away when an animal needed help, no matter how unlikely that she could save it. Not since that first tragic time.

One of the barn cats on the ranch had a litter of kittens, and Lorelei had been enamored with them. But when she'd made a nest in a water barrel and sealed the top tightly to keep the stable hand's pup from finding them, all six helpless babes had smothered. Lorelei cried every day for two weeks and wouldn't even look at another animal, much less go near it, for a full month.

Then something had changed in her. Maybe it was finding

the injured bird beneath the tree and successfully nursing it back to health. Ever since then, Lorelei had been drawn to creatures in need, and no amount of reasoning could convince her not to help.

By the time they'd been riding at least an hour, the endless rows of lodges between their path and the river had finally fallen away, and a small grove of trees stood ahead.

"Are we getting close?" She glanced at the man riding beside her.

Riley's hat brim was cocked up as he eyed the landscape before them. The strong lines of his face stood out in his profile. His nose just the right size, his strong chin not quite buried under the beard—every feature proportioned perfectly to form a rather pleasing picture.

But not a picture she should be staring at.

"I haven't been down this way since the tribe came to the rendezvous, but I heard we should see their lodges on the other side of those trees."

"That's what I heard too." Mr. Dragoon spoke up from behind her. "The Peigan are the only band of Blackfoot allowed to come to the rendezvous, as they tend to be more peaceable than the Bloods or the Blackfoot proper. Still, we all make sure to camp north of them. The Snake Indians and the Flatheads and the Nez Perce all camp farther above the trappers. They'd rather the Peigan not be here at all, but as long as they don't do their warring during rendezvous, the Peigan are allowed."

"How many Peigan Blackfoot are there?" Rosemary asked the question, but they'd all been wondering. Exactly how hard would the search be?

Juniper glanced again at Riley. A crease had formed

in his brow, and he didn't look like he was planning to answer.

Thankfully, Mr. Dragoon did. "Well . . . I don't rightly know for sure. Maybe a thousand? Most of the Blackfoot live north of here, up near the Marias River and beyond. Not sure anyone would really know the answer to that."

A weight pressed in Juniper's chest. "How far away is the Marias River?" They'd been hoping to find this woman here at the rendezvous, since they'd heard many natives came for the festivities. Then they could return East with the supply wagons. Clearly they'd far underestimated the situation.

"Three weeks' travel, at least. Depends on how far your mount can go in a day or how many saddle horses you bring along to trade off."

Riley finally made a sound, a snort that showed he disagreed with the assessment. "It's farther than that. And Blackfoot country stretches all the way up into Rupert's Land."

"Do you know if there's a giant boulder in the shape of a windmill in that area? Our father said it was quite an impressive spectacle. I have a sketch of the way he described it, but I left it back at our lodge. He said Steps Right's people were camped near it."

Riley slid her a look, and his mouth pressed as though he was measuring his words. "I've never seen anything like that, but it isn't likely to help much anyway. The Blackfoot travel with the food. There's not much chance they'll still be camped in the same place they were two decades ago. You said it's been twenty years, right?"

She fought the disappointment coursing through her and

did her best to straighten her spine, though her body wanted to wilt. But before she could answer, he lifted an arm to point in front of them.

A few lodges appeared ahead, nearly identical to the ones they'd just left behind. As they rounded a cluster of trees, the full camp spread out before them. Figures stood beside the dwellings, sometimes alone, sometimes in groups of three or four.

They rode closer, but by the time they reached the first of the lodges, no one had come to greet them. In fact, most of the natives had moved either inside their homes or behind them, though enough heads peeked out to show how curious they were.

Riley raised a hand and made a sweeping gesture. "Oki." That first word might have been in the Peigan language, or she simply didn't hear him correctly. But then he spoke in English. "I bring white women who wish to speak with you. Is there anyone who will come talk with them?"

Juniper scanned the figures she could see. All appeared to be women, with their black hair hanging in long braids. Most wore dresses that reached just below their knees, with some type of pants underneath that.

Two figures stepped from the shadow of the lodge in the second row. Their gait was slow, like that of the aged, and when the sun shone clearly on their forms, the difference between them became apparent.

The figure on the left must be a man, hair almost fully gray, but wearing a tunic much shorter than the dress of the woman on the right. She couldn't be much younger than he was, but her hair possessed more black than his did.

They came within a dozen strides of the horses, then

stopped. The man spoke in a gravelly voice. "I am father of Mountain Chief, leader of this band. You bring us visitors?"

The man was scanning her and her sisters, though his look seemed merely curious. Not intrusive like so many other looks they'd received since setting out with the supply wagons.

Beside her, Rosie began dismounting from her horse. These people did look peaceable. And with mostly women at home, she didn't think there would be danger in moving closer on foot.

Juniper leaned forward and slid to the ground too. Should they take their rifles with them? That certainly wouldn't show good faith. Their boot pistols would have to do for protection. Maybe Faith, Lorelei, and Mr. Dragoon would stay back here with the horses, keeping ready access to the rifles just in case.

Riley had already dismounted and was striding beside Rosemary, so Juniper stepped quickly to catch up as they approached the couple.

When they reached the pair, a sense of familiarity swept through her. The images her mind had formed of what the natives would look like had created a scene not too different from this. Yet now she could see the textures of the leather clothing, the deep shadows in the lines on their faces, the strands of their hair. She finally had detail to the fuzzy picture her thoughts had formed as a child.

When Rosie spoke, Juniper had to blink to focus on her sister's words. "I'm Rosemary Collins, and these are my sisters, Juniper, Lorelei, and Faith." She pointed to each as she said their names. "We've come looking for a woman our father once knew. Her name is Steps Right, and she is Peigan."

The man looked at the woman beside him, probably his wife. Her father had always said it was hard to tell what an Indian was thinking, that they wore a solemn expression no matter what. But this fellow's thoughts showed clearly in the confusion marking his features.

It was the woman who became hard to read. She gave an almost imperceptible shake of her head, and the man turned back to Rosemary. "We do not know this Steps Right."

Rosemary nodded. "May we ask the other women here?"

Several of the Peigan women had gathered a few steps behind these two, shy curiosity on their faces. But perhaps they wouldn't speak to outsiders without permission from the chief's parents.

Juniper offered a nod of deference to the couple. "Or if you'd rather take our question to them, we can wait. We think Steps Right is more than forty years old. We don't know much about her other than that."

This time it was the woman who assessed her, and Juniper met those dark eyes. They were small, though not beady. They certainly held wisdom, and maybe a bit of decisiveness. She must hold the matriarchal rule in the camp. Juniper gave her a sweet smile and waited.

At last, the elder barked something in high-low sounds toward those gathered behind her. One of the women stepped forward, shyness tipping her chin. Then the others followed with her and lined up beside this grandmother. The matriarch motioned to the women as she gave a nod to Juniper and Rosemary.

Rosie nudged Juniper's side and murmured just loud enough for her to hear, "Ask or move over."

Juniper stepped out of her sister's way. Rosie would want to do the talking, and all those expectant faces had made her mouth turn dry.

SIX

While her sister asked about Steps Right, Juniper focused on watching the women's faces. There were eight of them who had lined up beside the elder, and all wore basically the same style of clothing and long black hair in braids. That was where the similarities ended.

Many were lean and well-muscled, though a few tended more toward the stockier side. One of the women was nearly a head taller than those on her left and right. Some possessed darker skin color, while three of the women were lighter even than Riley. She'd not expected each of these women to be so unique. A scan of their expressions showed their personalities were likely just as different from one another.

But each was studying Rosie with intensity. Did they all understand English? Surely someone would translate if they didn't.

When she finished her question, the women began to murmur amongst themselves in their own language. Not a word of it sounded familiar.

At last, the tallest one took a tentative half-step forward. Her voice was soft and her words sharply accented, but she spoke English. "Not know Steps Right. There is Peigan grandmother in Gros Ventre camp." She pointed to the north. "Past white man meeting."

Juniper smiled to say thank you, and before she could turn to Riley to see if he heard, he murmured, "The Gros Ventre are another tribe camped north of the rendezvous."

She nodded understanding, then looked at her sister. Was there anything else they needed to ask these women? They might not again have such an opportunity.

Riley addressed the man before she could decide. "Do you know of any other Peigan camps in this area?"

The wrinkled lines of the older man's brow drew together. "I have seen warriors from Head Carrier's band on our way here." He held up both hands, all ten fingers splayed. "This sleeps."

Riley nodded, as though the words made perfect sense to him. "They were a war party or hunting?"

The question seemed to wipe the expression from the man's face, leaving it with lines sagging and no sign of emotion in those eyes that had been so expressive a moment before.

Riley must have realized he'd erred in his question, for he spoke again quickly. "I only ask if it is safe to bring these women." He motioned toward her and Rosemary.

The man's focus flicked to them, then back to Riley. It was hard to tell what he was thinking. "I do not know how Head Carrier's warriors will act. I only know my son, that he will be fair to all. Even the pale hair." His gaze moved to Juniper. Or more specifically, to her hair.

She had to work hard not to shrink back, or even raise a hand to cover her hair. She'd been wearing it in a single braid down her back for most of the trip. The first morning away from St. Louis, she'd realized how unmanageable hairpins would be on horseback all day, especially since none of them had brought a mirror.

The way this man's hand lifted a tiny bit gave her the feeling he wanted to reach out and touch her, though three or four strides separated them. If he did, should she allow it? Perhaps Riley would step in, or at least give her a sign of what she should do.

But the man didn't approach. Instead, he turned back to Riley. "My son, Mountain Chief, has gone with his young men to race the horses. If you do not find the woman you seek with the Gros Ventre, come back and speak to him."

Riley nodded. "I will." He shifted so his attention included the older woman. "Thank you for answering our questions."

The woman nodded, as regal as Queen Adelaide herself.

Then Riley turned and gave a single motion with his hand to show that she and Rosemary should walk ahead of him. Perhaps he did it to be a gentleman, or perhaps he did it to place himself as a shield while they retreated to their horses. Probably not the latter. Their reception here had been friendly. Hadn't it?

There'd been an undertone through much of the conversation, but the feeling seemed to have shifted several times depending on what was being said. This tribe certainly seemed to have a hierarchy among them.

What would it be like to live here with these Indians? It seemed the younger women held little authority to speak unless given permission, at least to strangers. This bold undertaking she and her sisters had set out on likely wouldn't be allowed. Would it? Yet perhaps adventurous women were lauded. Maybe that's how the grandmother had earned her standing.

An image of their own grandmama slipped in, the one who'd passed away only a year before Mama. She'd not been so regal as this Peigan woman. She'd been a doer, always stitching or working in the garden or visiting. When her granddaughters came to visit, even in her older years, she'd greeted them with a hug and kiss on the cheek and the offer of a sweet.

It had been a while since the weight of grief pressed so hard on her chest for Grandmama, but tears stung her eyes now even as she took her horse's reins from Lorelei and reached her boot up to the stirrup.

Silence settled over them again as they rode. Not true quiet, for the squeaks of their saddles and the distant thundering and whooping of race spectators maintained a steady noise.

But there seemed to be a tension among them that kept any in their group from speaking. She needed to talk with her sisters. To absorb each part of the information they'd just been given, to pick apart expressions and nuances and decide what was said without being spoken aloud.

Riley broke the quiet first. He rode on her left again, with Rosemary on her right and the other three behind, as they'd been on the trip out. "What are your plans now?" His voice didn't ring loud enough for the question to be directed at all of them. Perhaps to her and Rosie, though it felt more like he addressed her specifically.

She slid a glance at her older sister. Rosie gave the slightest of nods, communicating her opinion on two things—yes, they would pursue the lead they'd been given here and visit the Gros Ventre camp, and yes, she could give that answer to Riley.

She adjusted her focus forward again. "We'll go to the Gros Ventre camp they spoke of and ask if anyone knows Steps Right. Can you tell us how to reach that place? Is it directly north of the trappers' lodgings?" If several Indian camps were clustered upriver, they would need to know how to decipher which belonged to the Gros Ventre. Or perhaps they could ask when they got there. Yet could they count on every village having someone who spoke English?

Riley shook his head. "There are camps of several tribes. Your blue eyes and brown hair will fascinate them, and at the very least they'd want to touch your braid. You can't go there alone." His voice hardened more with each word, laced with solid determination.

The thought of strangers, especially natives, swarming around her and touching her hair made her want to shrink back. Was it truly the color that drew them—a much lighter brown than the others' raven-black locks—or the fact that she was a white woman? She couldn't quite believe the latter would make no difference.

Riley loosened the tight line of his jaw enough to speak again. "I will take you. Can you all be ready to leave an hour after sunrise tomorrow morning?"

Did he really want to accompany them again? They were hardly his responsibility. "Don't you have work to do instead of escorting us around?" He didn't seem to be helping them for amorous reasons. He didn't doff his hat or try to kiss the backs of their fingers as a dozen trappers had that morning before she and her sisters had retreated back into their lodge. He seemed curious, not lovestruck.

So why would he feel the need to ignore his own affairs and invest himself in theirs?

"Like I said earlier, some of the camps haven't seen a white woman in years, maybe even decades. And most of the natives never have. It's not safe for women to parade themselves through all these men."

Parade?

He clamped his mouth shut, as though holding back the rest of what he wanted to say. Still, he'd said enough.

And she could easily fill in his unspoken words. *You four must have taken leave of your senses to come out here without a host of men to protect you.* Or better yet, *You should have stayed home and stitched pillows or painted fire screens and sent your men to do the investigating for you.*

She forced herself to relax. To breathe in, then slowly out. And when her mare bobbed her nose, Juniper eased the tightness of her reins. Riley wasn't saying anything they hadn't been told by their father's solicitor, by the men with whom they'd arranged transportation, and by every fellow in the wagon train except Mr. Provost himself.

Perhaps they would've been better off if Mr. Provost had worried as much about their well-being as the others. Maybe they would have their own food to eat now.

She pushed that notion aside. They would find someone who would allow them to purchase food with coin. Perhaps even Riley, though if he refused payment again, this would be the last time she would ask.

She kept the tone of her voice strong. "Mr. Turner, do

you know of a place in the camp we can purchase food with money? Or perhaps a man who would go hunting in exchange for payment?" If it came down to it, she and Rosie could hunt. But she would have to be awfully hungry to look an animal in the eye and pull the trigger. Perhaps they could fish instead, if someone had a line they could purchase.

"I already told you our lodge has plenty of meat to share. You're welcome to take your meals with us, or I can bring it to you to cook for yourselves. You've already met Ol' Henry and Dragoon. The other man who camps with us is Jeremiah."

"And will you accept payment in gold coin?" That was the only condition with which they could take the food. She and Rosie were committed to that requirement. They couldn't allow a man to think he had a hold over them, or that they were in his debt. Riley didn't seem the type to use that for his advantage, but they still barely knew him.

His jaw had tightened again, but he managed a few words. "If I have to. And only if you have it to spare."

She nodded. "We do."

Quiet fell again as her mind worked through the next steps in their mission and what they would need to do before then for their own upkeep. Riley had said he could take them tomorrow morning, but they shouldn't wait that long. They only had a few days before the wagons returned east.

Every hour mattered in this search.

SEVEN

Juniper eyed Riley as he rode beside her. "If you wish to go with us to the Gros Ventre camp, that's your choice. But we need to go now. Today. Our hope is to find Steps Right before the supply wagons return to the States. We can't lose an entire afternoon."

He shook his head. "It's at least a half-day's ride to that area. There's no way we can get there and back this afternoon. Best to start out tomorrow morning. Besides, I need to do a little more trading today before all the supplies are gone. If there's something other than meat that you and your sisters need, let me know and I'll request it."

Why was he taking such pains to help them? Would this be normal behavior for men back in Richmond? Perhaps. If a man were already acquainted with their family, he might step in as Riley was doing to help when he saw a need.

But out here in this wild country? Riley didn't fit the appearance of a respectable gentleman—no tailored coat or elegantly styled hair or valet in sight. But perhaps he'd been such a man before coming west.

She slid a covert glance his way. "How long have you been a trapper?"

"About three years."

"And where is your home?"

"Wherever I lay my bedding and build a campfire." His tone sounded almost amused.

She pushed down a flare of frustration. "I mean where did you come from before? The States, right? Which city?"

"The States, yes, but no city. My parents had a cabin in Illinois, a few hours' ride from St. Louis."

A rural cabin. So he likely hadn't ever lived a gentleman's life. Yet the source of his manners no longer seemed as interesting as one of the words he'd spoken.

Had. His family had owned a cabin in an unsettled part of Illinois. "Where do they live now?"

"My ma has moved in with my aunt and uncle, a little house on the outskirts of Peoria. My uncle is a minister there."

Sounded like she must be a widow, which meant Juniper shouldn't ask about his father. Yet her curiosity about this man grew with every fact he revealed. The picture of his life that was forming in her mind wasn't quite what she'd expected. But she could imagine him coming from those roots. The hole in the image where his father should be still glared up at her.

She had to ask, but she kept her voice as gentle and unassuming as possible. "Is your father . . . ?"

"Dead. Nine years ago. He was a scout and guide for government surveying parties. Took sick after he was caught in a snowstorm and never fully recovered." His tone was matter of fact, not harsh as though he was angry or bitter about his loss. It sounded as though his grief had matured to the point that he was able to share the information as a simple part of his past.

"That must have been hard. How old were you at the time?" And why did she feel at liberty to ask so many personal questions of this man? "I'm sorry. You don't have to answer any of this."

He sent her a half-smile, then returned his focus ahead. "I don't mind. People don't often ask."

With all these hundreds of trappers spread out through this valley, no one cared enough to inquire about Riley's past? Perhaps they only spoke of work or weather conditions or game—or whatever else was of import for their survival in this land.

He spoke again to answer her question. "I was fourteen when we got the news that he passed."

A weight pressed in her chest for the image of the half-grown lad that formed in her mind. Struggling to grow up without the guidance of a man to help him through those challenging days. He must have had someone else to teach him.

Or maybe it was his mother who'd helped him. If so, she'd done an excellent job, from what Juniper had seen so far. And perhaps that accounted for why he was so protective of them, if he'd been the man of the house from such an early age, caring for and protecting his mother.

His actions back when they'd first met him now made sense, there at the boulders on the hill when he'd reprimanded Lorelei for chasing after a coyote pup.

Through this new perspective, she could see where they hadn't made things easier for him, leaving their lodge several times when he'd warned them to stay inside. Refusing food unless they could pay for it. Even allowing Lorelei to keep that coyote pup.

But there was another view of the situation that he would also have to understand, the reality that she and her sisters lived under. Perhaps it was time to be candid and create a clear understanding between them all.

She turned fully to him. "Mr. Turner, I can only imagine how hard those years must have been, for you and your mother both. I'm sure you were a great help and solace to her. And I think I understand a little better now why you're assisting us. We're grateful for what you've done so far and for agreeing to sell us food and guide us to the Gros Ventre camp. I think it will be beneficial for you to understand a few things about us too."

Juniper snuck a glance at Rosemary. How much should she tell? Only the most critical facts. "Our mother passed a few years ago, and our father died only months ago. We are four unmarried women on our own. But we're not incapable. Each of us carries weapons and has been well trained in how to use them. When we planned this trip, we discussed all the dangers inherent in women traveling alone into a wilderness such as this. We made rules for ourselves for our own protection. One of those is that we won't accept gifts or charity from any man for any reason, lest he think he has control over us or that we are beholden to him. Therefore, we will always insist on paying for any food or supplies we accept from you."

Hopefully that explanation had helped this next detail become abundantly clear to him. "Because of this, we will need to compensate you for your help as our guide and interpreter. We can pay with cash or provide a service for you."

As she spoke those last words, Riley's eyes narrowed.

"We could cook your meals, perhaps?" she continued. "If not, we wish to render payment."

He glanced at her. "Cook our meals?" More than a bit of surprise sounded in his voice, and he glanced over his shoulder at Mr. Dragoon. "We all take turns keeping camp. It's not hard to throw some meat on a rock to sizzle by the flame."

She leveled him with a look. Had he heard nothing she said? He really seemed smarter than that. "That was just a suggestion. If there's no other service we can provide you in trade, we'll insist on paying you."

He jerked at her words, and one brow raised above his scrutinizing gaze. As she replayed her comment in her mind, what he must have heard became far too clear. By *service*, he must think she meant . . .

No! Heat flooded through her.

Luckily, Rosemary wasn't too shocked and embarrassed to speak, as she was. "Upstanding services, she means. Things suitable for moral women."

Rosie's explanation only increased the pure mortification overwhelming Juniper. She pressed a hand to her face, covering her eyes.

Had she really just insinuated they would trade *that*? She could never again look Riley Turner in the eye. It took long moments of breathing in and out before she could force herself to part her fingers and see his reaction. What must he think of her? She peered his direction, keeping her hand plastered over her burning cheeks as she peeked through her fingers.

He stared straight ahead, as though he realized looking at her would worsen her embarrassment, if that were possible. But he also seemed to be fighting a grin—and mostly losing.

When he spoke, his voice definitely held a tinge of humor. "Thank you for clearing that up."

Did that mean he'd actually believed they might be women of questionable virtue? That thought sent a new flood of warmth, and the burning inside was beginning to affect her breathing. But surely not. He'd behaved too well-manneredly to think so ill of her and her sisters.

Still, if she was ever to collect the scattered pieces of her control, she had to put space between them. She tightened her reins enough to guide her mare to the other side of Rosie's. "I'll just move over here and keep quiet now."

Rosie rolled her eyes but settled into her new position between them. Juniper didn't have the nerve to look Riley's way again, and certainly not to glance behind and see what her other sisters and Mr. Dragoon thought of her faux pas.

Thankfully, Rosemary kept the conversation moving in a more businesslike direction. "What is an appropriate payment for your services as guide and interpreter, Mr. Turner?" She turned back to the man now riding immediately behind Juniper. "And for your time today, Mr. Dragoon? I'm sure our journey tomorrow won't warrant another interruption of your work. I suspect you have a great many things to see to during the rendezvous, but we thank you for your generous efforts taking us today."

"Of course, ma'am." Mr. Dragoon seemed to fully comprehend that he'd been released from any further obligation to help them.

Rosemary turned back to Riley, an expectant expression on her face.

"I suppose cooking our meals might be a fair trade," he said. "While we're in camp at least. We can pack cold provisions to take with us when we ride up to the Gros Ventre." Did Rosemary also question whether that was enough to exchange for his help? It didn't seem so, not when he was leaving his own business to see to theirs. But perhaps if they allowed him to finish his trading this afternoon, they wouldn't be imposing overmuch on his work.

She could leave that up to Rosie to decide. And since her sister didn't speak again until they reached the herd of horses where they would unsaddle and hobble their own, it sounded as though the agreement had been set.

Though the heat still flaming her neck meant it'd be easier to never face Riley Turner again, she'd have to be fully recovered and in control of herself by tomorrow morning, an hour after first light.

EIGHT

I don't think this was the best route to take."
The delicate female whisper pierced the morning
stillness that always hung over the camp when dawn
first brightened the horizon. Riley jerked his head up from
where he was nursing coals to life in their cookfire.

"Shh." Another woman's voice rose above the first, this
one a little louder than a whisper. "He'll hear us, and I'm
not eager for another scolding."

"Better a scolding from him than another offer of marriage from the men in that lodge we passed on the way to
the river. They sounded drunk. And it's not even daylight
yet." This was the first voice again, and her tone had risen
to match her sister's.

The two women stepped into sight, creeping along the
edge of the path between his lodge and the one opposite.
Miss Juniper and Miss Faith.

When the former glanced his way, she froze, grabbing
her sister's arm and halting her too.

He nodded a greeting, working hard not to let his frustration with them show. Before bidding good evening to the ladies yesterday, he'd told them he would be by at first light to escort them to a private place to take care of personal matters. It wasn't safe for them to walk through the camp without a protector. Not even in pairs, as they'd protested.

From the sound of things, their impatience had already exposed them to at least one unsuitable remark this morning. They couldn't have waited a few more minutes for him?

"Where are your sisters?" He needed to get all four women back inside where they could be shielded from the waking trappers.

Miss Faith nodded toward their lodge. "Cooking. We've been down at the river doing laundry." She hoisted a bundle he hadn't seen in the murky dawn light. Miss Juniper carried a second load, though it nearly hid behind her skirts.

He stood and strode toward them. "I'll carry those back to your lodge."

None of them spoke as he walked behind the two women. Even the dim morning light didn't stop his wayward gaze from noticing the way their skirts swished with each step they took. Miss Juniper's, especially, had an almost mesmerizing rhythm. He was doing his best not to let his focus rise higher than their hemlines, but many of the other men wouldn't work so hard.

They'd nearly reached the women's lodge when a voice called from a few huts down. "Morning, gals. It's been a month of Sundays since I've smelled anything as good as what's coming from that teepee. You have room for one more? I'll even bring a good rump roast for you to cook up."

Riley shot the man a hard look. "Fry your own roast, Caldwell. Leave these ladies alone."

"Who made you their keeper, Turner?" Caldwell grumbled a few more remarks, his voice just barely audible. Probably not things the ladies should hear.

The man was usually friendly enough. They'd trapped together in MacArthur's outfit a couple winters back. But the presence of women tended to make men do things they wouldn't otherwise. Exactly why Riley had to stick close to these four.

When they reached the ladies' lodge, Miss Faith pulled the door flap aside. "Mr. Turner carried our clothes—"

A screech from inside broke off her exuberant words.

He tensed, backing away from the opening. The women must not be prepared for a male caller.

But the words erupting from within were more panic than surprise.

"No! What are you—"

"Get him!"

In front of him, Juniper peered over Faith's shoulder, pulling the door flap a little wider. But then she squealed and scrambled to close the opening. Before she could press the partition shut, a furry blur shot past Faith's skirts.

"Stop him! Boots, come back." The cry from within was Lorelei's voice, carrying an all-too-familiar ring. Hadn't they just chased down that animal two days ago?

Riley spun to see where the troublesome coyote pup ran. It darted toward the hides stretched in front of his own cook fire. Juniper was already sprinting that direction, with Lorelei stumbling after her. He dropped the bundles of laundry and ran after them.

He'd been saying for two days now that coyote needed to be set loose, and clearly the animal agreed with him.

Now he just had to convince these sisters not to chase it all through camp.

His long legs caught up with the sisters by the time they reached the hides. "Let it go." He hissed the words as he tried to reach out for Juniper. "It needs to be free. You'll cause trouble chasing it through camp."

Both women ignored him as Lorelei darted between the frames and Juniper circled around them.

"Here. He's almost cornered." Lorelei's voice called from among the furs. "June, come up on the right."

Riley fought down his frustration as he followed after Juniper.

"I'll get him if he comes this way." That was a man's voice. Dragoon, it sounded like.

Riley breathed out his ire and tried to moderate his tone. "He's better off if you let him go. Wild animals aren't meant to be pets."

Finally, Juniper glanced back at him, acknowledging his comment with a nod. But the pleading in her eyes made him regret his sour tone. "Lorelei needs him. If you don't want to help catch him, at least don't scare him away."

Her words, the urging in her voice, made him feel like a cad. Certainly not a help to them. Just as crotchety as all these other trappers. He was right about the coyote, but that didn't mean he had to make the situation harder.

Juniper had already turned back to help her sister, and he quieted his steps as he followed her. When he rounded the last stretched hide, the coyote pup came clear, huddled against their woodpile. Lorelei knelt low, her hand outstretched toward the tiny thing. Dragoon crouched beside their campfire, arms splayed, looking every bit the frightening mountain man he could be. Juniper stood a little ways back, her presence keeping the animal from turning her direction, but not nearly as daunting as his brawny lodgemate.

"Here, little fellow." Lorelei was murmuring in a sweet tone, her hand outstretched with something resting on her fingertips. Meat, perhaps? Where had she found it? "Come, Boots. It's time to eat. Let's get you back to the lodge where you'll be safe."

The pup really was tiny, no longer than Riley's hand from nose to hind end. It wouldn't survive in the wilderness alone, no doubt on that score. In fact, it didn't look old enough to eat the meat she held out to it.

But the smell must be too tantalizing, for its posture changed from a crouch to an interested stretch. As Lorelei continued to murmur, the pup took one step forward, then a second. Finally, it closed the remaining distance and took the nugget from her fingers. As it worked to chew the bit, Lorelei stroked its neck, then ran a hand down its back, scooping up the pup with an easy motion.

Riley eased out a long breath, and they all straightened. Lorelei gave them all a weak smile. "Thank you for helping." She glanced from him to Dragoon. "We have a warm meal ready for you if you'd like to come for it."

"Yes, ma'am." Dragoon rubbed his hands together as though he'd not eaten freshly cooked fare in months. "We'll walk there with you."

Riley could retrieve the food easily enough by himself, but if Dragoon wanted to come along, it wouldn't hurt anything. It was unusual for the man to be up this early. Perhaps their female neighbors were a good influence on him.

76

Something else was different about the man today too. It wasn't until they were both walking back from the women's lodge, hands full of meat and biscuits, that he realized what it was. Dragoon had trimmed his beard. Instead of long scraggly ends, he'd cropped them close to his face with even lines. That must've taken quite a while with a sharp knife.

Perhaps he shouldn't say anything, but so much effort begged to be commented on. He sent his friend a grin. "Looks like you went to see the barber yesterday. Does that mean you're planning to go a'courting? I think they're a bit too young for you." The youngest, Miss Faith, couldn't be more than fifteen or sixteen.

The man's cheeks turned ruddy, and he kept his eyes focused ahead. "Naw, they're too fine for a mountain man like me. It's just that riding beside those civilized ladies yesterday showed me how much I've let myself slip."

That wasn't a point Riley could argue with, so he just nodded. At least he could trust Dragoon to be decent around the women and not pay them improper attention.

As they reached their campfire, Dragoon glanced his way. "You sure you don't need me to ride with you up to the Gros Ventre camp?"

Riley shook his head. Rosemary had made that point clear. "I think we'll be fine. They all carry rifles and say they can shoot them. Likely one more gun wouldn't make a difference."

Dragoon laid his food on one of the logs they used as a table. "I'll walk out with you to saddle the horses when you're ready to leave. Thought I'd run my Bessie a bit, get her ready for the race later this afternoon."

Riley held his tongue. The man had been racing his little

bay mare at every rendezvous since they'd known each other, and though the mare could run well, they'd not won a race yet. He had a feeling the horse might be fast enough to win, but Dragoon was not a small man. He'd never figured out a kind way to tell him that might be the problem.

Dragoon studied him, a faraway look in his eyes. What was he considering? "I wonder . . ." He tapped his thumb on the side of his pointer finger the way he did when he was contemplating something. "That gal who has the coyote pup. She seems to like animals an awful lot. I'll bet Bessie would run for her. She'd weigh a good bit less than I do. Think she'd ride for me? I'd give her a share of the winnings."

Riley shook his head hard. "Have you jostled your brain? There's no way I'd let her get in the middle of all those men drinking and betting. Not to mention the danger in the race itself. Don't you remember that boy who got trampled last year?" Maybe Dragoon wasn't as harmless as Riley had given him credit for being.

The man gave his head a shake, as though trying to bring some sense back. "You're right. Don't know what I was thinking."

"I'd say you're on the right track with finding someone small and lightweight to ride her. But not Miss Lorelei."

Dragoon started to enter the lodge. "I'll give it some thought." Then he turned back. "Did you hear another horse was stolen last night?"

Riley startled. "Whose? When?" Why couldn't men just be decent and stop coveting things that didn't belong to them? It seemed more horses had already gone missing at this rendezvous than the others he'd been to.

"Jurgen Sanderson's Indian pony. The one with the spots

on its rump that ran so well in its first race. It came up missing last night after you'd already bedded down, I think. Surprised you didn't hear the ruckus he raised. Swore he'd search out and cut down the scoundrel who took it."

Riley shook his head. "Good luck to him. With so many people here, finding the animal will be nigh on impossible."

"Don't I know it." Dragoon turned back to the lodge. "Yell out when you're ready to go saddle up and I'll walk with you. Better to have two of us to protect those women around these uncivilized varmints."

Riley moved to his pack and tried to focus on what else they would need for the day's travel. Dragoon was right that it might take more than him to protect the sisters. It seemed danger came even from the directions he least expected.

NINE

Juniper watched Riley from the edge of her vision as he glanced backward again. What was he looking for? He'd been doing that for at least the last hour, maybe longer. She'd forgotten to pin on her watch that morning, so she had no accurate notion of time.

They must be getting close to the Gros Ventre camp by now. They'd already passed one native village. Snake Indians, Riley had called them.

"Do you think it's on the other side of that hill?" Faith was the only one among them who had the nerve to ask how much farther they would have to ride, though thankfully this was only the third time she'd formed some version of the question.

Riley eyed the hill, as though searching for sign of what might lie beyond it. "Maybe. I haven't been to the camp yet. We'll see soon enough."

By the time they'd ridden partway up the slope, Riley had peered over his shoulder twice more.

She could no longer hold her tongue. "What are you looking for back there?"

He hesitated, like he was debating whether he should tell her the truth. Perhaps she could make answering easier for him. "Is someone following us?"

His gaze flicked her way, then focused forward again. "I'm not sure. Maybe."

So that was a yes. Only he didn't want to frighten her. Hopefully soon he would realize he needn't worry about their sensibilities. They had to know the way things really stood in order to make wise decisions. "Do you think it's an Indian?"

He glanced over his shoulder, barely turning his head. "They're usually better at staying hidden."

"Why would a white man follow us?" For that matter, the question had little to do with skin color. Why would *anyone* pursue them?

Riley huffed out a frustrated sound. "The same reason I asked you not to leave your lodge unless I'm with you. These fellows haven't seen a woman from the States in years, most of them. Some will do anything to . . ."

He didn't have to finish his statement for her to understand his meaning. But would men follow them this far out of camp when they had an escort? She looked over at Rosemary to see if his comment surprised her too. Rosie's mouth had formed a grim line.

She was saved a response as they climbed the crest of the hill and the valley stretched out below them. Lodges much like the one they were staying in formed a circle in the distance, with the Green River running along one side. Horses milled about on the grassland closest to the river.

"Is that it?" Faith's chipper voice broke the quiet as their horses began to maneuver the downhill grade.

"Looks like it." Riley showed a remarkable amount of patience with her little sister's many questions.

Rosemary frowned at the cluster ahead. "Are the lodges in a circle for protection?"

"Sort of. They bring the horses into the middle at night so they aren't stolen by other tribes or attacked by wild animals."

Juniper jerked her attention to Riley. "The Gros Ventre don't get along well with others?"

Riley shrugged. "Stealing horses is common among most tribes. It's kind of a pastime for many of the braves. Plus a way to grow their herds."

"They won't try to take ours, will they?"

As they reached level ground, several men stepped from the circle of lodges and stood waiting for them. Unease prickled in her middle. The Peigan camp had been mostly women, but that wouldn't be the case here.

As they rode closer, the features of the four men waiting for them became clearer as well as the numerous heads watching from just inside the circle of lodges.

Riley spoke in a low voice, his tone urgent. "The men might wish to speak with me alone. If they separate us, just do as they say. Be careful not to offend anyone."

Separate them? She glanced at Rosemary on her other side. How would she and her sisters know what to do without Riley to interpret?

Rosie gave her the slightest of nods, but it was firm enough to speak clearly. The four of them would stay together. Even if Riley was taken from them, she could rely on her sisters.

Juniper took in a slow breath, then eased it out.

They halted several paces from the men who'd come out to meet them. Riley made a sweeping motion toward the natives, maybe the same he'd done at the Peigan camp. "Hello."

The man in the center of the three men spoke several sounds and returned the same wide gesture.

"Do you speak the white man's tongue?" Riley accompanied the words with another series of hand movements. This must be the hand talk he'd spoken of that the tribes understood. She tried to catch some of the signs, but he moved too swiftly.

The speaker of the group answered with a word and a simple rocking of his fingers. Since he wasn't speaking English, was that a no to Riley's question?

Riley pressed on, talking slowly as he accompanied the words with gestures. "I am Riley. These women are looking for a friend. A Peigan woman named Steps Right. We have heard there is one from that tribe among you."

The man responded with a long string of sounds, though not as much as Riley had spoken. She looked from the elder to Riley, but neither face revealed what was being said.

When the brave finished, Riley dropped his voice to just loud enough for the four of them to hear. "He is inviting me in to smoke with him. You can try to accompany me, but I think his women will take charge of you."

"Did he answer about Steps Right?" Rosemary kept her voice low like his.

He shook his head as he dismounted. "Not yet. It's considered poor manners to speak business before he offers hospitality."

The unease that had prickled before now clutched Juniper's

throat as she and her sisters slipped from their mounts to the ground. "What do we do with the horses?"

Riley pointed to two lads standing to the side. "They'll water and care for them."

"Do we take our rifles?" Behind them, Lorelei already had her hand on the wooden stock poking up from her scabbard.

"No." Riley spoke a bit too loudly, and the urgency in his tone couldn't be missed.

But was it wise to send their horses and guns off in the hands of these Gros Ventre? If stealing was a pastime, it seemed the height of foolishness to hand over something so important.

Perhaps Riley guessed her thoughts, for he turned to them and spoke quietly again. "They'll return them safely. It's a matter of honor toward guests. As long as we don't do anything to anger them."

He handed his reins to one of the boys, who looked to be around ten years old. She and her sisters did the same, then they followed in pairs behind Riley as he approached the men.

The one who'd been speaking wore more decoration than the other two men, with feathers tied into both braids and several bronze-colored earrings in both ears. All three wore the buckskin tunic and leggings that seemed standard for most of the natives and trappers, but the first man also had beadwork ornamenting his shirt.

The man turned and walked through a narrow space between two lodges, and Riley followed him. Juniper stayed close behind, with Faith at her side. In possibly dangerous situations, she and Rosie each tried to stay close to one of the younger ones. Lorelei and Rosemary nearly tripped on their heels as the other two men fell into step at the rear.

As soon as they entered the circle of teepees, two women approached. They seemed to be walking toward Juniper specifically. When one of them touched her arm, she stopped, though Riley continued on, walking behind the men. He threw a look over his shoulder, but she didn't have time to read his expression.

The woman spoke in her own tongue, casting her glance at all four sisters and motioning to the side. Her words couldn't be deciphered, but she appeared to be directing them to follow her.

Juniper looked to Rosemary for guidance. The woman didn't seem angry or inhospitable, but Juniper didn't dare make this decision on her own.

Rosie gave the slightest of nods, then shifted to gain the woman's attention. Their host looked to her with a dip of her chin, then pointed to the side as she had before. Rosie returned the nod and took a small step forward. The woman waved them behind her as she began walking toward one of the lodges.

The four of them followed her, then two other women moved in beside them. Neither looked young, though one had more gray streaked through her hair than the other. Juniper did her best not to stare at the people, instead using her gaze to take in their surroundings. About ten lodges, some larger than the others. That made sense. Bigger families would need more space.

The woman led her into one of the lodges, and after Juniper ducked inside, she had to blink to adjust her eyes to the dim lighting.

A cook fire burned in the middle, certainly not necessary for heat with the sun so bright outside. Around the outer edge of the lodge sat various stacks of furs. Their host pointed to a section, then pressed her hands down as she spoke. She seemed to want them to sit.

Juniper led the way to that spot and began to ease down, watching the woman as she did for signs whether she was doing the right thing or not.

Their host smiled and nodded, then pointed for Faith, Lorelei, and Rosie to do the same. The other two women who had walked with them busied themselves by the fire.

Their host brought Juniper a bowl filled with what looked like water. It also smelled like water. The woman stood before her, smiling and gesturing.

Juniper smiled back, then took a sip. Yes, it tasted like water. The woman nodded again, pointing toward the bowl once more. Juniper took two more drinks as the liquid cooled her parched throat.

The woman stepped back, though she still stood before Juniper. When Juniper lowered the bowl, their host motioned toward Faith, then down the line.

Juniper nodded and handed the bowl to her youngest sister. She smiled again at their host. "Thank you." She had no reason to believe she'd just been poisoned, not if she went solely by the grace these people had shown since they'd arrived at their village. This woman had been kind enough to offer hospitality to strangers who'd appeared on her doorstep. And she'd offered it with a smile and a willing hand.

Their hostess turned to speak to the two women by the fire, and the younger of them rose and carried a platter

MISTY M. BELLER

toward Juniper. The woman didn't meet her eyes but dipped her head with a shy smile as she held out her load for Juniper to see. Four round cakes sat atop a plate that looked like it was made from bark or some other kind of rough wood. The woman extended it closer to Juniper and murmured something she couldn't understand.

Juniper took one of the pieces. "Thank you."

As the woman moved to Faith, Juniper lifted the cake near her nose. It smelled sweet, maybe like berries. She took a small bite.

There was a crust on the outside, protecting a warm, soft inside. The sweet aroma was definitely berries, and perhaps some kind of vegetable or root. Though it tasted like nothing she'd ever eaten, it was actually quite good. "Mmm. Very tasty." She said that more for her sisters than their hosts. These native women likely couldn't understand her.

Faith gave her a dubious look but bit into her own cake. Her brows rose, and she nodded. "It *is* good."

Juniper glanced at their main host, the one who'd led them in here, and caught the woman smiling at Faith's response. Good thing her sister liked the cake. Faith didn't always school her expression. If the food had tasted foul, her reaction might well have put them in danger. Or at least, displeased their hosts.

As they ate, new women came and went from the lodge, some casting quick glances at Juniper and her sisters as they spoke with the women by the fire. Others were more obvious in their perusal, staring mostly at her. Was it her blue eyes that drew so much attention?

A few looked like they were speaking to her. She couldn't say for sure, though, for one of their hosts always answered in the same tongue. It would be nice to have Riley here to interpret.

What was he doing now with the men? If only she and her sisters could be there with him, to hear what these people said about Steps Right. Was she one of these women even?

The thought should have occurred to Juniper earlier. As she studied each of the five faces currently in the lodge, all looked to be over forty years, except the one who had just entered. She appeared young, barely a woman. Perhaps Faith's age.

She studied them with as much curiosity as the others had, her focus roaming over Juniper first, then down the line to Rosemary, finally swinging back to Juniper. She murmured something to the other women and received a matter-of-fact reply. Then the newcomer stepped toward Juniper. She stopped an arm's length away and smiled. The expression brightened her face, and Juniper returned the smile.

The girl spoke to her, a slew of sounds that dipped low then rose high in quick succession. No clue of what she said, though. How should Juniper respond?

She smiled wider and managed a simple "Hello." Should they introduce themselves? The girl didn't seem to be doing that herself.

Then her gaze shifted to Juniper's hair, and her attention fixed there. She raised a hand as though to touch. But her fingers paused halfway.

Juniper took in a breath. Did she dare allow these people to touch her hair? If she offered the chance to this woman, the others might want to as well. As long as they only stroked

... If they didn't pull, what harm could it do? And allowing the liberty might endear her to them.

Moving carefully so she didn't startle the girl, Juniper reached up and pulled her braid around to the front of her shoulder, then held out the loose hairs at the tip for her to touch.

The girl's eyes sparkled, her full cheeks spreading in a smile. She fingered the ends of Juniper's hair, then moved upward to stroke the lower half of her braid.

After several seconds of this, the girl pulled her hands back and reached for one of her own braids, pulling it over her right shoulder and holding it out for Juniper to touch. The glossy black strands were secured with a leather strap, which was threaded with beads of several different colors and sizes. Another string of beads, entirely blue, dangled from that tie.

Blue beads. Like those of the necklace tucked in Rosemary's saddle pack, the one they were bringing back to Steps Right. These beads here looked different than the ones they had, a lighter blue and not as clear, but still. The fact that they were a solid string of blue ... did that matter?

This girl couldn't be old enough to be Steps Right. Could she be a daughter or granddaughter of the woman?

She was still holding out her braid, so Juniper reached and stroked the end. Soft, just as the glossy strands appeared. She let her fingers trail down to the string of blue beads and pause there. She sent another smile to the girl. "Pretty."

The young woman smiled and nodded, almost like she understood.

Juniper pulled her hand away, and the girl edged back.

That appeared to be a cue for the other women, and they swarmed forward, surrounding and moving in front of her.

Juniper held her braid up, and hands reached from all directions to touch it, sometimes pushing another away as the women clambered closer.

Most stroked her braid, but a few wove fingers through the hair closer to her head, mussing what she'd carefully secured that morning. The women's happy chattering filled the lodge. If this was what it took to earn their friendship, or at least their good opinion, it was a small price to pay.

After what felt like hours, a clap from the lodge door rose above the voices, and all turned to face their host, who stood framed in the opening. At her words, the women backed away, retreating to the other side of the fire. She motioned to Juniper, then again to the rest of her sisters. Perhaps the men were finally finished and Riley had sent for them.

Juniper gripped Faith's hand and stood, pulling her sister beside her as she checked to make sure Lorelei and Rosie came too. The woman in charge turned and stepped out of the lodge, then paused for them to follow her.

Juniper blinked in the brightness of the sunlight, then squinted across the courtyard to where the woman was taking them.

Riley stood beside two men at the place they'd entered the circle of lodges. He was watching their approach, but from this distance his expression was hard to read. Part of her was more than a little relieved to see him. To know that they'd survived and would soon be back together. But in truth, though this had been an adventure she would never forget, the women had been kind and quite hospitable.

Her attention snagged on a figure tucked behind the men

with Riley. The young woman who'd first approached and touched Juniper's hair. Why was she there with the men, standing so quietly?

When they reached Riley and their hostess backed away, his mouth held a twist of amusement. "Are you ready to go?" He glanced around at all four of them but came back to Juniper, as though he was speaking mostly to her. How had she suddenly become the leader in their group of sisters? This was Rosie's place, but the Gros Ventre woman and now Riley all seemed to look for her to speak for them.

She met his gaze, searching for any details he might share about Steps Right. "Did you learn anything?"

His tone dropped a little. "Not much. I'll tell you what they said when we're riding again."

He turned to the two men and spoke as he signed. "Thank you for sharing your campfire."

The other men answered with a few sounds and hand gestures.

Riley nodded, then turned toward the opening between the lodges as he waved for her and her sisters to follow. She sent a farewell smile to their host and the women who had gathered behind her, then moved in behind Riley.

She could only pray he'd learned something useful, for she had a feeling not every visit to an Indian camp would be so friendly as this one.

TEN

When Juniper and her sisters followed Riley outside of the circle of lodges, their horses were waiting there with the two lads, just as they'd left them. After they'd reclaimed their mounts and swung up into their saddles, Riley turned back the way they'd come.

She nudged her mare up alongside his horse, and Rosie came up on her other side. Rosie spoke before Juniper had a chance to. "What did they say?"

Riley kept his voice low, but loud enough the four of them could hear. "I met the Peigan woman who lives with them. She's young, too young to be Steps Right. She thinks she's eighteen winters old but isn't certain because she was captured from the Peigan eight winters ago and has been raised as Gros Ventre since then."

Disappointment pressed in her chest. An image of the young woman who'd touched her hair slipped in. Those blue beads . . .

She studied Riley. "You met her? What did she look like?"

He shrugged. "Like a young woman from one of these

tribes. She wore the same kind of dress the others did. Long black hair in braids."

Leave it to a man not to notice any details. "Two braids? Or one?"

He frowned. "Two, I think. Why?"

"Did she have any ornament on the tie that held her braids? Like feathers or beads?" Perhaps it didn't matter if the young Peigan woman was the one with the blue beads. Perhaps there was nothing significant about the color among that tribe. But it was the only possible connection so far.

"I . . ." Riley dragged out the word like he was searching his memory for images. ". . . think she had beads." He turned to face her. "Now will you tell me why it matters? Did you meet her? Did the women tell you anything?"

"Maybe it doesn't matter. We met lots of women, though none of them spoke English, so we couldn't communicate at all. But one girl about eighteen years old was bolder than the rest. She had a strand of blue beads hanging from one of her braids." She caught herself in time to keep from commenting about them being the same color as the strand they were returning to Steps Right. They weren't telling anyone about the necklace so they didn't risk it being stolen.

Riley nodded. "That was probably her. She was standing behind the chief when we left?"

"She's the one." Maybe she could ask about the beads as a casual question. "Are those beads special to the Peigan? Blue ones, I mean. Or beads in general, I suppose. I didn't see the Gros Ventre women wearing them." Though she hadn't really been looking for beads on the others. That blue strand had simply stood out.

He shook his head. "Women from all the tribes love

beads. And for some reason, the blue ones in particular. It's not specific to the Peigan. I don't know why the other women weren't wearing any. Maybe these people don't do much trading with whites, or maybe they simply didn't want to reveal them while you were visiting."

Their horses were climbing the hill now, and she leaned forward to help her mare balance on the slope.

Riley did the same, and when he finally sat up, he cleared his throat. "Anyway, the men told me something else that might be worth pursuing. They said there's a small band of Peigan camped a few hours north of here, on the other side of a Crow village."

"Then why are we riding south?" Frustration laced Rosie's tone.

Riley shot her a look, but he kept his voice measured. "I thought it best we follow our trail until we get over this hill, then we can circle around and ride north if we choose to."

That made sense, but Rosie still seemed of a mind to argue. "Why wouldn't we choose to? It took us a half day to reach this point. We should push on now instead of wasting a full day of travel going back to the rendezvous camp."

Riley raised his brows at her. "I'm willing to ride north now if that's what you wish, but I wanted to give you the choice of going back to the main camp before dark. I'm sure tongues will wag if you're gone with me overnight. I've been removed from civilization for a while, but I've not forgotten a woman's reputation is important." He spoke that last bit with a hint of censure in his tone.

Rosie waved the words away. "You think tongues didn't start wagging the moment we were spotted with the supply wagons? I'm not worried about what a bunch of hairy-faced trappers think. As long as you know how to keep an appropriate distance"—she pinned him with a look—"we'd rather make efficient use of every day."

Riley started to nod, but Rosie appeared not quite finished. "But you can be warned, Riley Turner. If you so much as touch one of my sisters, your life will end that very hour. I give you my word."

His brows rose again. He took a moment to speak, hopefully weighing his answer. Rosie wouldn't look the other way if he said the wrong thing now. "I understand, Miss Collins. I've no intention of touching any of you, as you say. I'm here to be your guide and protect you. I give *you* my word." That last bit was an exact copy of Rosie's comment, and it looked almost as if his mouth played with a smile as he said it. Thankfully, it was not enough to rile her sister.

Rosemary nodded. "Make sure it stays that way."

Their group stretched out single file as they turned eastward to ride on the opposite side of the hills that bordered the path of the Green River. Riley led, of course, with Juniper behind him, then Lorelei, Faith, and Rosemary bringing up the rear. It seemed she was always being positioned nearest Riley. His presence had begun to feel comfortable, no longer unsettling. Though she was still far too aware of him.

They crested the rocky peak and began to descend the other side. This wasn't a tall mountain, not like those in the distance on the other side of the Green River, but the sharp stones and boulders scattered over its side required the horses to pick their way. The slope didn't extend all the way down to a valley. Partway down it rose again into another small mountain. Riley turned them north before they reached the joining, and they wove between boulders along the trail.

None of them spoke as they rode, and the sounds of nature seeped in around them. Constant wind mussed Juniper's hair even more than the women's hands had back in the Gros Ventre lodge. Somewhere above them, the cry of a bird rose over the breeze. This place was so untouched by human hands, as though they were the very first to travel here. Every deep breath she took in filled her lungs, renewing her with its freshness, refueling her vigor.

The sound of running water rose above the wind, and she studied the land ahead of them. Water trickled down the mountainside on their left, a pretty little waterfall that collected in a dip of the rock so the horses could drink.

As they moved on, the path curved around the side of the mountain. Soon, a narrow valley stretched ahead of them. A bit of scraggly grass rose over the mostly flat land, and a small stream ran down the center.

Riley slowed his horse as he studied the ground ahead. The grass was short here, like it had been grazed very recently. Hoofprints had churned up mud in some places.

"What are you looking at?" Juniper asked.

"Horses have been here. A lot of them."

Rosemary was frowning at the ground too. "Horses? I thought it might be buffalo. Are they mounts from people coming for the rendezvous, do you think?"

Riley shook his head. "We're too far away from the main camp for it to be trappers' animals. And this is more than a group passing through. Horses were kept here for a while." He lifted his gaze across the length of the valley, maybe the distance of a city square before the mountains came together to close off the flatland. "This would be a good area to camp. The horses wouldn't be likely to leave this valley as long as there was grass and water. But I don't see outlines of lodges like a group stayed here."

"So you think horses were kept here, but the people lived elsewhere?" Rosie studied him.

Riley seemed to think through his answer before responding. "That's what it looks like."

Juniper glanced around the valley once more. "Do you think it has anything to do with our search? Is this unusual?" She couldn't imagine how that might help them find Steps Right, but Riley knew so much more about this land and its curious people.

He shrugged. "It's strange that horses wouldn't be kept right there with the lodges, especially with so many tribes around for the rendezvous. I don't suppose it matters to us though." Still, his tone sounded like it *did* matter. He was working so hard to piece together what these tracks meant.

As they continued riding, she tried to imagine possible scenarios. "Perhaps a group moved their horses here for better grazing, but the people had so many lodges they didn't want to move the entire village. Especially if the horses might eat all the grass here within a few days."

"Perhaps." But Riley's tone sounded more patronizing than seriously considering the scenario. After another minute, he shook his head, as though trying to clear his thoughts. "It doesn't really matter anyway. The tracks look at least a week old."

He seemed to be trying to put the questions behind them, for he turned to her with something like a forced smile. "So, your sister mentioned growing up on a horse ranch. Is that where you all live? Outside of Richmond?"

She shook her head. "Our land was several hours' ride from the city. When our mother died a few years ago, our father sold the business and moved us to town." She glanced behind to where Lorelei rode beside Faith and Rosie brought up the rear. She didn't think the others would mind her telling Riley this next part. "We, um, plan to start the ranch back up when we return to Virginia."

He shot a look at her. "You're going to buy your father's ranch back?"

If only. "That land has been turned into a silver mine. But one of our old neighbors is selling his farm. We have enough in our inheritance to buy it back." Now she really was giving too many details. One simply didn't speak of finances, not to a man they'd met only days before. Though it felt like she'd known Riley for years. Like she could tell him anything and he would look at her with that curious half-smile. The look that seemed to say he found her fascinating.

Her. The middle child in a family of girls. Papa had never made them feel like he'd rather have had a son than four daughters, but it only made sense that a male child would have been much more useful to him on the ranch.

The weight of Riley's gaze kept her from following that trail in her mind. She glanced at him, her brows raised.

One corner of his mouth tipped. "I was just thinking how it must be nice to have sisters to go into business with. You four seem pretty devoted to one another." The faintest hint of sadness laced his voice. He'd not spoken of any siblings the other day. "I'm surprised none of you have married yet.

Now I suppose it makes sense. Do you plan to be business-women instead of wives?"

She stiffened her spine. But his tone hadn't seemed condescending. Just . . . curious. Still. "Who said we couldn't do both?" She tipped her chin up and gave him another lifted-brow look. "If any of us chooses to marry, that husband is welcome to join us on the ranch."

Riley shook his head and grinned as he shifted his focus forward again. "As long as you have your priorities straight." But as the mirth slipped from his face, he spoke again. Softer this time, almost as though thinking aloud. "I do envy you a bit. Being as close as you all are. You don't often see siblings stick together the way you do."

A longing slipped through her. A need to tell him why her sisters mattered so much to her. Were the details too intimate? Did he really care to know their story? She inhaled a breath, then released it. "I suppose nearly losing one another will do that."

He didn't press her to tell more, but once again, the weight of his gaze sank over her.

She kept her focus on the grass and rock-strewn ground in front of them. "When Rosemary was ten, she took sick with an illness that left her weak and coughing all the time. Whenever she left her bed, she had trouble breathing, even just to walk down the stairs. Our local physic said the only way she would recover was if she went to this little town by the coast and took special treatments. If she didn't go, her lungs would continue to shrink until she wouldn't be able to breathe at all."

Her own chest constricted with the memories. That had been so long ago, and Rosie was healthy now. But she'd never forget the awfulness of thinking she'd lose her sister. Her best friend. Watching her struggle for every tiny bit of air was hard enough, but imagining Rosie dying that way . . .

Riley still didn't speak, but his full attention rested on her. She eased out a quiet exhale. "Mama took her for the treatments, and they were gone for about three months." Three months and four days, actually. She worked for something as close to a grin as she could muster. "I received a taste of what it was like to be the oldest, taking care of Lorelei and Faith while they were gone. Papa was there too, of course, but he still had his work on the ranch. And we had a woman who brought meals." But it had mostly been her and the younger girls, with her doing her best to entertain them and keep them from worrying as much as she did. Keep them from knowing there was a real chance that Rosemary might never return.

It was only when the wagon rolled into their yard with her older sister on the seat, looking far more like the old Rosie than she had since the sickness, that Juniper finally took her first full breath in months. And that was the moment she'd committed that she and her sisters would be a team. Whatever any of them needed, she would be there to give.

And now, they needed to return to ranch life. All four of them working together. Selling the land and moving to Richmond had been a mistake—one that stole their father from them. But now they could right their course.

"So I assume the treatments worked?" Riley's voice tugged her back to the present.

She nodded, the smile coming a little easier this time.

"I think her lungs are even stronger now than before she took sick."

He nodded. "Good."

Then, as if he realized she needed a change of topic, he raised his voice and motioned ahead of them. "We'll keep an eye out for the Crow camp over that rise and go around it if we can."

He'd spoken loud enough for Rosie to hear from the back of the line, and she called up to them, "Should we stop there and ask if they know Steps Right?"

He frowned. "I'd rather go to the Peigan camp first, since there's a better chance we'll find her there."

Her older sister nudged her mare forward and rode up alongside Juniper's mount. "Are the Crow dangerous?"

Riley's mouth pressed before he answered, and he kept his focus on the path ahead. "There's always that possibility when meeting with people of a different background and customs. I try to take the measure of each person individually instead of labeling an entire tribe as dangerous. There's good and bad in every village." Finally, he turned to look at Rosemary. "But I also have to take you on the safest path I know. It's more likely we'll find the woman we're searching for with the Peigan, so I'd rather not add a layer of possible trouble unless we need to. After all, this isn't a cultural sightseeing trip, is it?"

Juniper barely held in a snort. And a side glance at Rosemary showed she was also trying to contain a smile, though she was doing a much better job at it. This land and the complexities of the different tribes was proving much harder than she'd anticipated—not to mention all those trappers back at the main camp.

Yet as her mare climbed the slope of the next mountain and they rose higher and higher toward the wide blue expanse of the sky, she couldn't possibly regret coming to this place. Too bad she hadn't brought her paints to try to capture this view. Only one sketching journal and a pencil had fit in her saddle pack. But at least she could savor the scene now and try to re-create it later.

But as she breathed in the freshness of the air and let her gaze seek out the blending of shadows that cast such different colors on the land around them, her mind kept slipping to the man riding beside her.

One thing was for certain. They had much to thank God for in sending Riley to help.

ELEVEN

Riley left his horse with the women as he climbed on foot to the top of the slope to see if the Peigan village lay on the other side. They'd passed the Crow camp an hour ago, but something still had him uneasy. All those horses that had been grazed in that valley . . .

They weren't the Crows' animals. They'd had their horses grazing along the banks of the Green River near their lodges, as he'd expected. And the Crow village was small enough that they only had twenty or so mounts. From what the Gros Ventre chief had said, the Peigan camp they were riding to was even smaller.

But that valley had grazed a huge herd. There was no way he could say for sure, but he'd guess upward of fifty head. Who did they belong to?

Distant sounds of voices reached him even before he peeked over the top of this low mountain. Six lodges were nestled in the flatland alongside the river below. This had to be the people they'd come to see. Dusk had already begun to settle, which meant entering the camp would likely mean a long, drawn-out meal, and they'd be offered a place to sleep. Although with so few lodges, they'd be packed in closely with their hosts.

It would be wiser to camp out here and enter the village in the morning. The Collins sisters would see that wisdom, no matter how much they wanted to push forward. He eased backward, then turned and maneuvered down the slope to the women.

The sisters looked at him expectantly as he reached them and took his reins from Juniper. "That's where they are, six lodges by the river. It's going to be dark soon. Unless you'd like to spend the night in a Peigan camp, we should lay out our blankets in that flat spot down the slope and wait to go talk to them in the morning." He looked to the oldest Miss Collins for an answer. She was the one who seemed to take charge of most decisions like this. She was also the one pushing for them to move as quickly as possible.

As usual, she met his recommendation head-on. "You think it's likely Steps Right will be there?" Normally, she always seemed to be taking his measure, but this time something like hope brightened her expression.

He had to be honest. "It's hard to say. But if they're friendly, they'll want us to stay and eat well into the night. Then they'll insist on putting us up on their best buffalo hide couches while they sleep on the dirt."

Miss Lorelei's eyes widened a bit, and she tucked her coyote a little closer to her side. Miss Faith looked almost eager. Perhaps a bit too eager. She might have come to this country hoping for adventure, but she'd better be careful, or she'd find far more than she bargained for.

His attention swung to Juniper, as it so often did. She was different from her sisters. Certainly not innocent and naïve like the younger two. Well, naïve, yes, but she seemed to have a maturity about her. And she wasn't as suspicious and hard-driving as her older sister.

She was studying him now, maybe looking for his reaction. Or maybe thinking about something totally different. Who was he to think he knew the mind of a woman?

"How early can we visit their camp in the morning?" The older Miss Collins tugged his focus toward her. "Will it offend them or break some unspoken etiquette if we go a little after dawn?"

He raised his brows at her. "Would you drop in on a perfect stranger a little after dawn back in Richmond?"

She looked the tiniest bit embarrassed. Maybe she would realize how hard she was pushing.

"No, but people here don't take their morning meal in bed very often, I'm assuming." Her expression finally softened. "I don't want us to misstep and insult them. But I also don't want to waste any time, and we have a long ride back tomorrow. What do you think is the best course of action?"

Well, miracles truly did happen. He did his best not to let on how good it felt to finally hear her ask for his opinion instead of arguing each step of the way. "I think we should camp in that flat spot I mentioned. We have enough food we can eat cold so we don't have to build a fire and alert them of our presence. Then in the morning, we'll wait until enough mist wears off that they can see us coming. That way they won't think we're aiming to surprise them."

Miss Collins took her time thinking through his recommendation, then nodded. "All right." She turned and started walking down the slope. "Let's go clear the rocks, girls. And keep quiet. No giggling, Faith. And whatever it takes,

Lorelei, keep hold of that pup. The last thing we need is another cross-country chase."

The two younger girls led their horses after her, and Juniper waited to fall into step behind them. He caught her gaze as she stood there. She had her lower lip tucked between her teeth, the sparkle in her eyes showing she was trying not to smile. Did she realize how challenging her sister could be? She must.

He moved in closer to walk beside her, then spoke in a voice only loud enough for her to hear over the horses' hooves. "She would have made an excellent cavalry officer."

A smile spread across her face, lighting every pretty feature. "Only if they made her general."

Now he was the one who couldn't hold back a grin. He liked this woman, no doubt about it.

Riley knew everything about setting up camp on the side of the mountain. Juniper should have expected it—he lived in this wild land, after all. As far as she could tell, he didn't have a house and just moved from one camp to another, residing in lodges. But he made quick work of settling the horses, his movements sure and effortless.

Then, from one of his packs, he pulled out an oilskin large enough to be a tent. "This will go easier if I have a couple pairs of extra hands."

He looked Juniper's way as he said the words, and her heart did a little flip. She would gladly assist with this task or any other.

"I'll help." Faith jumped in.

Lorelei stepped toward him. "What do we do?"

Disappointment sank through Juniper. He'd said a couple people to help. That usually meant two, so if she offered as well, she would look overeager. She turned back to the food pack she was unfastening.

"Lorelei, come help me set out food." Rosemary was working on the other tie.

Juniper looked up at her. Was Rosie *allowing* Juniper time with Riley? She hoped she hadn't shown her disappointment on her face. And even if she had, they'd made a pact that none of them would form an attachment with a man on this journey. Rosie would hold her accountable to that commitment.

For that matter, she should hold herself accountable. It shouldn't count that he seemed so different from the other men. That he'd set aside his own work to help them, had taken on their protection as if they were his responsibility.

It shouldn't matter that her entire body came alive when he looked her way, that she sneaked glances at him every chance she could get.

She had to stop.

Lorelei knelt between her and Rosie, and their older sister began giving her instructions about splitting open biscuits and layering in meat. Rosie stopped midsentence and lifted her head. "Aren't you going to help Riley?" She glanced behind them, and Juniper followed her look.

Riley was on one end of the long oilskin, with Faith on the other. He was using his foot to hold a corner down while stretching to place the end of a branch under the center of the cover.

She stood and moved to them. Perhaps Rosie didn't want Lorelei near him. That seemed the more likely reason than that their overprotective sister would be offering Juniper the chance to assist him. Perhaps she thought Lor was developing a preference for him.

One more reason she'd better get herself under control.

"How can I help?" She stood before the oilskin.

"Can you hold this end over the branch while I tie a strap around it?"

She took the pieces from Riley and held them tight. As he lashed a cord around the end of the branch, their hands brushed. She tried not to react as tingles slid up her arm.

He was standing so close, his masculine hand wrapped around hers. No odor of pomade on him.

What must she smell like after a long day in the saddle? She'd washed up in the river when they did their laundry that morning, but that had been so many hours ago.

He finally pulled the knot tight and stepped away from her. Maybe now she could breathe again. Just as she took in a deep gulp of air, he slid a half-grin her way, then knelt to attach the bottom corner to his rope.

That grin washed heat all the way down to her toes and back up again. *Stop it, Juniper.* She turned her focus to the branch in front of her and kept it there.

"Keep holding that one upright while I get the other side secured, then it will stand on its own." Riley's words tried to pull her attention to him, but she didn't let them. Just kept her eyes honed on a chunk of bark that looked loose enough to scrape off.

Finally, they finished setting up the tent. Riley stepped back to examine their work. "It'll keep the dew off you. If you ladies want to gather some pine boughs from those trees down the slope, they make for a softer bed."

Juniper turned the direction he pointed. "Come with me, Faith." A bit of time outside camp was exactly what she needed.

The distraction worked, for by the time she and her sister returned with arms full of pine branches, she was exhausted and ready to collapse on top of them. Hopefully she could keep her mind off Riley long enough to sleep tonight.

TWELVE

T he tent was just wide enough for the four of them to sleep under its shelter, and Riley laid his bedding a few steps away. His bedding didn't consist of quilts as theirs did, but a fur to lay on and a woolen blanket to cover himself with, the kind that had been packed in the supply wagons.

Darkness had almost settled fully by the time they ate and packed away the remnants of food. Back home, they wouldn't have thought to retire this early. But from that first long day on the trail west, the moment work was done in the evening, Juniper longed to collapse onto her blankets.

Now, though, as she sat on her bedding at one end of the tent, she couldn't bring herself to lie down. This wasn't even a tent, really. More like a roof with a bit of oilskin hanging partway down the back. With Riley stretched out mere steps away from the front, he was right there. So very close.

Rosie and Faith had gone to the little trickle of water down the slope to refill their drinking containers and wash up for bed. She and Lorelei had already finished that task, and her sister now lay with the coyote pup tucked against her side, feeding it scraps of meat.

Riley sat on his blankets, facing uphill, which put his side to them. He was writing in a book, likely a journal. And maybe that was why she was having trouble settling into sleep. What was he writing in there? Only a description of what he'd done that day, or were they his thoughts? Maybe it wasn't a diary of the events of his life. Perhaps he kept a log of weather, or animals he saw, or his communications with tribes. He might even be writing a novel. There were at least a hundred things he could be penning on those pages. A thousand. Ten thousand. And that made her want to know all the more.

The only way she would ever know was to ask. Did she dare pry that far? Perhaps she could just speak of it in general terms. And better to do it now before Rosie and Faith returned to provide even more of an audience.

She picked up a strand of long grass and twisted it in her fingers. "Do you keep a daily log of things that happen during your time in these mountains? I would think you'd have a great many adventures to report." There, that didn't sound so much like she was nosing into his personal affairs.

He glanced up, his expression almost startled, as though he'd not felt her watching him. "No, but I've trapped with several men who did that, and I'm sure their journals would make for lively reading. My writing wouldn't be so interesting." He dipped his head back to his paper like he planned to say nothing more.

Disappointment pressed in her chest, and maybe a bit of frustration too. Perhaps it was rude of her to be curious, but it was just as ungentlemanly of him to ignore her veiled request. He must realize what she was asking. Though she'd heard men weren't always aware of subtle hints. Perhaps she should come out and ask the question straightaway.

She tossed aside the mangled grass blade and reached for another. "If not a daily log, what are you writing?" She managed to keep her voice casual, but breathing through the pressure in her chest proved harder. There was nothing that couldn't be considered nosy in what she'd just asked.

He lifted his focus again and raised his brows at her. A definite sign he realized she'd stepped too far. "I'm not writing much, just a basic description of the terrain. Mostly I'm sketching a map." He turned the book so she could see.

The weight on her chest fell away, and she sucked in a breath at the surprise of what he showed. "Really?" Of the long list her mind had conjured, making a map was not among the things she'd considered. In fact, drawing in any form hadn't been included. But why not? The forms of art usually weren't far from her thoughts. Though could map-making be considered art?

She couldn't see the map well, and the wording was too small to read from this distance, but what details she could make out looked very much like other maps she'd seen, with shading that could be mountains or trees. And a set of squiggly lines must be the river.

Yes, what he held up was definitely art, though not the same level of details as her own sketches. But he wouldn't be able to spend weeks on each drawing as she did.

She looked back to his face. "Have you been contracted as a surveyor?" Wasn't that the kind of work his father had done? Or maybe he'd been a guide for surveying parties.

Riley shook his head, turning the book back to face himself. "It's just for my own records. I traveled so much with the cavalry that I started sketching all the places we went to keep track of them. Then, when I mustered out and started trapping, I kept up the practice. It's kind of interesting to see how much of the land on either side of the Rockies I've traveled through." He dipped his head again and returned his pencil to the paper, but this time he seemed to retreat into the work, almost as if he was embarrassed about revealing so much.

"That's fascinating. Do you try to travel a different route every time you go somewhere so you can see new terrain?"

The corners of his mouth curved, and he glanced up at her. "If I have that liberty. If I'm traveling with a larger group, I don't usually get to decide our trail."

She dipped her chin. "Makes sense. Are there places you mark that you'd like to return to later? Maybe in a different season?"

Again, a hint of embarrassment touched his features, but this time he didn't return to his work. "Some. The Rockies have so many pretty spots. I mark the ones I like best, but like I said, I don't always plan my travels for pleasure."

This new side of him made him even more fascinating than before. "Are there any places you haven't yet been where you hope to travel to?"

A spark lit his eyes, then he dropped his gaze back down to the page on his lap. He didn't resume sketching, though, just seemed to be considering. "I'd like to go farther north. Follow the backbone of the Rockies as far as it goes. I don't know of another man who's done that, and there's definitely no maps for it. There are so many mountains and really high elevations, which means all travel would need to be done during the summer months. I think it would take more than one summer to follow them all the way north and sketch the land."

As he spoke, his tone took on an excitement it didn't normally hold. Not volume, for he still kept his voice low. But this dream meant something to him. He'd been thinking on it for a while, from the sound of things.

She tried to work through such a journey in her own mind. "That sounds like something that would be hard to do alone if the mountains are as numerous as you say. Traveling with a group would be easier, no?"

He gave a slow nod. "That's why I haven't done it. Any man who's trekked across the Rockies once knows how treacherous the journey is. Riding the crest for months at a time would be hard. But something about those mountains, being in the middle with peaks stretching as far as you can see in every direction . . . it makes you realize how small you are. It gets in your soul."

She could imagine what he described. This open land they traveled through already made her feel that way. What would it be like to take the journey he spoke of? To paint some of those majestic views?

The swish of quiet footsteps coming up the slope broke through their conversation, and they both turned to watch Rosemary and Faith approach in the near darkness. She'd forgotten about Lorelei lying on her blankets, hearing her conversation. There wasn't anything she *couldn't* overhear. But what did she think of Riley's dream? She had her face turned away as she watched their sisters' entrance into the little camp.

Rosemary sank onto the blankets on the other side of

Faith. "Lights out, girls. We need to be rested for tomor-row. Hopefully, we'll find the woman we've come all this way to meet."

Riley's belly clenched as they descended the slope on horseback the next morning, headed toward the little clus-ter of Peigan lodges nestled beside the river. It seemed too unlikely that one particular woman would be in this tiny village instead of the many, many others spread across this side of the Rockies.

After they inquired here, what next? They had to return to the main trappers' camp first, there was no questioning that. Not only would staying away another night seriously endanger the sisters' reputation as women of virtue, but he'd also left all the supplies he traded a year's worth of furs for back in the lodge. He trusted Ol' Henry, Dragoon, and Jeremiah, but it also wasn't their job to guard his belong-ings. Anytime they left the lodge, his things would be easy pickings for any man who hadn't brought in enough furs to procure his own supplies. Or who simply wanted to add to his stock without the hard work of trapping and scraping and stretching the skins.

But all that would come later. First, he had to navigate the meeting with this new band. If he were by himself, he wouldn't have minded stopping in a Peigan village to ask questions, or even the larger Crow band they'd passed yes-terday. Most of the natives were friendly and hospitable to a man or two coming into their village with peaceful intentions.

But having these four women in his care made the stakes

considerably higher. They were such a novelty to everyone in this land—trapper and native alike. It was hard to know how each man or group of people, or even the native women, would respond to the Collins sisters.

And he couldn't take chances that weren't absolutely necessary. His father had once said it was a man's responsibility to protect the women in his charge. He'd certainly not planned to take on that role with the Collins sisters, but they'd brought no one else to do the job, and he couldn't stand by when they needed help. Needed someone who knew the lay of the land and the ways of its people.

If only they would let him handle the search on his own. But they'd made it clear they wanted to be part of every step along the way.

When they'd ridden halfway across the valley, the stirring of figures in the lodges showed they'd been spotted. As they drew near the camp, two men stepped outside the circle of homes. One wore his long gray hair in a single bundle down his back, but the other looked much younger. Perhaps around twenty years old. With six lodges, he would expect at least ten men here, since extended families often lived within a single shelter. These two must be leaders among them. The chief, maybe, and perhaps his grandson, a young warrior being molded into a future chief.

Riley greeted them from atop his horse, using the hand talk, but he also spoke aloud in English for the benefit of the women. If only he'd spent more time learning the tongues of the individual tribes. The sign language had always seemed enough, since all the nations in this area spoke and understood it. The Blackfoot tongue, in particular, was said to be challenging—almost impossible to learn unless one lived among the tribe for years.

The older man responded with a stilted greeting, and his face showed wariness. He was mostly looking at the women, and his gaze drifted to Juniper far more than to her sisters.

Riley's body tensed more, but he did his best to show only confidence. "We are looking for a woman. Can we come into your village and ask about her?"

The younger man's hands hung by his side, but at Riley's words, the fingers on his right curled toward his palm.

Toward the handle of his tomahawk.

Riley didn't let his focus linger there but kept stock of the young man's movements as he focused on the elder's answer.

The older fellow gave a slow dip of his chin, then signed a response. *You are our honored guests.*

THIRTEEN

No lads trotted out from among the lodges to water the horses this time. Riley glanced over at Juniper and Rosemary, who'd been riding beside him, and kept his voice low. "They don't seem as friendly as the others, but they're allowing us to come in and ask. Why don't one or two of you come with me, and the others stay out here with the horses?"

Would it be better for Juniper to go inside where he would be nearby to protect her from the natives' curiosity about her piercing blue eyes? Or remain outside of camp with her sisters? These strangers might act on their curiosity either way. As opposed as he was to bringing her into camp, he'd feel better having her close.

Rosemary leaned forward to swing her leg over her saddle. "June and I will go with you. Lorelei, you and Faith stay with the horses. And whatever you do, don't let that pup get loose."

Heavens above, don't let the pup get loose. That would be the very last thing they needed. The animal had done pretty well on the journey so far, except for whimpering several times in the night. While they rode, it seemed content to stay tucked in Miss Lorelei's arm or walking alongside her with a cord tied around its neck and shoulders in a harness. He'd never have imagined a wild coyote could be tamed so well.

He led the way into the village, following the chief. Juniper and Rosemary stayed close behind him, and the younger man turned and strode after them.

It took everything in Riley not to stop and move the women in front of him, so he could be the protective barrier between them and the young warrior. But that would show fear on his part and lack of trust, both things that would lower their respect of him and make these hosts more likely to turn hostile.

The chief led them to a cook fire in front of one of the largest lodges and lowered himself to sit. The younger man stepped inside the lodge, disappearing into the darkness within. No women approached to take Juniper and Rosemary away, though many clustered at the door flaps of almost every lodge in the group.

Riley motioned for Juniper and Rosemary to sit beside him. They did so with a grace that showed their bravery, though they crowded close, both to each other and to him. Juniper's skirt touched his leggings all the way down.

He had to fight to ignore the warmth of having her so near. Had to work to focus on the leathery lines on the face of the man in front of him.

The chief drew out a long pipe decorated with feathers and braided leather. After he blew a long stream of sweet-smelling smoke, he handed the piece to Riley.

He'd never developed a preference for the taste of the kinnikinnick that many tribes in this area smoked, but the ritual of sharing the pipe meant peace between them—and he appreciated *that* a great deal.

After blowing out his own stream of smoke, Riley didn't offer the pipe to the women. Back in the world they came from, women didn't smoke, at least not publicly that he knew of. And in this culture, women weren't often invited to the council circle at all.

The chief reached to take the pipe back, and Riley handed it over. The man tapped his chest and spoke a sound too quick to understand. Then he signed the words *Son of Owl*.

Riley nodded and pointed to himself. "Riley Turner." He motioned to Juniper and spoke her name, then the same with Rosemary.

As he presented them, he kept his focus on the chief's face. This was a bold move on his part, introducing the women without their host asking. The man frowned, making the lines around his mouth and jaw sag even more. But he didn't reprimand Riley.

A short silence fell over them, and Riley held his tongue. Hopefully Rosemary and Juniper would also. The chief should be the next to speak, as the host. And he would likely want to discuss events in the area, maybe the happenings at the rendezvous, or even the weather, before allowing Riley to ask about Steps Right.

The man drew in another draft from the pipe, then blew it out as the younger man exited the lodge beside them and came to sit beside the elder.

A small bit of the tension in Riley's chest eased. At least he could see the fellow now.

That seemed to be what the older man was waiting for to speak, for he leveled his gaze on Riley. He signed without speaking aloud. *This is my grandson, Flies Ahead. What have you come to ask?*

It seemed there would be no small talk then. He glanced at the women and kept his voice low but made it clear in his tone he was interpreting. "He inquires what we've come to ask."

Without giving either of the sisters a chance to answer, he looked back at the man as he spoke and signed at the same time. "We have come searching for a Peigan woman named Steps Right. Do you know of her?"

The chief gave no visible reaction to the name, nor did the younger man, as far as Riley could tell. Riley kept his focus mostly on the elder as a sign of respect. Something about the younger fellow made him wary.

The chief shook his head in a slow yet sure motion. Then he signed, *There is no woman with that name here. Why do you look for one of the People?*

As Riley gathered the right response in his mind and how to translate it into signs, he slid a glance to the younger man. That was a definite frown on his face, almost anger. When the man saw him looking, the expression slipped away.

Riley looked back to the chief and formed the signs as he spoke. "The father of these women knew her many years ago. She helped him, and now they wish to repay the kindness."

The chief still showed no sign of his thoughts or any reaction that might make Riley think he'd ever heard of the woman. But the younger man's mouth had pressed into a thin line. Did he know of Steps Right and wasn't happy that they were looking for her? Or perhaps he was only displeased with one of his people helping a white man.

He might risk the chief's displeasure if he directed the same question to the younger man. But it might be worth a chance to get a better read on the fellow.

Riley kept his voice and expression as amiable as he could while he signed the question. "What of you, have you heard of a woman named Steps Right? She may be the age of the grandmothers." Perhaps not that old, but it would be a good estimate.

The glimmer that touched Flies Ahead's dark eyes and the slight twist of his mouth sent a shiver of unease through Riley. Like the chief, he signed his answer without speaking it aloud. *As my grandfather says, there is no woman by that name here.*

His choice of wording, though . . . Riley hadn't caught it in the grandfather's response, but now that he thought back, neither man had said they didn't *know* Steps Right. They'd only said she wasn't *here.* Had they used those words because they were the clearest to understand when signing? Perhaps not. The sign for *no* was simple enough.

Riley nodded understanding, then signed and spoke to them both. "Have you ever met this woman?"

The younger man lifted a shoulder in a casual move. *I do not think much of women I meet.* He probably meant he didn't remember much about them, not that he held a low opinion of them. Although perhaps both meanings applied to this man.

Either way, it didn't seem like Riley would get a straight answer from either of them. What were they hiding? There was a chance that they simply didn't trust white men enough to give details about one of their people. Was there a way he could test that idea?

He affected a lighthearted air. "We are on our way back to the trapper meeting to trade for supplies. Have you gone to trade as well?"

The older chief made a sound almost like a grunt, but it was his grandson who answered again. "We have come for that purpose, to trade with the white men who bring wagons. But the Crow dogs stole our horses. We have only last night taken them back. It is the sign that we should not have come to this place. We leave this day."

Well . . . finally a bit of detail, and it told him plenty, though not about Steps Right. At least these people trusted the whites enough to trade. And it sounded like it was a good thing he'd not stopped at the Crow camp yesterday. He might have landed the women in the thick of a rivalry, and that was the last place they belonged.

He nodded to the younger man. It might be best to avoid the topic of the Crows, for it seemed that was one that still stirred hot anger. Instead, he opted for a little more small talk. "There are many who have come to trade, even more than in past years. The supplies have gone quickly, but there may yet be some if you plan to go that route."

His words yielded only a single nod from the chief and nothing from his grandson.

If the tribe was planning to pack up and leave today, they were likely hoping their visitors would leave quickly. Better he ask his final question so they could be gone. "Thank you for sharing the pipe with us. Do you know where this woman Steps Right might be? Who can we ask about her?"

He may not follow their advice, but at least he'd like to hear how they answered. Since it didn't seem these men distrusted whites in general, it must be something about

Steps Right they didn't want to tell. Why would they hide details about her?

The younger man's gaze flicked to the fire, his expression saying the topic mattered little to him. The chief was the one to answer through sign. *I do not know. There is another group of our people who should be gathering to trade on the other side of the white man's camp. They may know of this woman.*

Those must be the first band they'd spoken to, the one south of the main trappers' camp.

Riley signed a thank-you, then prepared to stand. He glanced at Juniper and Rosemary with a nod to show they should do the same.

After a final farewell, they were ushered out of the little camp. The tension that hung thick in the air had to be more than just the unease of mixing two different races in an unsteady peace.

He could almost believe that the ordeal of having their horses stolen and fighting to recover them had made these two especially reserved and uneager to help strangers. But his instincts told him otherwise, and he'd learned never to ignore a feeling like this one.

FOURTEEN

Juniper's head ached as they rode back past their campsite from the night before. Riley had just finished relaying the full conversation between him and the two Peigan men. She and Rosie had listened to Riley's side already but hadn't known what the others were saying. And of course, Lorelei and Faith had heard none of it.

The tension that had grown thick in the air the longer the men talked had made her entire body tighten up, which was why her skull pounded now. That, and the little bit of sleep she'd gotten last night in between the coyote pup's whimpering.

"So what do we do now?" Lorelei asked the question Juniper hadn't yet voiced.

Before Riley could respond, Rosemary spoke up. "If you think they were hiding something, should we stay here and watch their camp? We may not be able to recognize Steps Right, but we could at least see if anyone rides in or out. Then we could find out for sure if they're packing up to leave today. That will help us know if they're telling the truth."

Riley's eyes lifted to the sky before he answered. "I'm not

sure that would tell us anything we don't know. I already don't think they were telling the truth, at least not entirely. And I need to get back to the rendezvous. A year's worth of supplies is sitting in my lodge unguarded."

He spoke the words casually enough, but they pressed the air from her lungs. "Oh, Riley. We didn't realize. . . ." Had he risked so much to bring them here?

Of course he had. She'd thought about how he'd set aside his normal work to help them, but she'd not thought about what that work might be. She knew he'd just traded, though. No wonder he'd been hesitant to come north to find this camp instead of returning to the rendezvous after meeting with the Gros Ventre. Given what he was risking, he'd been remarkably easygoing about their insistence.

He shook his head, as if flicking away her worries. "I asked Dragoon and the others to watch my things while I'm gone. I'd just rather not be away a second night." It would take them the rest of the day at least to reach the main camp.

"Let's start back, then." Rosemary's tone held a tinge of frustration, but hopefully Riley didn't know her well enough to catch it.

He motioned for them to start riding, and since the path downhill was wide, they rode two and three abreast for most of the slope. As they reached the bottom, Juniper's mare pricked her ears toward a group of cedars ahead. Beside her, Riley's hand tightened on the stock of the rifle he kept laying across his lap.

She studied the trees for any sign of movement. There must be something there that both Riley and the horses heard, but several pounding heartbeats passed before a horse emerged around the cluster. Its rider was an Indian, with a long black braid over one of his broad shoulders. A second horse and rider came behind, and the two continued their steady progression toward Juniper and the others.

She rode with Rosie on her right and Riley on her left in their usual positions, and she lifted her voice just loud enough for him to hear. "Who are they? Are they danger-ous?"

He hadn't lifted his gun, and neither of the natives held weapons poised, though it seemed very likely they had them ready.

"I don't know." He responded in the same quiet tone. "They look like they've been out hunting."

Large bundles were secured behind both riders. That must be the meat they brought in.

Riley halted them when the strangers stopped a half-dozen strides away. The second rider remained a little behind the first, but as he peered around his companion, realization swept through Juniper.

A woman.

Were they husband and wife, gone on a hunting trip to-gether? Was that done among these people? She'd supposed the men handled such details, and women stayed behind to cook and keep house and care for the children. But maybe that was only a white custom.

Riley was the first to greet them, and he spoke English while he signed, as he had all the other times they met with the villages. He probably did this so she and her sis-ters would be able to follow along with the conversation somewhat. His thoughtfulness continued to surprise her, not always obvious, but there in the smaller details that were so easy to take for granted. But without these little acts of kindness, she and her sisters would have been frustrated, lost, and maybe even in danger.

After Riley greeted the pair, he gave them his name and introduced the four of them as "the Collins sisters."

The brave in the lead responded with the sign she'd come to realize meant *hello*, or some similar greeting. Then he pointed to himself and spoke English, though broken and heavily accented. "White Horse." He motioned to the woman behind him. "Singing Water." He frowned as he seemed to struggle for words, then he formed a sign.

"She is his cousin." Riley spoke quietly to interpret for them, but loud enough the strangers could hear him.

White Horse nodded. "Cousin. The daughter of my . . ." Again he struggled for a word. "Uncle." His face seemed to question whether he'd found the correct term.

When Riley nodded, White Horse's expression relaxed. The man seemed amiable, especially compared to those they'd just left.

"You have come from the trading wagons?" Riley nodded toward the bundle behind White Horse.

The man shook his head. "Hunt buffalo."

Riley dipped his chin in understanding. He still signed as he spoke. "We are looking for someone. A woman who helped the father of these sisters. They wish to repay her kindness. Have you heard of a woman from the Peigan tribe who is called Steps Right?"

Something in the stranger's demeanor seemed to shift a tiny bit. In fact, Juniper might have imagined it. But his expression had seemed open and friendly at first, and now his bearing reminded her a little more of the Peigan camp they'd visited that morning.

Was it the mention of Steps Right? It had to be.

The man shook his head in answer to Riley. He signed a response but didn't attempt to speak it in English.

Thankfully, Riley again quietly interpreted. "He says he has no knowledge of where she is."

Juniper spoke in the same quiet voice he did. "Does that mean he doesn't know her?"

Riley hesitated, and she flicked her glance to him to see why. Did he think it unwise to press?

But then he turned and repeated her question as he signed to the Indians, and she focused on them too. She'd been mostly watching the man, but Singing Water caught her notice this time. The woman was staring right at Juniper, watching her.

Juniper met her look and tried to make her expression friendly. Singing Water didn't look angry, just . . . intense. As though she was searching for something in Juniper.

White Horse answered Riley with signs only, so she had no idea what he said. Riley didn't interpret this time. Part of her wanted to ask what had been spoken, but Riley would tell them if he thought it wouldn't hurt the conversation. He'd already proved that, and she had to trust him.

Riley nodded in response to the man's answer, then the two stopped speaking. White Horse guided his horse around them as he and his cousin started up the hill.

Riley motioned for her and her horse to start their horses walking. They all stayed quiet until they'd ridden far enough that White Horse and Singing Water could no longer see or overhear them.

She looked at Riley, and he shook his head. "It's strange. He was friendly until I asked about Steps Right."

"What did he say when you asked the second time?"

He frowned. "Not much. The signs he used were vague, but basically he said he hadn't seen her. I had planned to ask him if he was going to the Peigan camp we just left, but when he got quiet, I decided he might not take kindly to more questions."

She nodded. That made sense, and he would know better than they would. But why such secrecy about this woman? First from their father, and now from this group of people who were supposedly her own tribe.

"You think they're hiding her from us?"

At Rosie's question, Juniper turned to her. "But why? We only want to thank her and return something that belonged to her." Of course, they hadn't spoken that last bit to any of the people they'd met. Riley didn't even know about the necklace.

"I've been careful to make sure I state that you want to thank her for her kindness." Riley's voice sounded as perplexed as the rest of them felt.

Faith piped up from behind them. "Maybe she has a special power that they don't want white people to learn about. Or maybe she's deformed and they're trying to protect her." Leave it to their spirited little sister to come up with something so outlandish.

Juniper turned a look on her. "Maybe your imagination stretches a bit too far."

"There does seem to be something suspicious going on here." Rosie's murmur drew them back to the focus of the conversation. "But I doubt she has special powers." She sent Faith the same kind of look Juniper had, then squinted at Riley. "If the group we spoke with this morning was trying to hide her, where would she be?"

He glanced at Rosie, then shifted his attention forward as he scrubbed a hand through his hair and blew out a long breath. "Anywhere. She could have been one of the women poking her head out from a lodge. We don't know what she looks like, so we have no way of finding her unless she's willing to step forward and admit her name."

Rosie shrugged. "I suppose it's not likely they're holding her hostage. It's just frustrating not to have any leads."

A thought slipped in, clicking into place in Juniper's mind with new clarity. "What about the horses?"

Riley and Rosemary both turned to face her, but Riley spoke first. "We've been looking for the two animals you've described. The chestnut's coloring is so common, she'll be hard to find. But we've not seen any horses with the white ear bonnet you said the stallion had." He frowned. "Besides, the chances aren't great they'd both be alive after twenty years."

Determination pressed through her. "But maybe it will help us. We haven't focused on looking for the horses yet, so perhaps if we asked around, someone would have remembered an animal with that white ear marking. Even if the original stallion isn't alive, perhaps he passed that coloring down to his offspring. Maybe it will lead us in the right direction."

Riley looked so doubtful, she almost felt silly for the suggestion.

She threw up a hand. "We can try anyway. We should work from every angle we can. It won't hurt to ask about them, will it?"

His frown shifted into a thoughtful expression as he rolled his lips in. He turned his gaze forward again, staring into the trees and the low mountain ahead of them. "I don't know if it's a good idea to ask the natives or not. There's so much horse thieving between the tribes that strangers asking about horses tends to raise suspicion. Especially if they're already dodgy from our questions about Steps Right.

"It might not hurt to ask the trappers. There's been more horse thieving than usual of late, but most men think it's the Indians. They certainly know it's not you four. A lot of the fellows are newcomers within the last few years, but they may still have seen a horse with these markings in their wanderings. The old-timers might even have seen the original mare and stallion, but that probably won't help us know where Steps Right is now."

He still kept his focus forward, his brow dimpled as he was clearly working things through in his mind.

She offered a hesitant answer. "That sounds like a good plan. At least we have something to try. Especially since we've no more leads from the tribes we've visited."

Riley turned to her and Rosie. "The marking that's on your mounts." He dipped his chin toward her mare's shoulder. "Would Steps Right's horses have had that too?"

Would they have? They'd been so focused on the coloring, the brand hadn't entered her mind. She turned to Rosie. "When did Papa start marking his herd?"

Rosie was frowning back, clearly trying to think. "When we were little. I remember him drawing out several marks and showing them to us. Asking us which we liked best. You were barely toddling around, and you kept getting slobber on his paper and making the ink run." Her frown deepened. "It might've been around the same time he sent the horses with Mr. Sampson. Maybe. Within a year or so."

"Who's Sampson?" Riley's voice turned sharp.

Juniper stepped in to ease his concern. "Our father's partner on his journey West. They'd been hearing about the fortunes made by people who spent a winter trapping and hunting in the mountain wilderness, and Mr. Sampson talked Papa into going with him. Our ranch was still small at the time, and I think Papa wanted the money from the furs to build up his herd. Anyway, when they returned the next spring, Mr. Sampson came only to purchase supplies, then return West. Papa sent the horses back with him to take to Steps Right."

Riley still wore a frown. "How long did Sampson stay in the mountains the second time? Where is he now?"

She looked to Rosemary. Had Papa ever said where he ended up?

Rosie met her gaze, then turned to Riley with a shrug. "I don't think we ever heard."

He nodded, though his mouth had formed a grim line. "All right. I suppose we can start asking about the horses." His manner didn't seem like he thought this path would lead them to Steps Right. "When we get back to camp, I'll give you some paper to sketch out the marking so I can show it around."

As they started up the next hill, the hint of hope that lightened her spirit even gave her mare a quicker step. They had a plan, and if they worked hard enough and asked enough people, surely God would bless their efforts. They could finally find Steps Right and finish this impossible mission.

FIFTEEN

Though they'd pushed hard on the return trip to the main rendezvous camp, darkness had settled deep through the hills along the Green River by the time the flickers of campfires stretched before them. They were entering the valley at almost the same point as when Juniper and her sisters had first seen this place with the supply wagons, but how different the sight looked now.

Instead of hordes of ants milling around between the lodges, below them lay hundreds of flickering candles. The view seemed magical, like so many fireflies, or like the fairy stories Aunt Gertie used to tell them when she came to visit the ranch each summer.

Instead of aiming toward the campfires, Riley pointed them southward to hobble the horses near the rest of the mounts. All five animals picked up stride as they neared the herd.

Exhaustion weighted Juniper's limbs, and she couldn't find the second wind the horses managed. Too, they still needed to cook for Riley in payment for his services as a guide. It looked like collapsing onto their blankets and ignoring hungry bellies wouldn't be an option tonight. Not after he'd done so much to help them.

She glanced over at him. "As soon as we get the horses unsaddled, we'll get a fire going and a hot meal for you."

He shook his head. "The fellows at my lodge will have food cooked. We can all eat there tonight. They'll want to hear our story anyway."

"What story?" This from Rosie, who'd been silent for a while now. She was probably as tired as Juniper was. Lorelei and Faith looked almost asleep in their saddles.

"About what's happened to us on this journey." The moonlight cast a shadow beneath Riley's raised brows. "We've been gone a day longer than expected. They'll be looking for quite a tale from us. These mountain men don't have much to keep them occupied at night, so storytelling around the campfire is one of their favorite pastimes."

Rosie's voice took on a protective edge. "I'm not sure I want the details of our search spread to a hundred men by morning."

Riley shook his head. "It'll likely just be Ol' Henry, Dragoon, and Jeremiah. And we can choose how much detail we want to give. Just telling who we met up with and how we were treated can be built up into a story interesting enough to satisfy."

His voice turned serious. "I do think it would be good to tell Ol' Henry what we're thinking about the markings on the horses. He's lived in these parts long enough to have a lot of wisdom and experience. I'd like to get his thoughts on it all."

Rosie was quiet for a moment, but with the position of the moon, shadows hid her expression. When she spoke, her voice had softened. "I suppose it's fine to tell him. I know we'll need to ask everyone about the markings. I'm just not sure I want to spread our suspicion that Steps Right might be hiding from us."

Was this just Rosie's protective instincts rising up, or did her intuition tell her to keep that detail secret? Juniper softened her tone to match her sister's. "Do you think word could get back to Steps Right? Or is there another reason to stay quiet?"

"I don't know, June. It just seems like one of those details we should keep to ourselves—for now, at least. Riley can embellish the story of who we met with and how hard it was to get any detail from them. He can ask every man within hearing distance whether they've seen horses with markings like the ones we're looking for. But I think we should not mention the rest of it. Except to Ol' Henry. He seems trustworthy. And he certainly has been out here long enough to have seen the horses. I'd like to know what he says about it all."

They made quick work of unsaddling the horses, then each of them hoisted their saddles with packs still tied on to carry to camp. Riley propped his saddle upside down over his left shoulder, then reached for Juniper's. "I can carry one more."

Her body breathed a sigh of relief at the thought of handing over the heavy load, but it wasn't fair to ask him to do double the work. "I've got it."

He closed his grip around the pommel and pulled it from her hands anyway. Then, with a familiar motion, he flipped the leather upside down and lifted it to his right shoulder. "You can carry my rifle." He nodded to his feet, where moonlight glinted off metal.

That she could manage, and she wouldn't argue any more over giving up the heavier load. But as they started toward camp, Lorelei stepped close to her and muttered in a half-teasing tone, "Slug-a-bed."

Juniper shot her sister a grin, and on her other side, a soft chuckle drifted from Riley. She and her sisters stopped at their own lodge to leave their saddles and freshen up a bit while Riley went on to his camp.

The coyote pup had been sitting atop Lorelei's saddle as she carried it, but now the animal jumped down and stretched, then trotted around the lodge sniffing, as if finding all kinds of new smells. Had someone come in while they were gone? She glanced around the place. "You don't think people bothered our belongings, do you?"

Faith plopped down on the ground and lay back on the flattened grass where she stretched her bedding at night. "Why would they want to? All we left behind were a bunch of clothes. These men have no use for women's undergarments, I'm sure." She sprang up to a sitting position as fast as she'd flopped backward. "Let's go eat. I'm starved."

If only a bit of Faith's boundless energy would rub off on Juniper. She shook out as much of the dust and wrinkles from her skirts as she could. "Wash your hands in the water basin before we go. All of you."

As she straightened, she glanced at Rosemary and saw that her sister had been watching her. Juniper tilted her head. "What is it?" Was she thinking they should stay here instead of going to Riley's camp to eat?

Rosie studied her another heartbeat, and when she spoke, her voice held an unexpected seriousness. "It's been a while since we've discussed the rules we set for ourselves before we started on this journey. It might be good we take time to recall them. Especially the one about not allowing an attachment to form with any of the men here."

Heat flared up Juniper's neck. Were Faith and Lorelei staring at her as Rosemary was? She did her best to keep her nod casual. "You're right. We can't be too careful here."

Rosie returned her nod, then finally looked away, allowing Juniper a chance to catch her breath. She really did have to be careful not to grow attached to Riley. He was such a good man, but they'd formed these rules in advance so none of them would be swayed in the moment. There had been wisdom and sound reasons for each commitment they'd made to one another, though for the life of her, she couldn't remember those reasons now.

"Let's go." Rosie motioned them toward the door flap.

One by one, they stepped through the lodge opening to the warm night air outside. Juniper eyed the coyote pup walking at the end of its leash and harness. "I hope he doesn't squirm out of that and run. The last thing we need is to stir up camp chasing him down."

Rosemary sighed. "Sounds like the place is already stirred up." The volume of male voices certainly seemed louder than when they'd entered their lodge minutes before.

The four of them stood listening for a moment. Voices and conversation rose around them, along with the occasional shout or burst of laughter. In the distance, a group chorused a drunken song. There were so many men here, and their voices layered on top of one another to make quite a hum.

Rosemary must have decided there wasn't a particular danger right now, for she waved them all forward toward

Riley's camp. Juniper fell into step at the end of the line, and they all kept to the shadows until they approached the welcoming circle of light illuminating Riley, Ol' Henry, and Dragoon. Jeremiah sat with his back to them but turned as she and her sisters stepped into the glow.

All the men stood at their arrival except Ol' Henry, who waved instead. "Pardon me for not standing to greet ya ladies. My joints are makin' it hard today. We'll be in for a rain by morning, I think. Pull up a log and grab yourself some meat." He pointed with the stick in his hand at the food sizzling on the rock they used as a frying pan.

Rosemary moved in to take the log nearest Jeremiah, allowing the four of them to sit side-by-side around the fire. Juniper ended the row of sisters by sitting with Faith on her left and Riley on her right. He was already using the tip of his knife to spear slabs of meat and lift them onto plates. "These started cooking when I first got back to camp, so they should be ready now."

She took the two plates he handed her, and passed one for Rosie and Lorelei to share, then held the other for Faith to eat from as well. The meat needed to cool before they could pick it up with their fingers, but its aroma tantalized her insides, stirring her hungry belly to life.

"Riley says you gals have seen a bit more landscape than you planned these last couple days." Dragoon sat with his knees bent, one hand wrapped around the mug that rested on his leg.

Rosemary answered, of course. "We did. I'm sure he can tell the story best."

The three men turned expectantly to Riley, and Juniper slid a glance at him from the corner of her eye. Did he mind being put on the spot? But these were his friends, and he knew this tradition of storytelling far better than they did. He would keep their secrets, she had no doubt about that anymore.

He held a chunk of meat in the air, speared at the end of his knife. Probably letting his cool as well. "Well . . ." He drew out the word in the manner of every good storyteller. "We found the Gros Ventre tribe as we expected, two valleys north of here."

As he outlined the details of their journey, she watched the other men. They seemed to be soaking in every word, maybe picturing where they'd been and who they'd spoken to. Likely these trappers all had traveled to those same locations. Riley said nothing of all the horse tracks they'd seen in the valley, nor of the way the last two groups they questioned had clammed up when they'd mentioned Steps Right.

He did, however, become a bit more animated as he mimicked the Peigan chief's straight-to-the-point solemnness and the way his grandson's hand kept shifting toward his tomahawk. "They had nothing new to tell us in our search, so I figured we'd best get out of there while we still had everything we came with." The grin he sent Juniper and her sisters was clearly a show for the rest of the men, but it still did something funny to her insides.

That had been happening a lot when he looked at her, especially when the dimple pressed in his right cheek. And was it her imagination, or did his gaze hover a half heartbeat longer when it touched her, his eyes softening the tiniest bit?

But then he turned back to the men with a nod. "And that's about all there is to tell." He left out the meeting with White Horse and Singing Water completely.

Riley had been talking so much, he hadn't had a chance to eat even a bite yet. He lifted the meat to his mouth but paused just before biting into it and raised his focus to the others again. "Any rabid wolves come into camp while we were gone?"

Juniper sucked in a breath, and Lorelei let out a tiny whimper.

"Rabid wolves?" Faith sounded almost eager.

Ol' Henry chuckled, then poked a log with his stick, pushing it deeper into the flames. "That's a saying we've taken up that's kind of a way of asking if anything unusual happened. It started back in '33 when we actually did have a wolf come into camp. Sneaky thing she was. Crept in three nights straight, attacking folks, darting back and forth in the darkness so we couldn't get a clear bead on her. Finally, Skeeter plunged a knife into her just as she bit him. We'd suspected all along she'd been taken with the hydrophobia. When men started coming up sick and foaming at the mouth, we learned the truth. In all, twelve men were bit. All twelve died, as far as we know. Six of them here in camp. The other six wandered off into the plains and were never seen again."

A somber quiet settled over them as Ol' Henry's voice faded away. Even the volume of the camp around seemed to have dimmed. A weight settled in Juniper's belly as her mind tried to form images of the chaos such an event must have created. Men running from the creature, the booms of guns trying to stop it. Then all those dead bodies stretched out. Men who would have been vibrant and lively only days before. Men who may have families back East, waiting for their return, eager for a letter carried back with the furs on

141

the supply wagons. Had friends of the deceased sent notes back instead, sharing the sad fate of sons and brothers, husbands and fathers?

Her throat ached. She could have lost her own father that way when he'd come West two decades before. Lorelei and Faith would have never been conceived, for they were born after his return. The months he spent in this land were still such a mystery, but at least he'd returned home to his wife and daughters. Had he left part of his heart here with Steps Right? The idea soured the food she'd just eaten.

"Anyhow." Ol' Henry's quiet tone returned her to the present. "Nothing half so exciting happened while you folks were gone. A new group of Snake Indians set up camp last night. And Wallace's party showed up this morning. Weren't pleased to see supplies are down to slim pickins. They said they were held up when their horses were stolen. Bloods took them, they think. Never could find the animals, though, so they showed up here on foot with only leggings and a few shirts between them. Haven't seen such a sorry-looking group of men since Wyatt's party was robbed back in '34. It was nigh on to winter then, and more than one toe was lost to the frostbite."

Juniper nearly shivered despite the pressing heat from the fire and the warm summer night around them. Bears, hydrophobic wolves, thieves . . . Every detail brought forth some new danger.

Riley's sleeve brushed hers, as though he leaned toward her. Or maybe she'd moved closer to him and the safety of his presence.

His voice rumbled through her as he spoke again to the others. "Any horse races planned for tomorrow?" He must be thinking about how to start asking about the horses with their father's brand.

"First heat is scheduled for when the sun's two fingers above the horizon." Dragoon held up two digits sideways and closed one eye as if he was sighting a rifle.

Riley glanced her way. "That's how the natives tell time. It takes the sun roughly an hour to rise the width of one finger, and they mark it from the nearest horizon."

She glanced into the darkness where the sun would rise tomorrow morning and fought the urge to hold two fingers sideways. "Interesting." It made sense that the trappers would use the same method. Watches were likely not considered a supply necessary enough to transport over such a distance.

Riley turned back to Dragoon. "How'd your run go yesterday?"

The man's smile slipped downward. "Tucker's mare pulled ahead at the last. Won by a neck." He shook his head. "My Bessie is faster. She just got tired there at the end."

A corner of Riley's mouth twitched. "Maybe you could have one of these skinny new fellas ride her next time."

Dragoon's mouth pinched. "Thought about having that fellow they call Slim run her. He's not young, but he's short and wiry. A lot of the fellows have hired him to ride their races, and he wins about every other one, I think. Tucker got to him before I did, though. He's probably the only reason that nag beat my Bessie."

Again, Dragoon shook his head. "Tucker's horse went missing today. He even had her staked right near his lodge so he could keep an eye on his prize runner. Came back from watching the last race of the day and the animal was just gone. Rope sliced clean through, so's it had to be done on purpose. Tucker swore he'd been had by a thieving native, but I'm not sure how any could get so close to his lodge right here in the bright of day."

"Another horse stolen? It doesn't seem likely she could be taken from the middle of camp without being seen. Are you sure one of the fellas isn't playing a trick?"

Dragoon shrugged, then turned toward Juniper and her sisters, as if to explain the conversation. "There's been more horse stealing than usual at the rendezvous this year. Three or four of the mounts that won a race or nearly so have disappeared a day or two later. The boys are starting to stir up about it. Some are saying it can't be the Indians, not the way it's always the ones that's just proved themselves. Seems it has to be someone among us. No one's laid claim to knowing who."

"That sounds awful." Juniper glanced at Riley to check his reaction. His brow gathered in concern, and his eyes stared at the fire as though his mind was far away. If only she knew him well enough to read his thoughts. Was he scrolling through images of men who might possibly be horse thieves? Or was he remembering horses taken in the past?

Jeremiah spoke up, and she turned to better hear his quiet voice. "I heard Provost say the wagons might be headed back early, maybe in a couple days. Are you ladies riding along with them?"

Juniper's chest tightened. They hadn't even come close to finding Steps Right yet. Would they have to return East before they located her? But Papa . . . He'd nearly begged them to find this woman and return the blue beaded necklace to her and make sure she'd received the horses. They'd come so far, put their lives on hold. . . . They couldn't turn back without finishing the mission.

She met the quick glance Rosie sent her way. Her sister clearly felt the same, but they needed time to talk through the logistics of staying behind once their best chance for safe passage left them.

Rosie turned back to Jeremiah. "We'll speak with Mr. Provost tomorrow. I hadn't heard he was planning to leave so soon."

The weight of all they had left to accomplish pressed new weariness through Juniper. She mustered a smile for their hosts. "We thank you for the meal. I think it's time we retire for the night."

She glanced sideways at Riley. He deserved a much stronger thank-you, but one she'd rather not give in front of the group.

He met her look. "I'll walk you back to your lodge."

They all rose, even Ol' Henry this time, and Riley's lodgemates offered farewells as Rosemary led them through the darkness toward their temporary home.

SIXTEEN

J uniper strolled behind her sisters on their way back to their lodge, with Riley at her side. He seemed to enjoy her company, maybe almost as much as she did his. Or perhaps that was wishful thinking. Perhaps it was only habit that put them side-by-side more often than not.

The moon glowed above them, partially hidden by clouds. But even with the murmur of voices from the camps around and the glow of firelight in almost every direction, the expanse of sky made her feel as though they'd left the smothering feel of civilization far behind.

In this land, she could breathe.

It wasn't that she didn't love Virginia. Their ranch had been a wonderful place to grow up. A haven she still missed. And she and her sisters were planning to buy another ranch with their inheritance once they returned to the States.

But this wild territory was another kind of wonderful altogether. This place held a surprise at every turn and land-scape that filled her lungs with life. Animals that stirred both curiosity and respect. And a new breed of people—both native and trapper—who lived so differently from the rigid strictures required by so-called civilization.

She took a breath, held it deep within her body, then released it. Even laced with woodsmoke, the air still smelled fresh and invigorating.

"You look, um . . . happy about something." Though he kept his voice quiet, Riley's tone held a hint of humor.

Heat flushed through her. She hadn't meant to be so obvious. "Just enjoying the night air. It's so fresh here. Everything's far cleaner than back East. So much more wide open."

His raised brows could be seen even in the night shadows. "You think the trappers' camp is clean?"

He was teasing, but even so, she couldn't stop another blush. At least he couldn't see her turn red in the dark. "Not this exact spot. But the country around us feels so much freer. Not confining. Maybe it's because there aren't as many trees as we have back in Virginia. Makes me wish I'd brought my paints."

"You're an artist?"

She shook her head. "No. It's just fun to try to capture some of the beauty I see around us."

He didn't speak, and when she finally found the nerve to look at him again, he was watching her, his eyes intense.

His expression turned sheepish when she caught him, and he lifted his gaze upward, above the camp to the mountains beyond. His mouth formed a gentle curve. "I know what you mean. I've been out here three years now, and the sights still take my breath away. Then again, I'm not sure I could really breathe anywhere else."

They reached her lodge and paused as her sisters slipped

through the opening, one by one. This was her moment to thank him. The moonlight made the scene feel intimate. "Thank you again for all you've done to help us. I don't know how we would have managed if you hadn't set aside your own work to accomplish ours. I know it's been inconvenient, but thank you."

He studied her, his expression impossible to read. Maybe because shadows hid the nuances of his green eyes. His hand lifted, as though he wanted to touch her. She could reach out too, place her hand in his.

But he dropped his arm again, taking the possibility away. His throat worked. "I don't mind. I mean . . . I'm glad I can help. That is . . . I haven't really helped yet." He let out a laugh and looked away, then turned back a heartbeat later. "Sometimes when I'm around you, my tongue ties in knots." His mouth did that shy half-smile that looked so handsome on him, and she couldn't help grinning back.

He was attracted to her. Wasn't that what he was saying? Good thing her sisters had all disappeared inside the lodge, though they might be standing with their ears pressed to the animal hide, listening.

She raised her brows in a coy expression. But then she could think of nothing smart and sassy to say. With her mouth parted but no words coming out, she probably looked even sillier than she felt.

He noticed too, and the shyness in his look turned to humor. It seemed they were both struck dumb, and the humor of it bubbled inside her, spilling out into something far too close to a snort. She pressed her mouth shut, but the grin still tugged at her cheeks. His own chuckle soaked around her, filling her empty places with warm pleasure.

She let out a long breath. "I suppose you take my words away sometimes too."

His eyes glittered with humor as he spoke again. "You're a special lady, Juniper Collins. Not like anyone I've ever met." He cleared his throat. "Anyway, what I was trying to say is that we still have a ways to go to find Steps Right, but hopefully I can make some progress tomorrow. If you ladies can sketch the markings that might be on those horses, I'll show the page around at the horse races tomorrow."

Disappointment stabbed as he changed the topic back to business, but they needed to discuss it. To make plans. She nodded. "One of us can draw the brand while we prepare the morning meal."

He nodded, then stepped back, allowing her room to turn and step into the lodge.

She moved that direction, but in the doorway, she looked back at him. "Good night, Riley."

"G'night." He was watching her, so she turned away and stepped inside. Part of her wished he'd spoken her name with the farewell. Hearing it in his warm tones . . . Well, maybe it was better he didn't.

As the door flap fell behind her and she turned toward the interior, all three sisters stood before her.

She nearly jumped as her heart raced. She pressed her palm to the spot, then laid a finger on her lips to silence them all. Riley might still be standing outside, and the leather stretched over the lodgepoles couldn't be very soundproof.

She made the mistake of glancing at their faces, easily discernible in the light from the lantern one of them had lit while she was outside. Faith looked almost giddy, her hands propped on her hips, as though she was bursting to ask what had passed between Juniper and Riley. Nothing had, not really. But she couldn't stop the heat from rising into her cheeks.

Lorelei still cuddled little Boots to her chest, stroking the pup's soft neck scruff. Her expression was a bit harder to decipher, maybe a combination of schoolgirl longing and wariness.

But Rosemary . . . The frown Juniper expected to see there wasn't showing. Not a true frown, anyway. Dents bracketed her brows, but not from displeasure. More like from deep thought. Perhaps she didn't know what to think about Juniper's attraction to Riley either. They'd agreed nothing like this could happen with men they met in the West.

But they hadn't expected to meet Riley Turner.

At last, Rosemary's long sigh broke the silence. "Get ready for bed, girls. Morning comes early." She turned toward her own bundle of blankets.

Faith let out a laugh. "I'd rather hear about Juniper and Riley."

Juniper waved her off, then moved to settle in. "Go to bed, Faithy. There's nothing to tell." If Rosemary had decided they weren't going to talk about it tonight, Juniper was more than happy to put off the conversation.

⁕

Riley waded through the throng of men, searching for a familiar face. Anyone.

Maybe the races weren't the place to ask around if anyone had seen horses with the Collins' brand. It had seemed the best place to talk with the most people, but they were gathered so thick, it was impossible to start a conversation without being jostled too close or too far away to speak easily.

Maybe he was going about this all wrong. Maybe he should just hold out the paper with the marking drawn and start calling out like a street vendor. It might get him further than trying to squeeze through narrow openings and look for people he knew. And he had to start now, or he'd never make progress before the chaos of the race began.

He lifted the sketch. "Hey, fellas, looking for a horse with a marking like this branded on its shoulder. Have you seen anything?"

A few men looked his way and glanced at the paper in his hand. One only gave it a quick look, but the other two peered closer. All three shook their heads.

"Don't look familiar."

"That's different enough that I'd know if I'd seen it."

He nodded his thanks, then moved past them and raised his voice so another group could hear him. Mostly the same reaction there. One man thought he might've seen it a year or so back on a horse another trapper rode. He didn't know the man's name, though, and could only mark the place as "a couple weeks north o' here in the mountains."

Five more times Riley asked all within hearing distance as he lifted his voice over the rumble of the crowd.

Then a shout broke through his questioning. "Line them up, boys! Not a move till you hear the gunshot."

All eyes turned to the racetrack in front of them, including those of the men Riley had just been speaking to. He lowered the paper. He wouldn't get their attention again until after this heat had finished and all wagers were satisfied.

He was several rows back, but he could still see the horses in the distance that would be running. Four mounts in this race. Would Slim be riding one? Dragoon really should look into having the man run his little mare if he planned to race her again at this rendezvous. She might actually have a chance with a smaller rider.

The gun fired, and the horses sprinted forward. The crowd surged, shouts roaring all around him. The track wasn't long, just far enough to let the animals really stretch their legs for about a half minute. One animal fell behind near the end, but the other three finished close. There might be some arguing over who placed where.

After a few minutes of conversation, the murmuring among the onlookers rose. The talk sounded like friendly rivalry now, but if a winner wasn't announced soon, those who'd wagered the higher stakes might get impatient.

At last, a man led one of the horses from the group, its rider still sitting atop. The fellow on the ground waved his hat to the crowd. "She won, boys. My Liliana won."

A roar swept them up as trappers surged forward. The chaos would make it impossible for Riley to show the sketch to anyone else for a while, not until the men cleared the racetrack as they prepared for another round of races.

He ambled toward the starting line, where another set of mounts were being saddled. If he could talk with some of those who were paid jockeys, he might make some progress in the search. They saw quite a bit of horseflesh and were up close enough to notice a marking branded on the animal's shoulder.

A handful of men worked to ready the three horses that must be running in the next race. Only one fellow appeared short and lean enough to be one of the hired riders. He stood at the head of a paint mare, stroking it as someone else strapped on the saddle.

Riley walked toward him, and when the fellow glanced his way, recognition slipped in. Slim, the man who'd ridden the horse that beat Dragoon's mare. He would be a good one to ask.

Riley stopped a few steps back to allow the men room to work, but close enough to speak.

Slim shifted to look at Riley more fully. "You need something?"

Riley eyed him. "You're Slim, right? The one who's been riding so many of the winners?"

The man dipped his chin in a single nod. A hint of pride stretched in the set of his shoulders, but not as much as most men's would have after such a remark. He was watching Riley with a shrewd look. Maybe he thought Riley had come to hire him, but he didn't ask.

Riley pulled out the paper. "I have a question. For all of you, really." He glanced at the two other men working on the horse, then back at Slim. "I figure you've seen a lot of horseflesh. I'm looking for the owner of a horse who has a brand on its shoulder like this one. Two horses, actually, a chestnut mare and a paint stallion. Does this look familiar to you?"

The man studied the paper. His gaze flicked up to Riley for a single heartbeat before dropping to the page again. His expression seemed casual, maybe too casual, as he shook his head. "Horses in these parts don't usually have markings burned into their hide. A lot of what I ride are Indian ponies the trappers have traded for."

Was that a no? He hadn't actually said the word, though his statements had implied it. "So you haven't seen a horse marked with this symbol?"

Slim lifted his focus to Riley, and his mouth curved in a sympathetic smile. "Can't help you. Sorry."

A ripple of frustration pressed through him. He'd known this was a long shot to find the two horses. He turned to the other two. "Do either of you recognize this?"

The burly man studied it, then looked at Riley, much as Slim had done. But this time his eyes roamed down Riley's form and back up again, as though taking his measure. "The horse been stolen?"

It was a likely question, especially with so many animals going missing at this rendezvous. But something about the way the man asked it tightened his gut. He shook his head. "No, just trying to locate the owner. Have something to give back to them."

The fellow nodded. "Haven't seen the animal. Titus, that marking look familiar?"

The man on the near side of the saddle shook his head. "Not to me."

Riley fought to keep his frustration from showing. "Thanks for your help." Or lack of it.

He turned his focus to the group of men gathered around the next animal and moved that way. It seemed he had a long day ahead of him.

SEVENTEEN

Juniper kept her gaze trained on the supply wagons she and Rosemary were approaching. A lot of the trappers must be among those lining the raceway, but enough sat around the cook fires in camp that she and Rosie had to be careful as they made their way between the lodges.

Occasionally, slurred voices rose above those around them. She'd never seen so many intoxicated men in one place, except for in a saloon. Of course, she hadn't actually been in any saloons, but she'd glimpsed the crowds inside through the windows.

None of the men here at the rendezvous had physically accosted them, thank the Lord, but enough drunken voices called out questions and offers as they passed to keep her nerves dancing. What a difference it made to have Riley walk with them. The trappers had stopped bothering them at all when he accompanied, which was why she hadn't expected as much this time either.

A few even mentioned him when making their offer. *"Your feller finally decided to share with the rest of us?"* and

155

"How did you sneak out without your guard, sweethearts? Don't worry, I'll protect you."

They finally reached the row of wagons and easily spotted Mr. Provost standing at the rear of the second one. He was riffling through the contents, but as they approached, he straightened and turned to them with the smile she'd learned to trust on their journey here.

"Good morning, ladies. What a pleasant surprise. I haven't seen much of you since we arrived." His mouth tightened with that last bit, probably as he remembered the shocking news he'd delivered to them that first day.

"Good morning." Rosie made a show of scanning the first few wagons. "It looks like your supplies are almost gone."

He nodded and glanced down the row. "The trading's progressed faster than we expected. More men here than usual. This is definitely the biggest rendezvous so far." He turned his focus to them. "I was going to come by and tell you we're hoping to finish up today or tomorrow at the latest. We'll be leaving two days from now, early in the morning." His eyes searched them. "Have you found your father's friend?"

They hadn't told him much about their mission, only that they'd come to find someone their father once knew. They hadn't given Mr. Provost the details because he wasn't from this area. He was part of the eastern branch of the partnership who organized the supplies for the rendezvous, and he also managed the wagons traveling West.

Rosie stayed quiet, and she didn't look Juniper's direction, so it was impossible to read her thoughts. In fact, it seemed like she wouldn't answer at all. Was she expecting Juniper to? Rosie always did the talking for them.

Juniper moved forward so she could nudge her sister's arm, but Rosie finally spoke. "We haven't found her. We'd hoped to have a few more days before starting back."

Mr. Provost's brows raised. "It's a her?"

Rosie still wasn't looking at Juniper, so she couldn't signal with her eyes. Perhaps they should at least tell him about Steps Right. Who knew whether he'd crossed paths with her in his travels?

Juniper nodded to Mr. Provost. "She's a woman from the Peigan Blackfoot tribe. Her name is Steps Right, and our father met her when he traveled through here twenty years ago. We don't know much more than that, except that she should also have two horses he later sent to her. They might have the same markings that are branded on our horses. Do you know of anyone that might describe?"

His lips rolled in as he thought. "That's not much to go on. I've met quite a few Peigan at the various rendezvous, but not many of their women. None that stood out to me so much I'd remember their names." His gaze turned apologetic. "Sorry I can't be more help."

He paused, then added, "Do you still plan to travel back with us?"

Juniper looked to Rosemary, and her sister lifted her chin. "We'll need to discuss it. I'll let you know our answer to-morrow."

Mr. Provost nodded. "I understand. Sorry things haven't worked out the way you'd hoped."

They made their farewells, then headed back to their lodge. The men's comments as they walked no longer made her nervous. Frustration simmered within her. Nothing was going as they'd hoped. Even with Riley's help, they'd exhausted every lead with the natives, and now it looked like they would be losing their safe passage home. On top of that, these ill-mannered trappers couldn't manage to hold their tongues.

Maybe Riley's day was going better as he showed the sketch of the brand around. *Thank you, Lord, for Riley.*

As their lodge came into view, two people standing in front of it caught her notice. That might not have stood out normally, for men always seemed to loiter around their door flap during daylight hours. But one of them was Lorelei, her periwinkle-blue dress obvious even from a distance. It was the prettiest one she'd brought along, though still plain compared to what she usually wore back home. Who was she talking to? And why were the two standing so close?

Juniper's chest tightened. They'd given Lorelei and Faith strict instructions not to leave the lodge. Surely she would only break that rule if Riley came. And if he was back so soon, did that mean he had news? *Good* news?

She and Rosie both increased their pace, but as they drew near, they saw the man speaking to Lorelei wasn't Riley. Mr. Dragoon spun toward them as she and Rosie approached. Lorelei held the pup in her arms. Maybe he'd gotten away again. But he wouldn't have if they'd kept the lodge flap secured.

"What are you doing, Lorelei?" Rosemary barked.

Was it Juniper's imagination, or was that a blush creeping over Lorelei's face? What was going on with those two? A knot coiled tight in Juniper's belly.

Mr. Dragoon looked friendly as always. "Hello, ladies. I stopped by to check on you all since Riley's at the races.

See if you need any water carried or wood brought in. Miss Lorelei said the two of you went to learn what day the wagons are leaving."

His words didn't explain what he and their sister were discussing when they'd approached. Water and firewood certainly wouldn't make Lorelei blush. Had she developed an attachment to him? Dragoon was older than Riley by at least five years. Maybe ten. And Lorelei was only eighteen. Certainly women her age and younger married, and sometimes to men far older. But Dragoon wasn't the one for her. Nothing about the match felt right.

Juniper stepped forward even as Rosie answered the man with a curt "We did." Clearly she didn't like the thought of what they'd come upon either.

Juniper reached her younger sister and touched her arm. "We're having a family meeting, Lorelei. Come inside."

Rosemary moved in behind them, like a mother hen shooing her brood toward the lodge door. "Good day, Mr. Dragoon."

Thankfully, the man didn't try to waylay them any further. Just tipped his hat with a "Good day, ladies."

When they stepped inside the lodge, they could see Faith lying on her pallet with a book. What did their little sister think of Lorelei stepping outside with that man?

Once she'd secured the door flap, Rosemary spun on Lorelei. "I thought I made it clear neither of you were to leave this lodge. What were you doing out there?"

Lor dipped her chin, her cheeks turning pink. "He came by to ask about water and wood, like he said. Didn't he, Faith?"

"He did." Faith looked somewhat amused.

Lorelei turned back to Rosemary. "I needed to let Boots do his business, so I stepped outside to answer Mr. Dragoon. I didn't think you wished him to come in here to speak to us." She lifted her brows with that last bit.

The situation she described sounded possible and much more innocent than the two had looked. Juniper worked to keep her voice level. "Why were you speaking so close to him?"

Lorelei's ears turned cherry red. "We weren't close."

Juniper frowned. "There wasn't more than an arm's length between the two of you. What was he saying to you?"

Lorelei rolled her lips together, clearly hesitant about whether she should speak truthfully.

"Tell us, Lorelei, just say it." Rosie softened her voice. "We promised not to keep secrets." They were all one another had, and they could only accomplish their mission in this wilderness among all these men if they stuck together.

Lorelei's expression relaxed, then her eyes grew bright. "He asked if I'd be interested in riding his horse in a race tomorrow. He said he'd seen how I am with animals and he thinks I'd have the perfect hand with her. We'd be certain to win."

A new tightening clenched in Juniper's middle. "What did you tell him?"

Lorelei's eyes narrowed. "You interrupted before I could answer."

"I'm sure he realizes the answer is no." Rosemary turned to the area they used as a dressing table and began organizing the brushes and bottles.

"But why should it be no?" Faith set her book aside and

sat up. "That sounds thrilling, and you'd be so good at it, Lor. He's right. You could coax any animal to its best."

"She's not going to be a spectacle before hundreds of men." Rosemary's voice held her don't-argue-with-me tone.

Lorelei crossed her arms. "But what if I *want* to ride in the race?"

Rosie spun, a comb in one hand and a ribbon in the other. "You want to parade yourself in front of all those hungry eyes? Think, Lorelei. We're trying *not* to stir up too much notice. That would do just the opposite."

Lorelei's eyes widened. "But I wonder if I could use it as an opportunity to ask about the horses, or maybe even about Steps Right. If I win the race, I'll have the attention of all those men. I can explain what we're searching for. They'll be eager to help, I'm sure." She gave a little hop of excitement. "That's it. That's how we can find her."

"No!" Rosemary's nostrils flared. "Not even to find Steps Right would I make you a showpiece in front of all those trappers. It would put you in untold danger. Absolutely not."

They needed to calm things before the girls raised their voices too loudly. Juniper took a step forward. "Anyway, we need to talk about what we learned from Mr. Provost. We've a decision to make."

Lorelei's shoulders eased. "What did he say?"

Juniper moved to her bedding and motioned toward the blankets Rosemary and Lorelei both used. "Sit. Family meeting."

Once they'd all settled cross-legged, Rosie took the lead. "Mr. Provost plans to head out with the wagons the morning after next. We need to decide if we're going with him or if we stay here to find Steps Right."

"We have to find her." Faith looked surprised they would consider the opposite. "That's the whole reason we came here. We can't leave without finishing. I know we'd planned to get back in time to buy a ranch and be settled by winter, but we have to see this through. The entire trip would be a waste if we don't."

Rosie nodded slowly. "That was my thought, but we need to consider some things. The wagons were to be our safe passage back. If we don't go with them, do we hire someone else to travel with us? If so, who? And do we have enough money?"

"Riley, of course." Faith shot Juniper a look when she said it. "I doubt he'd take our money willingly, but if we insist, I'm sure he'd only accept what we had to give."

Juniper opened her mouth to respond. It seemed like she needed to defend herself, though what she should say escaped her.

Rosie relieved her of the need. "We talked about that before. We won't accept gifts from anyone, not even Riley. We'll pay a fair wage for every service we accept. The last thing we need is a man to think we owe him something that he can receive payment for in any way he chooses."

Now it wasn't herself she needed to defend, but Riley. Yet Rosemary was only stating what they'd all said before setting out on this trip. What they'd agreed to. Still . . .

Juniper straightened. "I do agree that's the best way to handle our business, though not every man would take advantage like that."

Rosie shot her a look that said she wasn't helping matters. "Of course not every man would do it, but we must keep to that policy in all situations. It will only protect us, and there's no reason not to. We brought sufficient coin." Sewn into the hemlines of every garment they'd brought and tucked in a number of other unlikely places. They'd certainly packed enough money, though a man who tried to rob them would have a hard time finding it all.

"None of that is really the point." Lorelei's voice seemed more cautious than usual, probably because she'd no desire to be under scrutiny again. "We're trying to decide how we would gain safe passage back to the States without the wagons. I agree we should ask Riley. Maybe he could gather a group of men he trusted, enough for protection should we run into danger." The pup had curled in her lap, nestled in her dress as she stroked a finger down its fuzzy side. That little coyote might never agree to leave her when it was time to release him.

"We should talk with Riley and make sure he's willing to take on the task. Just because he's dropped everything to help us these past few days doesn't mean he'll be able to continue for several months of travel."

Several more months with Riley . . . The idea held far too much appeal. Yet the time would end with saying goodbye to him. Forever. She had to remember that. Had to keep her heart from becoming too engaged in their friendship.

Rosie let out a breath. "The other thing we need to consider—*earnestly* consider—" she moved her gaze around the group to land on each of them—"is whether we'll actually find Steps Right. Now that we know the situation here better, are the chances of us locating her too small?"

It was hard to tell from Rosie's expression what she

thought of the question she'd just asked. Juniper shivered. "Do you think it's a hopeless cause?"

"I don't know. It seems like either she wants to remain hidden, or her people don't want us to find her."

"I still think she's being held hostage." Faith sounded almost excited about the prospect. About the adventure of it anyway.

And the adventure of a lengthy search did sound appealing. Sort of like when she and Rosie were girls and they would set out on horseback for a full day of riding through the pastures—except this would be on a much grander scale.

Of course, there was no Peigan woman being hidden against her will on their escapades.

Could that really be the case now? Out here, thrilling scenarios seemed more likely than back home.

Rosie looked uncertain. "I suppose we can mention the idea to Riley again. See if he thinks we should pursue it." It was remarkable how much they all relied on him now. Perhaps he should have been invited to their family meeting. Juniper pressed her lips together to keep her smile in.

"And if she's not being held hostage, do we still think we'll find her?" Lorelei's quiet question wiped away the humor from Juniper's spirit.

Would they? It was impossible to know for sure.

"June, what are you thinking? You haven't said much." Rosie was studying her.

Juniper swallowed and glanced around at her sisters, ending with Rosemary. "We can plant the seed in the sunshine and water it, but only the Lord can bring the crop. I don't think we can know for sure. We'll just have to try. Put everything we have into the search, and pray God leads us to her."

Smile lines fanned out from Rosie's eyes, but her mouth stayed solemn. "All right, then. If Riley agrees, we'll stay and finish what we started. And pray God does what only He can do."

EIGHTEEN

This search was more exhausting than spending all day scraping hides. Riley's bones ached as he trudged back toward his lodge. It must be the disappointment of receiving one no after another that wearied him so. Either that, or the sheer number of men he spoke with that day. He hadn't talked to so many fellows in the last three years combined.

He'd received plenty of strange looks and heard at least five stories of horses stolen recently—those men likely thought he was hunting stolen horses too. Only one fellow said he'd definitely seen the brand before, and the sisters would likely be interested in his comments.

He couldn't help hoping the ladies would be sitting around his campfire when he came within sight of it. They would probably be coming to cook, after all. That's what they'd done that morning, though other times they'd simply taken the food back to their own lodge to prepare. They were probably getting tired of meals made with only meat and what few greens Jeremiah and Ol' Henry had brought in. But he didn't dare use up what little flour he'd managed to trade for, not before the year even began. Plenty of trappers had made hoecakes to celebrate the rendezvous, but flour was so very precious.

The top of his lodge came into view, and his heart picked up speed. Foolish thoughts were to blame for that. He couldn't let himself get so upended over Miss Juniper Collins. Not only was she far above his station, but she and her sisters would be leaving soon. He'd never see her again. This was the life he'd chosen—the life he loved. He couldn't let his head be swayed by a pretty face who didn't plan to stick around.

But as he finally approached near enough for a clear view of the figures in front of his lodge, the leap in his chest ignored every rational thought.

The four women sat around the campfire, and Juniper's hair shone in the evening light. She knelt beside the stone they used for cooking, and that angle outlined her comely form far too well. She was beautiful. He couldn't ignore that fact no matter how hard he tried.

Her inner beauty definitely added to the appeal. The way she was so devoted to her sisters. The intelligence she so often showed in her questions and quiet suggestions. She didn't push her opinions or crow when she was proved right, just offered her quiet presence as support. The younger sisters definitely looked up to her, and that alone said much. Yet did they realize what a treasure they had in her? He had a feeling they didn't.

And she could even cook over a campfire. How much more could he ask than that?

He struck the thought aside as he stepped into the camp.

Several of the women looked up at him, but it was Juniper's sweet smile that drew his notice.

Her gaze searched his face. "Are you hungry? The meal should be ready in just a few minutes."

Now that he thought about it, his belly had been grumbling for a while. Yet the aroma drifting from the fire wasn't mere *food*. This was a meal, a delicious experience. A stack of meat was laid to the side, and Juniper worked with something that looked an awful lot like johnnycake.

His belly gave a fresh leap, and his mouth watered of its own accord. "You got flour?" Apparently he'd been fooling himself about the need to ration his supply. They could gladly scoop from his flour barrel to make food that looked and smelled this good.

"Mr. Dragoon brought us some and asked us to use it in the meal this evening." She looked hesitant, as though she thought she might have done the wrong thing.

He grinned. "Good. Wish I'd done that myself."

A shy smile brightened her face, but she covered it by turning back to the food.

He moved his own focus to the others just in time to see Rosemary watching him. Her expression looked as wary as a mother elk protecting her young. Not trusting, and not about to back down. She'd shown herself to be protective of her younger sisters, a fierce leader of their group.

When he was looking at Juniper, he must have shown something of his thoughts in his expression. Either that or she suspected her sister was partial to him. Did she not approve of him, then?

But even if he did admire Juniper, she would be leaving soon, so he couldn't let himself grow attached. The sisters had plans back in Virginia, and he was content here among these mountains. Rosemary had nothing to be concerned about.

He ignored the pressure in his chest and shifted his focus to the other two. Faith was working a needle through the bunch of cloth in her lap, and Lorelei sat with the coyote, stroking its fur.

Riley nodded to the animal. "Looks like he's grown in these few days."

Lorelei looked at the pup with a smile that bordered on besotted. He appreciated the companionship of animals as much as the next fellow, especially working as a trapper through the long winters, when he liked his horse and pack mule a lot better than his campmates some days, but her attachment to that pup seemed a bit extreme. Maybe losing both parents made her look for that connection in animals. He well knew how the pain of loss could bring on irrational thinking. He'd watched that happen with his mother. Thankfully, Miss Lorelei didn't seem as affected as Mother had been.

"Have you learned anything about the horses?" Rosemary's voice broke into his thoughts.

He lifted the sketch, which had wrinkled with the day's activities. "I showed this at all the races. I think I must have spoken with half the trappers here at least. Maybe more."

She lifted her brows. "And?"

"Most said they'd never seen the brand. There was one old fellow who remembered a trapper who rode a horse with a marking like this on its shoulder, but he said it was at least two years ago when he saw it, maybe three."

Eagerness spread across Juniper's face. "Could he describe the horse?"

Riley hesitated. "Not really. He said he thought it might've been sorrel. I'm thinking the white bonnet would've been something he'd notice, so it must've been the mare."

Rosemary frowned. "How would the trapper get one of the horses from Steps Right?"

He shrugged. "Traded, I imagine. That's pretty common."

Faith let out a dramatic sigh. "So you're saying there's almost no chance Steps Right still has both horses. And it's quite possible the two horses aren't still together. We'll spend all this time and effort looking for them and simply find two grizzled old trappers."

Juniper turned to her sister. "It's actually Riley who's put in all the time and effort today." She looked back at him. "Did you even stop to eat?"

It'd been forever since he'd had a woman worry about whether he missed a meal. He let himself rest in those blue eyes. "I took food with me."

She nodded with a little smile, then dropped her focus back to her work. Since her gaze no longer held him tight, he turned to Faith. "There's a good chance you're right. It's impossible to say for sure, of course. But I'm far less confident that seeking out the horses will lead us to Steps Right." And he'd not thought it a strong possibility to begin with.

"What then?" Lorelei finally raised a tentative voice. She certainly was the quiet one in the group.

He released a long breath. "That's what I've been thinking through. It seems the most likely way to find her is the way we'd started off searching. Go from one camp to the next, asking if anyone knows her."

"Do you think they'll tell us the truth?" Rosemary looked doubtful.

All he could do was shrug. "Can't say for sure. We'll have to look for signs that they're not. I'd suggest we seek out that small Peigan camp again. Maybe watch them for a while and see if and what they're hiding."

Rosemary nodded, but her mouth still held a thin line. If she didn't like that idea, she might be even less pleased with his next suggestion.

He did his best to keep his voice level. "Searching is going to take time. And it won't be safe for white women. We'll have to go much farther north into Blackfoot country. I know you were hoping to find her before the supply wagons went East. Why don't you ladies travel back with the wagons? I'll keep looking, and when I find her, I can give her whatever message you leave with me. Once I locate her, I'll come East to you and tell you everything. I'll even bring her to you if I can get her to come, though I don't think that's likely."

All four women had stopped what they were doing to watch him as he spoke. But now a look moved between them. Clearly they'd already discussed something like this. Was there a chance they might actually return home and let him finish this mission on their behalf? They'd been so determined to be with him each step of the way, he'd not thought it possible they would hand over the entire project to him, though he'd had to ask. If he knew they were safe, he would gladly travel every square mile of this mountain wilderness to find the woman they sought.

Rosemary lifted her chin. "We spoke to Mr. Provost this morning and he said the wagons will start East the morning after tomorrow. We discussed it among ourselves, and we don't plan to travel with them. We'll stay and find Steps Right as we set out to do."

Her posture softened a little. "You're wise, though, when you said it's not a good idea for four women to travel through the Indian camps alone. You've been more than gracious to help us so far, and we appreciate everything. If you're amenable to continuing the search, we'd like to hire you as a guide until we find her. Even once we find her, though, we understand it might not be advisable for the four of us to travel back East alone. We'll pay you, or men you recommend, to escort us until we reach a place where we can procure safe passage."

She'd been watching him with that shrewd gaze throughout her speech. "We realize this may take a while. Weeks, at least, to find Steps Right, then months to take us East and return here if you wish to. We've already taken much of your time, so we understand if you can't continue with us. But we respect your opinion and hope you can direct us to men who would be willing to guide and protect us for compensation."

There was that notion of payment again. His gut roiled with everything she'd said. There was no way he'd hand them off to another man, not when he was around to do the job himself.

But spending several more months with these women? Sharing meals and long rides and night after night of camping under the stars . . . He wasn't sure he could keep himself detached through all that. Juniper's charms would be far too strong to resist with so much time around her. Not that he would do anything untoward, but he had a feeling his heart might not come out of this unscathed. He'd have to ponder what to do about that.

But for now, there was only one answer to Rosemary's question. He gave a single decisive nod. "I'm willing. Let's make a plan."

NINETEEN

I can't believe he would dare ask her."

Juniper watched as Riley stalked from one bag of supplies to the other. Rosie had taken the younger girls to the river to catch up on washing before they set out in the morning for their journey northward, while she helped Riley pack the food they'd need.

These few minutes alone finally gave her the chance to tell him about what happened when she and Rosie found Dragoon and Lorelei talking. He seemed as upset about it as they'd been.

He jerked the leather tight on the bundle he'd just rolled, and she pressed her finger over the strap to hold it secure while he tied the knot. "He'd already mentioned to me the idea of asking Lorelei to ride, and I said absolutely not. That would put her in far too much danger, both from the horses and the men. I thought he agreed. I can't believe he still asked her."

She prepared to pull her finger away from the leather as he jerked the strap hard to secure the knot. They'd worked together like this on four other packs with no problem, but he'd not been nearly so riled with those.

"I'm sure Lorelei would do well in the race and could handle the horse with no problem, but Rosie and I both agree it's not a good idea for her to be paraded in front of the men like that." Did she dare say what had really bothered her about the situation?

This was Riley. If she could trust anyone, she could trust him. "I think what troubled me most about their talking—and why I wanted to tell you—is the way they looked and acted when we first came upon them. They'd been standing close together as they spoke, and when we called out, Lorelei acted flustered, like she'd been doing something wrong. Maybe it was just that she'd actually been considering riding in the race."

Riley was watching her. "You think Dragoon might have other intentions toward your sister?" He didn't say it as though he discounted the idea. Nor like he'd already thought of it. He sounded as if he respected her opinion and was thinking through this new possibility she raised.

She turned her focus to his question. "I'm not sure. I just . . . thought you should know. To help watch them."

He was still studying her, though he seemed mostly thoughtful now. "Do you think I should tell him not to come with us on the search? Would you be uncomfortable having him so near her every day?"

He would send his friend away just because she asked it? When they'd made plans for the journey north to search among the Blackfoot camps for Steps Right, they'd decided it wise to add a few more numbers to their group. So they'd invited Riley's lodgemates to come along. Jeremiah had already made plans to head toward the Yellowstone River with a different trapping party, but Dragoon and Ol' Henry agreed to come.

If they now asked Dragoon not to accompany them, would he be angry? Hurt, for sure. And he didn't seem a bad sort in general. They would just have to watch him and Lorelei more closely. After all, the entire situation may have only been about racing the horse. Animals were certainly her sister's weakness.

Juniper shook her head. "As long as you think he's trustworthy, we'll just keep an eye on him and Lorelei."

Riley nodded, and his throat worked as his attention dipped to the next bundle he was rolling. He seemed to be considering something, maybe even battling over a decision. "I *thought* he was trustworthy. I know him as well as I do anyone out here, and I don't think he would do anything to intentionally bring harm. It's hard to know anyone for certain."

He looked up at her, his eyes so earnest. "Even when you think you know a person, sometimes they change." There was a sadness in those green depths that made her chest ache. He seemed to be talking about someone else. Someone who'd hurt him badly. Was it a woman? Is that why he'd become a trapper in this remote wilderness, so far from civilization?

She shouldn't pry, but every part of her longed to know more about him. Not just the facts of his life, but the deeper moments that made him who he was today. How he felt about each step in his journey. Maybe she could start with a question or two and let him answer as much as he wanted. She would be grateful for any morsel he offered.

She kept her voice gentle. "What made you come to these mountains? It's so remote. So far away from people, and from what you've described, the work seems like it might be lonely."

Something in his expression shifted. Maybe from surprise, or maybe he was simply thinking through his answer. She didn't try to hide that she was watching him.

Whatever shutters had shielded his gaze before now slipped away. A sad smile touched his eyes. "The happiest time I can remember was back when I was a young boy and my father would take me out riding. Sometimes we'd hunt, and other times we'd just explore. He would talk to me, though, and teach me about the land. About how the animals acted and why. I was only five or six, so I'm sure he couldn't have gone into very much detail, but I remember being fascinated on those rides. Each time, I would feel like I understood the animals and the frontier around us so much better. We didn't have mountains in Illinois, but he would take me up to the tops of hills and we'd stare out at the country around us. He'd show me how to read the terrain by looking at the trees. I guess maybe that's why I like to add markings and shading to my maps, to show what the land really looks like."

An image formed in her mind of a little boy riding a big horse beside a tall man with Riley's strong outline, and the burn of her own memories formed. Growing up on the ranch had been a wonderful place. Their father had been busy with the stock and his wranglers, but he'd taken time to teach his girls to ride. To love the adventure of discovering. She and Rosie had explored for hours at a time. They'd been older than five or six, though.

His mouth pressed in a painful-looking twist. "When I was six and we were on one of those rides, we got separated. A man and woman found me and told me they'd take me to my father, but instead, they took me home with them. They wouldn't let me leave, no matter how much I cried. It was almost three weeks before my parents found me. I don't remember much from that time, except crying for my family and begging to go home. They didn't hurt me. I remember them feeding me. Later on, I pieced together that they had lost a son and wanted to raise me as their own. But I mostly just remember being so helpless and scared."

A bit of hardness crept into his tone. "I was never so relieved as when I heard my father's voice outside that cabin. He and some of our neighbors had been searching for me the entire time, and finally they found me. While the other men rounded up the couple who had kidnapped me, I ran to my father. I wanted to climb into his arms, to sit with him in the saddle on the way home and know we would never be separated again. I think he probably did hug me, but nothing felt right. It was like he changed during the search and put up a wall between us. I was only home for a few days before he left for his first surveying trip. After that, he didn't come back very often, and we never went out riding together. Not ever."

A lump of emotion clogged her throat and tears burned her eyes, though she swallowed them down. She would never have imagined he'd endured all that at such a young age. And then after he'd been found, why would his father begin a job that took him away from his family so much? It seemed like the man he described before would be overjoyed to have his son back.

Riley had already shared so much, maybe he wouldn't mind another question. "Why did your father leave after he found you? I would think he'd want to stay even closer to protect you."

He shrugged, as if the answer didn't matter. It had to, though. She could see it in his eyes. "I think he thought me being taken was his fault because we got separated while I was riding with him. At least, that's what my mother said once." It sounded as though he didn't believe her.

She studied him, doing her best to imagine how she would feel after enduring something so awful, then practically losing her father all over again. "At least you still had your mother. You two must have been close."

Something shifted in his gaze, as though the shutters settled back over his eyes. Had she said something wrong? He'd said his mother was still alive, she was sure of it. She was living with his aunt and uncle.

"Mother is . . . well, we're not close. Her mind started to grow weak, and she became a different person. She hasn't felt like a mother for a long time. I do have a vague memory of her reading to me, of sitting on her lap while she sang and played with my hair. But I was very young at the time."

A new ache welled in her chest. "Did she change when you were kidnapped too?"

He shrugged again. "Maybe. I'm not certain, but when I was old enough to realize she didn't always think clearly, I looked back and realized some of the changes started around the time my father began guiding the surveying groups."

"And your father left you with her? Did you tell him what was happening?"

His throat worked, and his features seemed to harden. "She wasn't dangerous. I was the man of the family, and it's the man's job to protect the women in his care."

A surge of anger shot through her. "Your *father* was the man of the family. You were just a boy. Their *son*, whom *they* should have protected and cared for. Not the other way around."

He gave her a tight smile. "I was older by the time things started to get hard with Mother. Twelve, at least. I was used to taking care of things. The next year was when my father went missing in a snowstorm. The spring after that, we received news of his passing."

She shook her head. She'd assumed his intense protectiveness toward her and her sisters had been ingrained in him after his father died and he was left to care for his mother. She'd had no idea the extent of the responsibility he'd shouldered from such an early age. Six years old.

She reached out and touched his arm, letting her hand rest there. If only she could do something to make things better for him, to go back and erase the hard times and fear and helplessness he must have felt as he struggled to grow up so quickly. "I'm so sorry you had to experience all that. And with no siblings. Even when things were difficult in our family, when our mother died, I had Rosie and Lorelei and Faith."

The darkest time in her life had been much earlier than Mama's death, back in those months when Mama and Rosie left. She'd floundered without her elder sister and best friend, but that sounded like a trifle compared to Riley's story.

She squeezed his arm. "You have us now too. No matter how hard things get, we're here for you."

His mouth tried to smile, but his eyes didn't manage it. "For now, anyway. You'll be going home when we find Steps Right."

A new pain pressed inside her. He'd said *when*, not *if*. And somehow, that confidence that they'd complete this mission only made her feel worse. How could she ever leave this man? Yet she and her sisters had a plan. A horse farm to purchase. A new life to build.

Feminine voices sounded, drawing her from the painful thoughts. When her sisters rounded the corner of the lodge, clothing bundles in hand, Faith was chattering about the upcoming horse race.

She flashed Juniper and Riley a smile. "Are you finished? We can already see the men lining up along the raceway."

Juniper nodded as she glanced at Riley, but he'd returned his focus to the final bundle he was rolling. "You can go put your washing in your lodge. I'll finish this last piece and walk with you up to a place we can watch away from the commotion."

He didn't look her way, and she had the distinct impression he was telling her to go with her sisters. The reminder that they would only have these few weeks or months together seemed to have made him pull back.

She should do the same. Yet the idea of closing herself away from Riley brought a physical pain in her chest. Her lungs ached.

She pushed to her feet and turned to accompany her sisters but couldn't quite manage a smile as she fell into step with them.

TWENTY

J uniper was just stowing her clean clothes in her pack
when Riley tapped on their lodge door flap only a few
minutes after they had reached it themselves. "We need
to get moving so we can reach the spot before the races
start. I don't know which heat Dragoon's mare will run in."

They were ready, and Rosemary pushed back the door
flap to step out. "Did he get that Slim fellow lined up to
ride her?"

Riley's gaze flicked to Lorelei for half a heartbeat before
he answered. "Not sure. He was hoping to."

He seemed especially reserved as he led them through
the camp southward, then around the horses being readied
to race. Dragoon stood beside his horse, speaking to two
men as they passed. The mare wasn't saddled yet, so maybe
she wouldn't be running in one of the first few heats.

Riley looked as though he planned to walk past the animal without stopping, but Lorelei veered toward the horse
like a compass needle to north. The rest of them paused a
few steps behind her.

Dragoon was so engrossed in his conversation, he didn't even seem to see them. Was Mr. Slim one of the men he spoke with? Both possessed lean forms, but one stood a head above the other.

The taller man slid a glance at them, then nodded at Dragoon and sauntered toward the mare. He stopped at Bessie's head and stroked her muzzle as he took in Lorelei. He didn't look lustful, just curious.

For Lorelei's part, she ignored the man as she stood at the horse's shoulder, crooning and scratching one of the places horses usually loved best. Juniper stepped nearer her sister, keeping her focus mainly on the man.

Riley came to her side. "Ladies, this is Slim . . ." He paused and looked at the man. "I guess I don't know your last name."

The corners of the fellow's mouth tipped. "Folks just call me Slim." He took them all in. "You must be the Collins girls." His chin dipped in greeting, and it was refreshing not to see any hint of lasciviousness in his eyes. Odd that he called them *girls* instead of ladies, but perhaps that was because they were probably three decades younger than he was. He looked to be around Papa's age.

Dragoon stepped up beside Mr. Slim and clapped a hand on the man's shoulder. "I see you ladies have met my secret weapon. Slim here can win on any animal he climbs aboard. He's been racing Indian ponies out here for nigh on twenty years."

Slim sent Dragoon a tight smile. "Not quite that long. But I do appreciate good quality horseflesh."

Dragoon chuckled. "You've a good eye, for you win nearly every race you run. You and Bessie together will earn me a heap with all the wagers I have going."

"That means we'd best find a place to watch." Riley's voice held a hint of impatience with his friend.

After giving their best wishes to the men, they turned toward the base of the hills that lined the other side of the raceway.

Riley pointed partway up the slope. "There's a cluster of rocks that make a nice place to sit and watch. They're protected enough that not many can see you there."

It didn't seem possible to have a clear view of the goings-on without being easily seen themselves, but the boulders allowed enough space in between that Riley proved right. The five of them settled, with Riley at one end, then Faith and Lorelei in the middle, where Lor would have the best view. Juniper and Rosie were positioned on the other end from Riley. Perhaps it was best she gave him space.

It's what he seemed to want from her. Though she ended up watching him more than the races.

It was also fun to see the pleasure on Lorelei's face as she kept her eyes glued to the animals. They hadn't been wrong to stop her from riding in the contests, but perhaps they could find another way for her to experience the pleasure of a race. Maybe once they were on the trail, Mr. Dragoon would allow her to ride his mare. Someone else could ride one of the others horses and allow Lorelei a real race—far away from all these rowdy onlookers.

"There she is. There's Bessie." Faith rose up on her knees and leaned forward, making herself far more conspicuous to the spectators below.

Three horses lined up in the starting position, Bessie on the far left. There were no turns on the track, so none of the animals would have the advantage of the inside position.

Watching from so far above gave them the ability to see the start and finish lines equally well, though they couldn't see expressions on the riders or handlers, nor hear what was being said. Not well enough to decipher words, anyway.

Juniper's insides bunched as the crowd quieted in expectation of the pistol shot. When the bang sounded, the horses sprinted forward. The one in the center, a dark gray with a black mane and tail, took the early lead. Bessie settled in, with her nose positioned by the lead rider's leg. The third horse fell a full length behind, and its rider snapped a whip to urge it forward.

This track wasn't as long as the other raceway her father had taken her and Rosie to when they were younger, but the horses here still had plenty of room to stretch out in a gallop for a strong competition. When only a quarter of the route remained, Slim bent lower over Bessie's neck. Even from this distance, she could see the way he urged the horse forward.

And Bessie responded. Her stride lengthened. She seemed to flatten to the ground even as she stretched out.

The effort worked, for she gained ground on the leader. By the time they surged over the finish line, she'd pulled half a neck ahead of the gray.

Juniper squealed and clapped as her sisters did, but their sounds were lost in the roar of the crowd below. Even Riley grinned and raised his hat in victory.

After Dragoon led the horse and rider back down the track in the victor's walk, the spectators finally settled down and another group queued up to race.

Lorelei pointed to a cluster of rocks at the bottom of the hill. "I'm going to move down there where I can see the horses better. I can't get a good look in their eyes from up here."

"Not by yourself." Rosie straightened. "I guess I can come with you." She eyed the boulders Lorelei meant with a frown. There were probably still enough rocks to protect the two of them from the ogling eyes of men.

"I'm coming too." Faith rose to a crouching stand and strode to the path down the slope.

Rosie let out a long-suffering sigh.

"Should we all come?" Juniper gathered her feet beneath her to stand.

But her sister shook her head. "There's not enough rocks to cover us all. I'll just go make sure those two behave. Lor can watch a couple races from there, then we'll walk back up here."

Juniper nodded and sank back to sit on her heels as Rosie ducked low and followed their younger sisters. Though noise from the men sounded in the distance, a kind of quiet awareness settled between her and Riley as they watched Rosie, Lorelei, and Faith perch on the rocks below.

Thankfully, a new group of horses were almost ready to race. A welcome distraction. Three horses would run in this match—a compact bay, a sorrel with a splash of white over one eye and a rear leg, and a roan with spots covering a patch of white on its rump.

Riley pointed toward the animals. "See that one closest to us with the blanket of spots on its hindquarters?"

She nodded to show she saw the horse.

"They call animals with spotted markings like that Palouse ponies. They're bred by the Nez Perce villages across the mountains."

She glanced toward the peaks he meant, as though she could see the natives who lived beyond. Then she focused back on the horse. "It's striking. How did they get those markings?"

He shrugged. "Not sure. But those animals are also known for their speed and endurance. If I were wagering in this race, I'd put my bet on that mare."

The starting gun sounded, and she sucked in a breath when the horses charged forward. The roar of the crowd drowned out the thundering in her chest as the animals tore down the raceway. As Riley predicted, the Indian pony pulled ahead and held that position, winning by over a horse-length.

While the crowd whooped and cheered, she sank back on her heels and turned to Riley with a grin. "You were right."

His eyes sparkled, and his teeth flashed white. "I've never seen one of those horses that doesn't stand out when tested. They can be feisty, though, some of them."

She studied him as she thought of his own riding horse, a simple bay with no unusual markings. "Have you ever owned a Palouse pony?"

He shook his head, his expression growing thoughtful. "They're more expensive to trade for, and I don't do much buffalo hunting, which is where they really excel. Maybe someday."

There was a hint of wistfulness in his tone that reminded her of his other *someday* dream. If only she could help him accomplish at least one of these secret hopes.

Was there a chance they . . . ?

It might not work out, but perhaps. She had to ask. "When we head north tomorrow, is it possible we could travel through the mountains, over the . . . What did you call it? The spine of them?"

His eyes softened, and his mouth curved in a sad smile. "The backbone of the Rockies. And that would be too far west from where we need to travel, and the terrain too rough for what we're looking for. We want to find all the native camps we can, and those will mostly be on the plains or in the valleys."

Disappointment pressed through her, though she'd known it would be unlikely. Still, what other way could she help him accomplish the dream? Maybe simply planning it out would give him the start he needed to carry it through.

She adjusted her seat so she was perched on the ground instead of on her legs, which had grown numb from her weight. This moved her a little closer to Riley, which would make it easier to talk without raising their voices over the men's shouts from below.

She turned to him. "I guess it may not work for you to start the trip this summer, then. You said the travel would have to be through the spring, summer, and autumn months? And that it might take more than one year? So it would be better to start off next spring. What month is best to set out? And where would you leave from?"

The sadness had left his eyes, replaced by a glint of humor. A half-chuckle even shook his chest. "Well . . . yes and yes to the first two questions. I want to start from the lower end of the Rockies, the place where the soil loses its red coloring. The snow likely melts earlier there than in the larger mountains farther north, so I might be able to set out at the beginning of May. Maybe even late April, though that might make the going hard at first."

Something like hope and maybe even muted excitement had crept into his expression and voice. But it fled now, his features settling into resignation. "It would be too hard to make the trip alone."

She shifted toward him, coming up on her knees again as she had to work to keep her frustration contained. "You don't have to make it alone. You have friends. I suspect Dragoon would think it a fun challenge. Ol' Henry might even want to join you. I'll bet a dozen men would jump at the chance if you only asked them."

She would love to go, if only to see Riley come alive as he fulfilled his dream. But the idea was too far-fetched. She couldn't leave her sisters and their plans for such a lark.

Riley shook his head, as though he could hear her thoughts. "The cold and hard travel might be too much for Ol' Henry. I'd never say it to him directly, but the harsher elements are getting to be hard on his body. He's not a young pup like he was when he first came to this land."

The weather did seem to affect his ease of movement, poor fellow. "I'm sorry things are harder for him now. But I still think you could have your choice of companions if you only asked around. Who would you choose to go with you?" It might be a while before she had another chance to speak alone with Riley, a time like this when he would be willing to dream and make plans with her. She needed to accomplish as much as possible now to ignite the spark of action.

The corners of his eyes crinkled in what could almost be a smile, but their depths held little pleasure. "I don't know. I'm not sure there's anyone I could count on to stick with me. It'll be a hard journey through much of it. There are so many things they could do that would be far more enjoyable." His attention had shifted to the rocks beside them, as though he could no longer meet her eyes.

Her heart ached for him. Why would he think others wouldn't jump at the chance? Was this because of his father? She had a feeling his love for adventurous journeys had been planted in him back in those early days. But had his father's choice to leave him made him think everyone else would too?

She reached out and laid her hand over his, curving her fingers around his palm. "Riley, look at me."

He turned back to her, his gaze finally meeting hers. His eyes held no sign of confidence, only a hint of worry. Could he really not know how special he was? How remarkable he'd proven to be in only the single week she'd known him?

She infused her voice with certainty. "You are amazing. I'm sorry your father—both your parents—were so caught up in their own struggles they couldn't help you see that. You're a remarkable person, a man anyone would be honored to call friend. If you let yourself lower your barriers a little and allow others to get close to you, you won't always get hurt. I promise."

He studied her, his eyes unreadable. Then, beneath her hand, he turned his wrist and wove his fingers through hers. His throat worked like he was preparing to say something. Her own eyes burned with the longing to take away his pain. To make him feel as fully loved as he deserved.

At last he spoke, his voice low and hoarse. "You're the remarkable one. I wish I could see the world the way you do."

Disappointment sank through her, and she closed her eyes as she gathered herself to answer. It would take more than her words to convince him. But what would need to happen for him to see the truth for himself?

She opened her eyes again to study him, and he was watching her. His gaze had darkened, its intensity far stronger than seconds before. It was almost as if . . .

Then his focus dropped to her mouth, and a flare of desire washed through her. Was he going to . . . ? *Yes, please.*

He leaned forward and closed the distance between them, his breath brushing warm over her skin before his mouth took its place. His lips were warm and supple, a caress that made her shiver all the way to her core.

Her eyes sank shut as she relished the taste of him, the way he made her feel treasured. Safe.

Seen.

Like she stood out from her sisters, from every other woman he'd known. It couldn't be possible, not her. But as his hand came around her neck, wove through her hair with the gentlest of touches, she never wanted the moment to end.

TWENTY-ONE

I t might be a huge mistake, but Riley couldn't regret kissing Juniper. Not when she was the only person in the world who seemed to believe in him. She would leave him too one day, but for now, in this moment, he simply wanted to say thank you. To relish the admiration he'd seen in her eyes and now felt in her kiss.

And oh, she tasted like . . . better than anything he'd ever savored before. She was sweetness and innocence and fire all wrapped up in an exquisite package.

He had to stop. Had to pull back, no matter how much he wanted to sink into this moment forever. Her sisters would return soon, and things might not go well if he was caught kissing Juniper like she was his last breath of air.

In truth, she was more like the first clear breath he'd taken in a long—*very long*—time.

It took all his self-control to ease back and break the link between them. He kept her close, though, near enough to feel her warm air on his skin as she worked to catch her breath.

He brushed his fingers over her cheekbone, down along

her jaw, moved his thumb over the red bloom of her lips. A rush of desire sluiced through him to taste her once more, but he moved his focus upward to her eyes.

Something like gratitude welled inside him. He had to acknowledge this, to somehow put to words what he was feeling, what she'd done for him. He swallowed so he could speak. "Thank you." His voice came out raspy, like he hadn't used it in a week.

Her eyes shone with the inner light he loved so much. "For what?"

How could he put into words this overwhelming feeling inside him, this sense of being accepted without the need to *earn* her favor? "For being my friend."

Her eyes widened, and she pulled back a little. In his mind, he thought back through what he'd just said.

Friend.

No.

He shook his head frantically. "That's not what I meant. I mean . . ." He gripped her hand. "What I mean is . . ." His breath came in short gasps as he struggled for words, any words that would take away the hurt now clouding her eyes.

He forced himself to slow down, to take a deep breath and gather his thoughts. "What I was trying to say is that with you, it feels like I can let my guard down. That you don't hate what you see in me. I don't have to be someone different around you or be careful about letting you see who I really am." He'd never felt so exposed as now, saying these words to her, stripping away every bit of pretense.

But the hurt in her expression slid away, replaced by a warmth that made every difficult word worth the effort.

He moved his hand to hers and wove their fingers together. "I'm sorry I'm not very good at finding the right words."

Her eyes turned glassy, and she hiccupped as she smiled. "Those were beautiful words. The most lovely I've ever heard."

The desire to kiss her again built up inside him, but the sound of female voices coming up the slope cleared away the possibility. He gave her hand a gentle squeeze, then released it and pulled back.

Camping with Mr. Dragoon and Ol' Henry as part of the group proved far different than "dry camping"—as Riley had called it—with just him on the mountainside.

Juniper's body ached from riding hard all day, but they'd made good progress. Around noon, they'd passed the valley where they'd visited the small Peigan camp. The place was deserted now, but ashes still marked where their campfires had blazed, and the grass was cropped short where the horses had eaten.

They hadn't seen any other people after that, but they'd spotted what Ol' Henry called *Indian sign* the last hours they'd ridden. It was basically hoofprints and dried horse droppings that looked to be a couple days old.

Now, as they sat around the low blaze of a campfire, bellies full from the deer meat and dumplings she and Lorelei had cooked, something like a contented silence settled over the group. Would they tell stories as Riley had said was a favorite pastime for mountain men in the evenings? Before that began, it might be good to ask the questions that had been taking shape in her mind as they set up camp.

She glanced across the fire at the three men settled there. "Does it seem likely the tracks we saw this evening are from the smaller Peigan band we met with? The leavings looked about two days old, you said, and it's been three days since that group told us they were packing to head out. Do you think they gave us the wrong timing on purpose?"

Riley's face took on a thoughtful look. "That's possible, but with women and children, they'd be traveling slower than we are. They said they'd be starting late in the day too, so they might not have passed through here until two days ago." He shrugged. "It's also possible the tracks are from a completely different group. We won't know for sure until we catch them."

Rosie leaned forward. "If we push hard tomorrow, do you think we'll reach them by the end of the day?"

He looked hesitant. "I doubt they're moving that slow."

Ol' Henry sat upright, a sparkle lighting his eyes. "Reminds me of the time back in '32 when I was trappin' with Suttler's group. We were campin' on a little prairie surrounded by mountains, on our way up to the Marias for the fall season. We'd heard that a party of Bloods had set out on the warpath, so we were on the lookout. Some of our hunters found a buffalo cow that had been brought down real recent, but apparently abandoned in haste. That told us whoever'd hunted her had fled quick-like, probably runnin' from somethin.'"

He leaned into the story, his forearms on his knees. "We set a watch that night, but nothing happened. So, the next morning, we broke camp like we'd planned to and started north up the river about three miles. Along the way, we found a fire still burnin' and the remnants of another buffalo cow that had prob'ly only been killed early that morning."

His brows drew down. "It seemed like we might be walkin' into danger, so we took a vote about whether we should keep going or turn west and look for a plentiful lake among the mountains. Suttler was determined to winter near the Marias, though, and he wanted to stake out his claim and get settled afore the cold weather hit."

Ol' Henry shook his head. "The vote was split, so Suttler got to choose, an' we pushed on. We found signs of Indians following a buffalo trail up along the margin of the river, so that made us think we were following a simple hunting party, not the Bloods on the warpath. From the tracks, we figured there weren't more than seven or eight in the group. The hills around us were covered with herds of buffalo grazing peacefully.

"Then, all of a sudden, the thunder of a thousand hooves shook the earth. That's a feeling you'll never forget, the ground trembling so hard it vibrates your insides. Through a break in the mountains to the east of us, a mass of brown beasts surged like the waves of the ocean up onto a hill and along its crest. I knew in my gut what was happening."

He shook his head. "I'd heard of buffalo jumps, but I'd never seen one till then. At the edge of the hill, a cliff dropped down, and the natives had positioned themselves on either side of the top to direct the herd over the precipice. It made my belly hurt to see all those animals jump to their death, but then a swarm of people gathered around at the base to harvest the meat and fur and all the other parts they use. I suspect they took in all they needed to carry them through the winter."

The story, in all its drama and horror, might've cast a pall over their group, but then Ol' Henry raised his brows at her and her sisters. "Did you see a bunch of herds on your way across the grassland? There aren't as many these days as there once were."

Juniper glanced at the other girls, but no one seemed ready to answer, so she turned back to him. "We saw several herds, but always from a distance. The hunters in our group supplied us with plenty of buffalo meat." She glanced at Lorelei. Her sister had kept away from those men for the most part. She knew they had to eat, of course, but couldn't bring herself to be part of the process.

Across the fire, Riley looked concerned as he slid a glance at Lorelei. He might realize too how the story would upset her tenderhearted sister.

He straightened and spoke to the group. "Speaking of food, that was awfully good dumplings you made tonight. Reminds me of the meal my aunt made the night before I left for the cavalry. She cooked dumplings with pork, something I'd never heard of, nor tasted since. It was awfully good, though. Have you tried it?"

Bless Riley for changing the conversation to something so benign. As Rosemary answered, Juniper sent him a grateful look, and he met her eyes with a slight tip of his mouth that showed he understood.

Of course, looking at his mouth reminded her too vividly of that kiss yesterday, and her entire body heated. They hadn't had a chance to talk alone afterward, what with so many preparations to leave this morning and her sisters always around. What would she say to him? He was winning her heart far too quickly, and she'd never met a man whose company she enjoyed so much.

But their worlds were so far apart. She'd committed to building the horse farm with her sisters, and even if she were at liberty to change that plan, they needed her. Faith wasn't even of age yet, and she couldn't leave the burden of raising her to Rosemary. Juniper simply wasn't free to marry and abandon them.

Would Riley be willing to move East . . . back to "civilization"? That idea seemed just as wrong. He loved this land, these mountains. His dreams lay in this place, and she wanted to *help* him fulfill them, not ruin his chances. Taking him away from these mountains would be selfish.

Her chest ached, and her eyes stung. She couldn't see a happy ending here, and the thought of losing him made her want to cry. Maybe an answer would present itself if they gave the situation a little more time. For now, they could simply focus on finding Steps Right.

Weariness from the day settled over her, and her raw emotions stole the last of her strength. She straightened and managed a smile for the group. "I think it's time to turn in, at least for me. The morning will come soon, and who knows what adventures we'll find on the morrow."

TWENTY-TWO

Riley stared at the horses in the early morning fog, counting them once more. Still only nine, if he combined horses and mules in the number. Maybe the mist was concealing one from him or muddling his mind.

There was his own gelding and mule, and Ol' Henry's mount and pack mare. Dragoon's spotted pack mule too, but where was Bessie, his prize-winning mare? All four of the sisters' horses were accounted for, but no Bessie.

As he approached the animals, his gut tightened. They'd all been here last night. He'd been the one to make sure their hobbles were secure before he'd bedded down. He moved in between them, brushing his hand down backs and letting them sniff his palms. Bessie wasn't hiding in the middle of the pack.

He turned and looked around the valley where they'd camped. The Green River bordered on the left, and steep slopes blocked off the right and behind them. Ahead, there was a narrow path between the rocky mountainside and the river's edge. If Bessie had managed to break her hobbles, she might have wandered out of the valley that way. It seemed unlikely she'd leave such plentiful grazing.

He moved away from the animals and looked around the valley once more, seeking out every rock or bush she might be hiding behind. Nothing.

The knot that coiled in his belly had doubled, but he had to return to the tents and tell Dragoon.

He trudged back to their little camp where Juniper, Rosemary, and Ol' Henry worked around the fire. Rosemary was nurturing a flame while Juniper worked among the food bundles. Ol' Henry poured grounds into his coffeepot.

Juniper noticed him right away, and the sweet smile she offered him fell into a frown. "What's wrong?" She straightened.

He shot a look toward Dragoon's tent, where the sound of low snoring could still be heard. Then he turned back to Juniper. "Dragoon's mare is missing. I'm going to see if I can find her tracks, but I thought he'd want to know too."

The snoring had ceased, and the shuffle of blankets sounded before the man poked a sleepy-looking face around the oilskin flap. "What's that you said?"

Riley gave him a grim nod. "Bessie's not with the herd. I'm going to look for tracks."

Dragoon blinked as though trying to take in the words. "Where did she go? You think she wandered off?"

His head disappeared back inside the tent before Riley could answer, then a muffled voice sounded within. "Hold on, I'm coming."

Juniper rose to her feet. "I can look for tracks too."

He should tell her to stay here and finish her work, but she was just as capable of spotting prints. "The easiest way in or out of this valley is upriver, so I was going to look there first."

Ol' Henry pushed up to his feet with a groan. "We'll see to breaking camp. I'm sure Dragoon will want to head out if you don't find her."

Dragoon nearly stumbled out of the tent, slapping his hat on his head. "Let's go. Where have you already looked?"

After Riley gave the details, the three of them searched for prints on their way to the pass between the river and the cliff. There was nothing that looked fresher than a few days old.

When they reached the pass, Dragoon spun and scanned the entire area. Thankfully, the fog had completely lifted, so there was no doubt about what they saw. And Bessie definitely wasn't there.

Dragoon planted his hands at his waist. "We need to spread out. I'll look along the river. Miss Juniper, keep about twenty strides away from me and search the ground on either side of you. Riley, you work on the other side of her."

Dragoon seemed to be thinking clearly now, though he had a desperate air about him. Riley nodded, and as Dragoon turned away, Riley shifted his focus to Juniper. Did she feel confident she could do what Dragoon asked?

She must have read the question in his eyes, for she gave him a firm dip of her chin. But then her look turned troubled. "Do you think she was stolen?"

He glanced toward Dragoon, who was already scouring the river's edge. "I'd say there's a good chance. She was here with the rest of the horses when I checked them last night, and Dragoon just made new hobbles when we were camping at the rendezvous. There wasn't a storm that would make her panic and run. Though why someone would come in and grab just her doesn't make sense. When the natives steal horses, they usually take the whole herd."

She tipped her head as she watched him. "You think a white man stole her? Because she won the race?"

Juniper had just put into words the suspicion that was growing in his mind since he first counted the horses that morning. "I hope that's not the case, but it seems likely." And that meant the man had been following them these past two days.

Watching. Having far too much access to the women.

He turned his gaze southward, the direction they'd come from. The mountain had been steep enough that they'd chosen to go around it by riding through the river. Had their stalker come through the water as well, or up over the peak? And which way had he taken Bessie out of here?

He turned toward the section Dragoon had assigned him to search. "We'd better get started."

Juniper moved to her section and began studying the ground as Riley did the same with his. Dragoon had already covered a great deal more ground than them, but Riley didn't rush his search. About halfway down the length of the valley, he found hoofprints from where all the horses had grazed through the night. The hobbles allowed them to move short distances so they could shift to new grass, and the fodder in this area had offered a rich supply.

From ahead, Dragoon turned and called back to them. "Looks like the herd moved to water there in the night. It's hard to tell, but I didn't find any tracks that looked like a single horse walking without hobbles."

202

Riley nodded and looked over at the river. It stretched wide here, far wider than a horse would usually choose to wade. The animals might even need to swim through the deeper center.

But a rider could certainly push a horse to cross to the other side. If they couldn't find where Bessie had left this valley, they should cross to the other side of the river and look for tracks there.

By the time he, Juniper, and Dragoon had scoured the valley with no sign of unusual prints—either horse or human—the others had broken camp and saddled the animals. When he shared his thoughts about crossing the river with Dragoon, the man agreed.

They mounted and prepared to cross over in the spot that looked most likely to offer shallow passing. Dragoon rode his pack gelding, though being forced to do so must rub raw the wound of having his prize mare stolen from beneath his nose.

He struck out into the water first, and Riley settled in to ride through with the middle of the group. The sisters had already proven themselves capable horsewomen. They'd clearly spent many long hours in the saddle, and more than just the journey West. Growing up on the horse ranch had given them an advantage there.

Ol' Henry would bring up the rear, as he usually did when they crossed a river. He might be the oldest in the group, but he'd experienced more mishaps on the trail than any of them and could usually spot a situation about to go awry before anyone was hurt.

Rosemary nudged her horse into the water behind

Dragoon's gelding, and she motioned for her sisters to follow. "Lorelei, come in behind me. Then you, Faith."

That would allow Juniper to bring up the rear of their group. He'd noticed the two older sisters always kept the younger ones between them, protected like the shelter of a mother hen's feathers. Juniper would make a wonderful mother.

But he couldn't dwell on that thought, couldn't allow himself to imagine what their children might look like. If he looked too far down the road, he might only find heartache. Today brought enough to focus on. He could worry about the rest later.

"See any sign of the horse?"

Juniper turned her focus to the ground along the bank, now that everyone was out of the water. Dragoon had already begun scouting upriver, scrutinizing the land in front of his mount.

She glanced at Riley. "Should we divide our group and go both upriver and down until someone finds the tracks we're looking for?"

He was studying the ground but nodded. "Yeah." He lifted his focus to scan the people already spreading out. "Ol' Henry, why don't you take Miss Rosemary and Miss Faith southward, and the rest of us will follow the river north? If anyone finds tracks, send a rider to alert the other group. If none of us find them in three hours' time, turn around and meet back here."

He gave orders like the cavalryman he'd once been, and even Rosie turned her mare to obey without even a question. She did send Juniper a look with a significant glance toward Lorelei.

Juniper returned a nod. Of course she would watch over her sister. Did Riley include an older and younger sister in each group on purpose?

Once they caught up with Dragoon, they spoke little as they all focused on the ground and searching for any sign of hoofprints. There were plenty of tracks—deer and smaller markings that Riley said were beaver, otter, and muskrat. But none were the right size and shape they were looking for.

The tension emanating from Dragoon hovered in the air, tightening her muscles and making it hard to enjoy the beauty of the scenery around them. The land rose in a steep incline at one point, with a sheer cliff wall that descended to the river, as though the water had cut through the slope many years before. She couldn't help but imagine how this land had changed with each century since God first created it all those millenniums ago.

Riley was right. Something about these grand mountains and wide-open plains made her feel closer to the Lord. So clearly seeing the beauty and craftsmanship of His creation here drew her to reach out to Him. To clear away the muddle of heartaches and disappointments that she'd allowed to block out His voice in her ear.

I'm sorry, Lord. I'm so sorry I've let these barriers come between us. Help me hear your voice. Show me what you want me to see.

They rode for what felt like an hour, and when the others weren't looking, she raised her hand to measure how many fingers above the eastern horizon the sun had risen. Three. If the sun rose around six o'clock, did that mean it was now nine? It felt closer to ten, but she couldn't be certain.

She turned her attention back to the ground, but she'd barely focused when Dragoon jerked his horse to a halt, bumping her mare's chest into his gelding.

He was staring even more intently at the ground. "That's them." He motioned to the place where the bank dropped sharply down to the water. "Two horses came out here. And that's my Bessie's tracks, I'm sure of it. The size and shape are just right."

He slipped from his gelding and crouched by the prints.

She studied them too, as did Riley and Lorelei. There did seem to be two sets of horse prints, one slightly smaller than the other. Could Dragoon really be certain one of the animals was his stolen mare?

He stood, following the tracks as they turned northward along the riverbank. He didn't take his eyes off the ground when he spoke. "Someone ride back and tell the others. I'm going to press on."

Riley turned his saddle horse, then looked at Juniper. "I'll ride back. Can you keep my mule here?" He held out the tether line for his pack mule.

She took the rope, and he spoke louder for all of them. "Stay here until I get back. I'll move quickly."

Dragoon was settling back in his saddle and waved a hand toward Riley as though swatting away a mosquito. "The women can stay here. I'm going to follow the trail while it's still warm. You all can catch up with me."

"No." Riley bit out the sharp remark. "Stay here." Though his eyes blazed, Dragoon wasn't looking his way to see them.

Riley must have realized it, for he turned to her and Lorelei. The hardness in his tone shifted to something more
pleading. "Stay here. Please. I don't know what's ahead, and
I don't want the groups to be spread too far apart."

Juniper gave a firm nod. "Go. We'll be waiting."

TWENTY-THREE

J uniper watched Riley and his mount lope away, then she leaned forward to dismount. "I suppose it'll be a while before they come back. We should let the horses rest."

Lorelei slipped from her horse too and lowered the coyote pup to the ground. Thankfully, his harness and lead were fastened securely around his shoulders, though the pup hadn't tried to escape for several days.

Dragoon still sat on his horse's back, studying the ground. After a moment, he looked up at them, then downriver the way Riley had disappeared. "I'm not going to sit around and lose my race winner while we wait for them. Every minute, that scoundrel's getting farther away with her."

She could remind him what Riley had just asked of them, but Dragoon had heard him just as well as they had. He would do what he felt he must. And part of her agreed that his thinking seemed right. A man on horseback with one animal tethered behind would be able to move quickly. Far faster than they'd been traveling as they searched for tracks.

Dragoon gave them one more look. "You'll be safe enough here waiting for the others. Tell them where I've gone. Once I have Bessie, I'll wait for you."

Then he nudged his horse into a brisk walk as he searched the land in front of him.

The sun was already heating the day, so she and Lorelei sat near a cluster of aspen trees to wait. The horses enjoyed the opportunity to graze, but she couldn't help the restlessness that made it hard to sit still.

The pup lounged in Lorelei's lap for a while, then stood and stretched. It turned to her, and if a coyote pup could grin, that animal surely was. Its tail wagged just like a dog.

"You want to go for a walk?" Lorelei spoke in a singsong voice.

Juniper reached for the lead. "I'll take him if you hold the horses. I need to move around."

They traded ropes, Lorelei taking both of their riding horses as well as Riley's pack mule. Juniper stood and tugged the pup away from the bigger animals. "Come on, little fellow. Let's enjoy the sunshine." They strolled toward some low boulders half buried in the ground to form a low platform.

When she stepped up on the stone, memories swept in of the area where she and Rosie used to picnic on the ranch when they were younger. The place was a couple hours' ride from the house, so they didn't go there often, but its unique surface and the trees that grew up from the rock provided a host of opportunities to play. Sometimes the stone floor would be a stage from which to sing or dance. Other times they would ride their horses over the surface, hooves clopping loud as they pretended the animals were trained for tricks. They even played cat-and-mouse sometimes among the low shrubs.

No such growth rose up from this stone floor, though its curved surface formed a number of cracks and crannies. Boots lowered his nose and sniffed as he walked. She followed him, letting him lead in a meandering path. After pausing overlong to sniff a dirt-filled crevice, the pup raised his head and whined.

"What is it, boy?"

He began to tremble, something she'd not seen him do since those first days after Lorelei found him.

She crouched beside him. "What's wrong?"

He made another high-pitched whine.

As she stroked his back, a sound slipped into her awareness, like rough sand being poured into a tin cup.

She glanced up to find its source, and her heart stuttered into her throat.

A snake lay coiled a dozen strides away.

The creature was thicker than her fist and a brownish color, not much darker than the rocks but with a pattern of lighter stripes down its back. Its head rose only a little from the stone, but its tail waved higher as that awful sound came again.

A shiver slid through her, and her body pushed into action. She gripped the pup and lifted it to her chest as she forced herself to move slowly as she stood and backed away. Her heart pounded in her ears, but the last thing she wanted to do was frighten the creature into striking.

Could snakes leap far enough to cover the distance between them? This was no small animal—longer than a man lying down, probably.

As it released another of those heart-stopping rattles, she reached the edge of the rock and stepped down.

Only then did she dare take her eyes from the creature long enough to glance around for any others. She'd heard of rattlesnakes but had never seen one in person. Did they gather in groups?

She could see no others, which meant she should be able to safely turn and run now. As she did, she called out to her sister, "Lorelei, mount up. We need to get out of here."

Her sister stood as she approached, concern marking her expression. But the urgency tightening Juniper's chest kept her moving.

She grabbed her mare's reins and the mule's tether rope from Lorelei, then pressed the coyote pup into her arms. "There's a huge rattlesnake on that rock. We have to get out of here."

They mounted, and she didn't take the time to fasten the tether strap to her saddle, just gripped it tight and turned her horse. She'd promised Riley they wouldn't go ahead without him, so it looked like they'd be heading downriver. At least far enough until her heart stopped pounding and they saw no sign of venom-filled creatures.

The moment Riley spotted Juniper and Lorelei downriver from the place he'd left them, his heart began to pound. What had happened to make them retrace their steps, and where was Dragoon? Had he left them and they'd grown afraid?

Riley should've known better than to think Dragoon would have stayed. Despite the fact he was generally a decent fellow, no one could be counted on to follow through with their responsibilities when something else seemed more important. Or when that responsibility proved too hard. His parents had taught him that truth long ago, so why had he lost sight of it now, when Dragoon's actions might have put Juniper and Rosemary in danger?

He spurred his gelding into a canter until he reached them. "What's wrong?"

Juniper had been frowning until he spoke, then her expression smoothed out. "Nothing's wrong now, at least not with us. We saw a rattlesnake where we were waiting, so we decided to move away from it."

Part of the fear coursing through him eased. They'd not been hurt. *Thank you, Lord.* "Rattlesnakes are fairly common in this area during the summer. They like to sun themselves on rocks, so you have to be careful."

They'd likely been terrified. He'd experienced that throat-clawing panic at coming face-to-face with a rattler prepared to strike, and it wasn't something he wished on anyone, especially not Juniper and Lorelei.

He looked over them from head to toe. "You're not hurt?"

Juniper shook her head. "I backed away before it could strike."

So *she'd* been the one in danger. His pulse picked up speed again, making it harder to breathe. "Where's Dragoon?"

Juniper's mouth pinched. "He went on ahead to follow the tracks. He said for us to catch up with him if we can, or he'll wait for us once he gets Bessie back. He was afraid to let the thief get any farther ahead."

Epithets he'd never let himself speak rose up in his mind. He should have expected this. But for some reason, he'd trusted that Dragoon wouldn't leave when Riley had asked him to stay. He well knew how suddenly danger could attack in this land, and two women alone . . .

"We'd best get moving." Ol' Henry's steady voice dragged him back from his anger. At the moment, Dragoon didn't seem worthy of them pushing hard to catch up with him.

But Dragoon's worth or actions weren't the reason for Riley to follow through on his word. He'd committed long ago that when someone depended on him, he would fulfill his obligation, no matter what it took.

He wouldn't be his parents. He would be better.

He nodded, then reached out to Juniper. "I can take the mule back."

She gave the long-eared fellow a stroke down his forehead. "He's fine with me."

He nodded and pushed his gelding forward. "Let's go, then." He couldn't let even Juniper's kindness and her sweet smile distract him from his commitment. And right now, he had a wayward companion to help and a stolen horse to find, then they'd have to return to the much greater challenge of locating a Peigan woman who may be determined to remain hidden.

By the time darkness settled over the rocky ground, they still hadn't caught up with Dragoon. Riley eyed an area of mostly flat ground that would work for their camp. The horse droppings they'd last found looked only a couple hours old, but though a half-moon shone bright, there was too much chance they would miss important details in the dark.

Hopefully Dragoon had also stopped for the night, and if they rose early and pushed hard, they would reach him tomorrow.

He reined in at the camping spot and dismounted. "Let's spend the night here." He didn't dare look at the others. He was pushing them, yet no one had uttered a single word of complaint.

Should he give them the option of separating into two groups tomorrow? A slower party and a few who rode fast to catch up with Dragoon? He'd had too much time today to imagine what might be happening with the man. The thief could be part of a larger gang, either whites or natives. If the man reached his cohorts before Dragoon caught him, his friend could be up against far more than he was able to overcome.

Dragoon had already proved that his desperation to get Bessie back could trample his good sense. He might try to sneak her out and wind up in the midst of a den of rattlesnakes—either figuratively or literally, as Juniper had experienced that day.

Thank you, Lord, for saving her. Loving someone made you far too vulnerable to the pain of loss, whether they left you by choice or through injury or sickness. He'd not let himself acknowledge that this richness growing inside him was love, but he could no longer lie to himself. No more than he could keep from giving his heart to her. He'd known Juniper less than two weeks, but it felt like she'd always been a part of his life.

But that didn't mean he had to act on the feeling.

She would be leaving, heading back East, and he would have to let her go. This was the home he'd chosen, the land he loved. He had dreams here that were beginning to feel like he might actually accomplish them. It was better to let Juniper go now before anything more happened between them than to lose her later, after she'd rooted herself permanently in his heart.

"Since it's so late, might be best not to worry over a fire." Ol' Henry's tone showed his weariness. "We can pitch the tent for you ladies, then fill our bellies with cold meat and call it a night."

"We don't need a tent." Rosemary sounded as tired as his old friend. Maybe Riley really had pushed them too hard. "We can lay our blankets on the ground and sleep under the stars as well as you can."

That notion felt wrong, letting ladies sleep without cover. But he was learning not to argue when Rosemary Collins made a proclamation.

He would just have to work with her decision and find ways to protect them anyway. Not that he expected much harm would come from not pitching a tent over the Collins sisters' bedding, other than a little dew on their blankets and faces maybe. At least he could bring in some pine boughs to make their sleep more comfortable.

Once they'd settled the horses and he'd handed over enough bunches of evergreen needles for the four ladies to spread their blankets on, he accepted a handful of cold smoked meat and settled down onto his bedding. The six of them ate in silence as the night sounds filled the air around them. The fare tasted like the bull elk he'd brought down and smoked in the spring—gamy and tough. The animal must've been ten years old at least.

But the food filled his belly, and he should be content.

Juniper's warm, savory meals simply made it harder to appreciate this cold fare that he used to think perfectly adequate.

Faith's voice broke the quiet. "This reminds me of that night before we went to that smaller Peigan camp, the ones who were hiding something about Steps Right."

Juniper's voice held a smile. "It does. We didn't want to build a fire that night either. I wonder where that group is now?" She turned to him, though the moon's shadows didn't let him see her expression. "Do you think we've missed them completely? Are we going the right direction now, or will we need to backtrack after we find Mr. Dragoon and Bessie?"

If only there was an easy answer to those questions. He glanced at Ol' Henry to see if he had any wisdom to impart. His expression was hard to read in the dark too, but he nodded for Riley to answer.

"We're going northward, which is the same general direction I'd planned before, though the route we're taking is a little more to the west than I think that little Peigan band seemed to be aiming. Maybe once we find Dragoon and get his horse back, we can turn east until we pick up the trail of that band again." Assuming it didn't rain and wash away their tracks between now and then, or a herd of buffalo didn't cross the path to cover sign of the Indians.

At least the sisters had realized this may not be a quick search. He knew without them reminding him how much they wanted to find Steps Right quickly and fulfill their father's last request.

If his own father had left him with a mission like this, would he be as determined to carry it out immediately? He'd like to think so, but it was hard to imagine. Ward Turner had left his family in spirit years before he left them in body. When they finally received word of his death, there were never any last messages or final words to his wife and son.

He straightened. Thoughts like that would only send him to a place he didn't need to go. "I guess I'm ready to turn in. If you're all up to it, we should be in the saddle at first light."

They had much ground to cover tomorrow, and they'd need every bit of strength they had to accomplish it.

TWENTY-FOUR

The sun beat down on Juniper relentlessly as they rode past the morning hours and into early afternoon. Dragoon's tracks—and those of the horses he'd been following—had been winding around several mountains, staying to the lower rocky terrain.

Now they'd begun to climb upward.

Ahead of her, Riley's horse let out a whinny, the high-pitched sound shaking the animal as it pricked its ears toward the top of the slope.

She eyed the place. Something must be up there. Had they finally caught up with Dragoon, or was this a stranger?

Another nicker drifted down from the peak, and Riley's gelding responded immediately. The two animals seemed to know each other.

A moment later, a horse and rider appeared on the top line, silhouetted by the sun at their back.

Was that Dragoon? Maybe, but from this distance she couldn't be certain.

"There he is." The relief in Riley's tone couldn't be missed.

Dragoon rode down the slope to meet them, and as he

came close, his scowl clearly showed the outcome of his search.

When they drew up, Riley spoke first. "Find her yet?"

Dragoon's pressed lips disappeared beneath his beard as he shook his head. "I keep thinking I'm getting close, then I lose the tracks completely and it takes too long to find them again. Whoever has her is a master at covering his trail."

He glanced back over his shoulder toward the top of the slope. "I might've lost the tracks again on these rocks."

Riley nudged his horse forward. "Let's get looking, then."

Juniper guided her mare behind his pack mule as before, and with the horses pushing hard, they soon reached the top of the incline.

Dragoon reined his gelding in and pointed to the ground. "See, here's the last track I found. I went downhill a ways but don't see another yet. Sometimes he doesn't take a straight path but turns left or right through a section where the ground won't pick up his tracks. Confounded rascal."

After glancing at the ground a minute, Riley lifted his head. "Let's spread out as we move down the hill. Stay two or three horse-lengths away from the person on either side of you."

They followed his instructions, and with Ol' Henry on one side of her and Faith on the other, Juniper searched the ground.

Dragoon had dismounted to see better, and his voice carried over the hillside. "Look for any marking that could have been made by a horse, more than just tracks. A scratch on the rock, a wet mark, even a spray of sweat."

They traveled a quarter of the way down the slope before Lorelei's voice rang out. "I found something."

Dragoon moved her way but called to the rest of them, "Keep looking until we know for sure this is from them."

Juniper turned her focus back to the ground, but she couldn't help regular glances at her sister and Dragoon as he crouched and examined the ground. Seeing the two of them together brought back the time she and Rosie came upon them outside their lodge. At least there hadn't been any more hint of an attraction between the two. At the moment, Dragoon seemed far more focused on the ground than on her sister.

Within moments, he stood and stepped gingerly downhill, scrutinizing his path as he moved. "There's another one. This is definitely their trail." He turned to his horse and mounted as he called out to the rest of them. "We found it."

Dragoon's restless tension had begun to affect them all now that they'd been back with him a full day. Juniper took in a deep breath, then released it slowly, consciously loosening the tightness in her shoulders as she sat up straighter in her saddle. The man had barely agreed to camp last night and only conceded after it became clear they would need to ride through a patch of trees that were too dark to see hoofprints.

They'd been back in the saddle as the sun lightened the eastern sky, then pushed hard all morning. Riley made sure they allowed the horses to rest every so often, especially as the day heated and harsh rays beat down on them.

She glanced over at him where he rode beside her. He was watching her with worry creasing his brow. He looked like he wanted to say something but didn't speak right away.

She gave him an expectant smile. "What is it?"

He shook his head. "Just wondering if keeping this pace is too hard for everyone. Maybe I should tell Dragoon to go on ahead."

Was that what he *wanted* to do, or was he making a sacrifice because he thought the challenge too hard for them? "If it's my sisters and me you're worried about, we can manage. I know riding so long and hard in this heat is challenging for the horses, but they're all hardy animals. We're giving them rest and making sure they get water, so I think they're handling the journey well."

He nodded, though his eyes still looked worried. When he turned his gaze forward, he seemed to be looking into the distance, as though his mind was far away. He was such a good man, always thinking of others and sacrificing his own wishes and hopes for their good. If only she could reach out and take his hand, but she didn't dare with so many people around. Especially Faith and Lorelei riding just behind.

She and Riley hadn't had any time alone since that kiss, though sometimes he would send her a look that warmed her all the way through. Other times, he would brush her arm with his hand in passing, sending a tingle all the way up to her shoulder. Once, when he'd brought her saddle over and hoisted it onto her mare, he'd taken advantage of the horse as a shield and placed his hands on each of her upper arms, then pressed his lips to her hair in a kiss so tender she wanted to melt right there on the hillside. But Rosie had been approaching, so Riley stepped away and moved to his own mount.

It was this and so much more that made her feel cherished any time he was near. The way he looked at her, she felt not only *seen* but *loved*. Could she possibly leave her sisters and their plans and stay here with Riley? Would Rosie and the others understand if she chose a man over them? She'd always thought she'd find a husband who would be willing to work the ranch too, so she wouldn't have to abandon the plans they were so close to fulfilling. But she couldn't ask Riley to leave this place he loved so much, to abandon his own dreams.

Ahead of them, Dragoon's hand flew up like an alert flag. Their entire group fell silent, and she strained to see what had caught his attention. He wasn't looking at the ground, and his horse still plodded forward around the base of the mountain they were maneuvering.

Then, at the curve of the hillside, a flash of motion grabbed her attention. A horse and rider.

Riley nudged his horse up to Dragoon's side. He should be in the lead to speak with whoever was approaching them, but not having him beside her left an empty spot somewhere deep within.

She focused on the stranger ahead. Two of them actually, and both appeared to be native.

As they came within twenty strides, a jolt of recognition flared in her. The front rider was the younger man from the smaller Peigan village. The grandson of the chief who'd sat with them at the fire. Flies Ahead.

Maybe they'd found that group after all. Though now they wouldn't be able to watch the village from a distance. Their presence here had been discovered.

She glanced at the second man to see if she might recognize him too, and another flash of realization sluiced through her.

White Horse? They'd wondered if the two were part of the Peigan band, and now seeing these two men together confirmed it.

Riley's voice murmured as he spoke to Dragoon, but his words were too quiet to make out. He was likely telling him who these men were.

Then Riley turned in his saddle to see Ol' Henry, who still rode in the back of their group. "These are Peigan. Will you come interpret?"

A leap of something like hope rose in her chest. She hadn't realized Ol' Henry spoke that language, more than just the hand talk. Why hadn't they taken him along before? He obliged now, guiding his horse forward to come alongside Riley.

As the two groups met and halted their horses, Riley raised a hand in greeting, then spoke the word he usually used as a hello. "Oki."

The two braves both nodded, either in acknowledgment or greeting. Flies Ahead eyed them with the same wary look as he had before, but White Horse watched them with something like curiosity. His gaze swept over the men quickly enough, then moved back to her and her sisters. Before reaching the rendezvous, she hadn't fully realized how much of a curiosity white women would be in this land.

As before, Riley spoke and signed at the same time. "These are my other companions, Dragoon and Ol' Henry." He motioned to each man as he said their name.

Ol' Henry spoke in a string of sounds that must be the Indians' language.

Flies Ahead responded in kind, motioning to himself, then to White Horse.

Ol' Henry spoke in a quieter tone as he interpreted. "He tells me his name is Flies Ahead and his companion is White Horse." This they already knew, but Dragoon wouldn't be aware yet unless Riley had told him. Interesting that White Horse had spoken to them in broken English before, but he seemed inclined to let Flies Ahead speak now. As the chief's grandson, maybe that was the way things were done.

"Ask him about my horse." Dragoon didn't try to hold back his eagerness.

Ol' Henry spoke to the men again in their language, motioning to Dragoon as he did so. He even pointed to the ground, maybe showing the tracks they'd been following.

A horrible thought jolted Juniper. Since White Horse and Flies Ahead had also been riding this path, would that make it harder to follow the thief's trail? Maybe.

And were they really following the trail of the man who'd stolen Dragoon's mare? These two proved it just as likely could be two men out riding together. Or an innocent trapper and his pack horse. Two sets of hoofprints could mean any number of scenarios.

God, help us find her. Lead us on the right trail. They needed to find Steps Right too, but it seemed she should address one problem at a time.

Flies Ahead answered Ol' Henry, and from his expression, his response seemed to be no.

But then White Horse spoke, addressing Riley. "Which tribe you think the thief is from?"

"We don't know. He could be white." Riley shrugged. "It would be a man with two horses, one a brown mare with black mane and tail."

White Horse studied Riley so intensely that everything

around him seemed to pause. What was he looking for? To determine if Riley told the truth? Or whether Riley really thought the thief could be white instead of automatically blaming the natives?

One thing she'd learned about Riley during their early acquaintance was his fairness toward different races. In a way, he seemed to treat them all—even whites—with wariness. He certainly held no prejudice for or against any one particular race or tribe.

Flies Ahead spoke again in his language, breaking the thick silence of the moment. He seemed to be asking what had just been said, and White Horse responded in the same tongue. Flies Ahead nodded, as though satisfied with the answer. Then he spoke once more and nudged his horse forward, guiding the animal around their group.

White Horse followed his companion, but as he passed by, his gaze met hers, then moved down the row to each of her sisters. The look didn't feel like it held malice or anything improper.

It seemed almost . . . questioning. Like there was something he wanted to ask.

But he didn't.

TWENTY-FIVE

What had White Horse been holding back? Juniper stared at the man's back as he and his companion rode away. Something about Steps Right? It must be. When they met him last time, he'd been so friendly . . . until they'd asked about the Peigan woman their father sent them to find. And now, something in his bearing told her he wanted to speak. But with his companion there, and with all the questions about Dragoon's stolen horse, there hadn't been a chance to talk privately.

Maybe she should ask Riley. Perhaps the two of them could follow White Horse and speak with him. Should they do it now? She had a feeling Rosie wouldn't like the idea, not without her coming along too. And it didn't feel safe to leave Faith and Lorelei with only Ol' Henry and Dragoon. The latter had already proved he was far too distracted with finding his stolen horse to see to their safety.

"Let's keep moving." Dragoon nudged his horse forward as he studied the ground. "Tracks will be harder to tell apart now."

As Ol' Henry turned his horse and rode back down the

line to his position at the rear, he caught her watching him and winked.

She couldn't help but smile. Even with all the questions and concerns clogging her mind, his grin and good humor were impossible to deny.

Riley reined his horse in beside hers again, but he didn't speak right away. Should she ask him about finding White Horse? She had to.

She slid a look at him. "Did White Horse seem . . ." How best to put the feeling into words?

"Like he wanted to ask something?" One corner of Riley's mouth tipped.

She smiled. "Yes. He seemed to be looking for something in us. Do you think it had to do with Steps Right? The way he changed when we asked him about her before . . . Maybe he's had time to think about it and has questions for us. Maybe he knows her and is trying to decide if he can trust us."

Riley shrugged. "It's possible."

Before she could analyze the situation any further, Rosie rode up along her other side. Juniper looked over to see what she needed, and her sister was wearing that shrewd expression as she asked, "What did you think of White Horse's behavior?"

Juniper almost grinned. She should have known Rosie wouldn't miss that detail. "We need to talk with him. I don't know if he'll speak in front of everyone. If a couple of us ride back and catch up with him, do you think he would be honest with us if Flies Ahead is there listening? Or do we need to somehow get him by himself?"

Riley nodded, the motion a little distracted as he seemed

deep in thought. "It does seem like he would talk more freely without Flies Ahead present. I'm not sure how we can get him away, though, unless we catch the two already separated." He grew quiet for a moment. "They didn't say where they were headed, but they're most likely out hunting. If we follow them, we could find a time when White Horse is alone. But the chance of us tracking them without them realizing we're there isn't very great. The natives are masters at recognizing animal sign, and the animals would give us away. Besides, it might take a while before we get White Horse off to himself. Maybe not until tomorrow morning."

Rosie lifted one brow in a look only she could manage. "And who do you think should go?"

Heat swept up Juniper's neck before she could stop it, probably turning her ears red. She'd planned to announce to her sister that *she* wanted to go, but with Rosie eying her like that, she couldn't manage to be so bold. "I think either you or I should stay with Faith and Lorelei."

Again, Rosemary dipped her chin. "I agree." Were the corners of her mouth twitching like she was holding in a grin? Then she lifted that brow once more. "So *I'll* go?" It came out more a question than a statement.

This was Juniper's chance to say she wanted to be the one. Before she could work up the nerve, Rosie spoke again. "Riley should definitely be the other person. White Horse seems to trust him." She nodded at him on the other side of Juniper.

Juniper didn't turn to see how he accepted the compliment, but those final words gave her the push she needed to speak up. She lifted her chin. "I want to go meet with White Horse."

Her sister eyed her. "You and Riley alone?"

That was the hardest question, wasn't it? Not whether White Horse would finally give them information to help in their search. Not when they should leave or how they would get White Horse off by himself. Not even a defense for why Juniper should be the one to go instead of Rosie. After all, her older sister had always been the leader of their family and the one to speak for them all.

"It might be best for someone else to go with us." She thought back to what Riley had just said. "Maybe Ol' Henry?"

Rosie rolled her lips together in thought. "Maybe Ol' Henry." She looked past Juniper to Riley. "What do you think?"

A quick flash of surprise flared in his eyes, then he glanced back at the older man. "White Horse didn't seem uneasy about him. Most men take a liking to him right away, both white and native. And it helps that he can speak one of the languages White Horse and Flies Ahead both know."

"That wasn't Peigan he was speaking?"

He shook his head. "Snake Indian. It's easier to learn, so a lot of the tribes and trappers use it to communicate."

Good to know. But better to focus on the decisions at hand. She glanced back at Rosie. "Will you and the girls be safe with only Dragoon? Are you going to ride on with him? I'm sure he won't sit around and wait for us to return."

She could feel Riley's uneasiness, though she didn't look his way as she waited for Rosie's response.

Her sister did look to Riley. "Will you be able to find us if we go on with Dragoon?"

"Yes, but . . ." He didn't finish the sentence right away, and Rosie didn't give him time to linger.

She turned back to Juniper. "Then yes, we'll go on with him. Go and learn as much as you can from White Horse. Will you follow him now?" This last question she directed to them both.

Riley glanced back toward Ol' Henry. "Probably. Let's talk with everyone first." He raised his voice. "Need to halt a minute."

Dragoon looked back with a scowl. "What is it?"

Riley reined in his mare and motioned for everyone else to do the same. When they'd all gathered around, Riley glanced at her, silently asking if she wanted to give the details. She nodded for him to share them.

After he announced the plan, Dragoon eyed him, his hands fidgeting with the reins. "Would you rather all of us go with you?"

There was the Dragoon he knew. One who didn't lose his mind so completely over a horse that he lost sight of more important things, like protecting those in his care.

But Riley shook his head. "We think it's better if only the three of us go. More than that might keep White Horse from talking."

Dragoon's features eased, though his hands never stopped moving as they slid down the leather of his reins.

Riley turned his focus to Ol' Henry. "Will you ride with us? You might be able to keep Flies Ahead occupied while we talk with White Horse. And your translation skills will be welcome."

The older fellow gave a single nod. "I'm always up for an adventure. Sounds like I might get one no matter who I'm ridin' with."

"Good. We—"

His words cut off as the boom of a gunshot split the air.

TWENTY-SIX

One of the girls screamed, and the moment Juniper's mind registered the sound as a rifle shot, she ducked.

"Get back to the trees!" Ol' Henry shouted, and Riley's horse nearly plowed into hers as he spun his mount and pushed them back.

"Take cover!" Riley waved them toward the woods.

The men all had their rifles raised to fire, though Riley continued herding them back toward the cluster of cottonwoods twenty strides behind them.

Her gun. As she reined her mare along with the others, she worked her Hawkins out of its scabbard. Getting the long barrel out proved a challenge, especially while moving. She and her sisters had practiced shooting, but not pulling the rifle out in the midst of danger.

Finally, they clustered behind the trees, peering back in the direction they'd come for some sign of the shooter.

"Who was it? Did you see them?" Rosie's voice had taken on her hard-edged protective tone.

"Don't see anything yet. Heard the wind from that bullet by my ear though." Ol' Henry studied the landscape through the trees as though he was one of the spectators watching a horse race at the rendezvous.

Rough breathing beside her made her glance over. Riley held his gun tucked into his shoulder in firing position, but his face wore a grimace and he seemed to be struggling for air.

She opened her mouth to ask what was wrong, then a patch of red caught her attention.

His arm.

She sucked in a breath. "What happened?" His shirt was ripped just above his elbow, and a circle of crimson had begun to spread from the torn fabric outward. The spot was the size of her fist, and blood pooled at the frayed edges, threatening to drip down to the ground.

Riley darted a glance at her, then refocused through the trees ahead. "Bullet grazed me."

She moved her mare closer so she could see and touch his arm. "You were shot?"

"It's not bad. Just brushed the skin." Riley's neck flexed as he tightened his jaw. He kept his focus ahead, scanning for danger. It didn't look like he would let her check the injury until they'd identified the threat.

She glanced at all three men, then shifted her focus past the trees. "Any idea who it is?"

Ol' Henry answered in a calmer voice than she would have expected. "Just one shot, so it might've been someone out hunting. Sounded like a fusee, which means it could've been Indian or white. Those are the guns most traded for by the tribes."

"Look. There." Dragoon's hoarse whisper sounded just as Juniper caught a movement around the side of the slope.

A mountain man appeared, riding toward them on a bay and leading a white-gray pack horse. She studied his animals. Neither was Bessie, no doubt about that. The bay he rode was far too long-boned, with an angular brow and a curved Roman nose. The gray pack animal was the wrong color altogether. The man carried a rifle across his lap and seemed to be scrutinizing the mountainside.

"Who is he?" Rosie whispered just loud enough for their group to hear.

The stranger's gaze caught on their trees at that moment, as though he'd heard her words. He couldn't have, but he must have seen them through the leaves, for his rifle lifted from its resting place. Not aimed, exactly, just at the ready.

"He's seen us. Best we meet face to face." Ol' Henry turned his mount to maneuver out of the woods.

Riley finally shifted his attention from the newcomer to Juniper. "You four stay back here."

She gripped her reins tighter to keep from reaching for his arm. "Do you think he's dangerous?"

"Probably not." Riley glanced toward Ol' Henry and Dragoon, who'd already left the cluster of trees, riding toward the stranger. Then he looked back at her. "You'll be safer here, and there's no need to come out."

He was probably right, and as he rode after the other two, she glanced at Rosie. Her sister's expression held a bit of worry and that intense look that showed she was thinking through the possible dangers and how to cut them off before anyone could get hurt.

The men met the stranger on the slope, the newcomer positioned uphill. She couldn't make out their words, but when Riley motioned to his bloody sleeve, the hunter's eyes grew wide. He pulled off his hat and flopped it on the saddle as though shocked. It looked like he must be apologizing as he pressed a hand over his chest.

Just a hunting accident. No malicious intent.

The conversation continued, and Dragoon became the main speaker. He must be asking if the fellow had seen any sign of the horse thief they'd been following.

After a good deal more talk and hand gestures pointing a multitude of directions, the man flopped his hat back on his head and nudged his horse forward. Riley, Dragoon, and Ol' Henry turned to ride back to the trees where she and her sisters hid.

Ol' Henry's face held its usual pleasant expression, but Riley's mouth was pressed into a grim line. That could be from pain, though, now that the threat of danger had subsided.

Yet the dejected slope of Dragoon's shoulders clearly showed that something the stranger said didn't bode well for them.

She pushed her mare forward to ride out of the shelter of the trees, and her sisters followed behind. As soon as they reached the men, she studied Riley's face. "What is it? What did he say?"

Dragoon released a snort, then lifted his own hat and wiped his brow with his sleeve before replacing the covering. It didn't seem like he planned to answer, so she looked back to Riley.

"He's a trapper who just came from the rendezvous and

he's out hunting. He rode up the same trail we did and said he shot at a deer he saw. He'd come back to get it." Riley grimaced. "I guess I was that deer."

She looked back down at his sleeve, but the red circle didn't look like it had widened any farther. *Thank you, Lord.* They still needed to clean and bandage it.

"What else did he say?" Nothing Riley had described so far should have affected Dragoon so.

Riley shook his head. "That's mostly it. But if he came up the same trail we did and he has two horses, it seems like his tracks might be the ones we've been following."

Realization sank through her, pooling in a lump in her middle. No wonder Dragoon seemed frustrated. If they'd been following the wrong man, the real thief must be far, far away by now.

She swallowed down the knot in her throat. "Is it too late to circle back and find prints from whoever took Bessie?"

Riley glanced from Dragoon to Ol' Henry as he shook his head. "If there was a trail left to follow, it would be nearly impossible to find now. We had enough trouble staying with this one."

Weight pressed in her chest as she turned to Dragoon. "I'm so sorry." Maybe not saying anything would be better, but it seemed she should acknowledge his loss.

He only nodded, his mouth a thin line and deep wrinkles fanning out from the corners of his eyes.

Quiet settled over them, with each person deep in their own thoughts.

But Faith never was one for silent contemplation. "So what now?"

Juniper straightened. "Now we take care of Riley's arm."

He sent her a glance, then released a long sigh. "I guess the horses could use a break."

Juniper slid from her mare's back as the others dismounted. She and Riley and Ol' Henry needed to set out after White Horse soon, but she couldn't let that mission endanger Riley's health.

Riley worked to keep the pain from showing on his face as he began rolling up his sleeve for Juniper to clean the mark left by the bullet. It couldn't be too bad, for he could still use the arm without trouble. The wound simply burned like he'd held the spot in a flame for a full minute.

She sat beside him, giving orders to her sisters while she waited. "Faith, could you refill our water bags from that creek down the slope? Lor, I know I'll need a bandage and the salve. Might as well bring the whole pack."

She hadn't given Rosemary a task. He glanced over at the older sister, who was speaking with Ol' Henry. She didn't look his way at all. Their conversation seemed mostly small talk about the waterways in this area, not anything that should hold her fascination so well.

"Oh my."

He'd finished rolling his sleeve up above the wound, and Juniper now leaned close, studying his arm. Concern turned her blue eyes almost gray. As nice as it was that she cared enough to worry over him, he wanted only to bring her smiles.

"It's not bad. Just bled a little. Once we wipe that off, it might not even need a bandage." Though they should definitely wrap it if they had clean cloth. Out here, a gash could fester quickly, enough to do a man in. With no doctors and very little medicine, more men had died from cuts than could be counted.

Juniper brushed her fingers across the clean part of his arm, sending warmth up the limb. Her touch burned even more than the wound, and he'd much rather focus on her face. But he needed to see what they were dealing with.

He lifted his arm to examine the mark the bullet had left behind. The blood smeared all over his skin could leave a man queasy, but once they cleaned that up, he knew only a gash would remain.

He would live, especially if Juniper Collins helped with the effort. He shifted his focus to her face. She was the prettiest thing he'd ever seen, even more so now than when he'd first met her. The corner of her lip was tucked between her teeth as she studied his arm with such tender concern.

His chest ached far more than the sting on his arm. He couldn't lose her. What would she say if he asked her to stay? Would she think him worth the challenges of living in this country, so far from the comforts she'd always known? He'd said he would never trust his heart to someone who could break it when they left him, but he'd already advanced past that point with Juniper. When she eventually went East with her sisters, she would take his heart with her. So why not risk asking her? There was a chance—maybe only a tiny one, but still a possibility—that she might love him enough not to leave.

Miss Lorelei and Miss Faith returned, and the women fussed over his arm for a while—the three younger ones, anyway. Rosemary still lingered with Ol' Henry and Dragoon. The one glance she'd sent his way had seemed to leach the color from her face. She must not handle the sight of blood well. Surprising, given that she faced every other obstacle head-on.

At last, Juniper finished, and he accepted the bit of smoked meat tucked in a cold biscuit Lorelei handed him.

"You need food to replenish the blood you've lost." She seemed as capable a nurse as Juniper, maybe from tending the animals Juniper said she was always nursing back to health.

Ol' Henry wandered over to him and nodded toward the bandage. "Think you'll live?"

Riley gave him a solid nod. "Couldn't ask for better nursing care."

A sparkle lit the man's eyes as his teeth flashed a grin. "I'll say." Then his smile eased. "We're coming on dusk. Won't get far tonight before it's too dark to see their tracks. Think it's best we make camp now, then set out first thing in the morning to catch up with White Horse."

A new weight pressed on him as he eyed the sky. Their light would disappear within a half hour. How had it gotten so late? He'd been so caught up in thoughts of Juniper, he'd lost focus of this important thing she'd asked of him.

He turned to look at her and saw the worry on her face. All he could do now was try to ease her concerns. He closed his hand over hers. "We'll leave at first light. They're not trying to cover their tracks and they weren't moving fast, so we should find them easily."

She nodded, then seemed to gather herself. "I suppose we should make camp, then."

TWENTY-SEVEN

A s they all began the tasks required to set up camp,
settle the horses, and prepare a meal, not even
Dragoon's sour mood could pull Riley's focus from
what he planned to say to Juniper. Maybe it was too soon
to speak with her, but now that he'd set his mind to it, he
had to ask.

Had to know her answer.

If she said no, how much harder would that make the rest
of their journey? Tense, perhaps, but he would be a bundle
of nerves by tomorrow if he didn't settle this tonight.

Getting her alone long enough to ask would be a challenge, but maybe he could find a reason to walk with her
after the evening meal. Or maybe he wouldn't look for an
excuse.

He could simply invite her to stroll with him. The request
would raise brows, but it might give her an inkling of his
intention. Just so his question didn't shock her.

He didn't manage to eat much of the meal, and of course,
Juniper noticed in her usual attentive and caring manner. As

she began gathering used dishes, she frowned at the meat left on his plate. "Is your arm paining you a great deal?"

He shook his head. "I barely feel it." He glanced at the stack in her hands. "Are you taking those down to the creek to wash them? I'll come with you." He hadn't exactly asked for a courting stroll, but this opportunity presented itself too easily.

Concern marked her features, and she hesitated. "I guess you can walk with me."

That didn't sound very eager. His question might be doomed long before he asked it.

While she turned to tell Rosemary where they were headed, he scooped up the pot the women used to heat the food and piled the dirty cups inside it. When they'd gathered everything, he hoisted the pot in his good arm and a stack of plates in the other.

She reached for the latter. "I'll take those. You don't want to use that arm or it'll start bleeding again."

He gave her a smile instead of the dishes. "That bandage you put on will keep it safe."

Hopefully the scowl she sent him was in jest and he hadn't actually angered her.

As they left camp, he could feel the others' gazes following them. Did everyone else realize this was more than a stroll to the creek to wash dishes? He needed to prepare himself. To shore up his defenses in case Juniper said no.

With the light of the campfire fading behind them, he could finally see the stars overhead and hear the evening sounds, especially the crickets that chirped nearly all night long through the summer months.

Beside him, Juniper released a breath that felt full of

tension. Hopefully that meant she was letting the tightness flow out of her body. If he didn't have his hands full, he might have reached over and woven his fingers through hers.

She looked over at him, and the moonlight cast a glow on her sweet smile. "I was just thinking how much has happened today. There's certainly not a dull moment on the trail, is there?"

He returned the smile. "There can be quiet times, especially in the winter. But you learn to expect surprises." Maybe this was his opening. "What do you think of this land now that you've been here a few weeks? Do you like it?"

Her countenance lifted, removing the shadows from her eyes. "It's beautiful. I completely understand how these mountains and the open country can weave through your heart."

Now was his moment. He gathered a breath for courage. "And has this land found a special place in you? Would you like to stay here? With me?" He was such a coward. He'd meant to tell her how much he loved her. How the thought of living without her was becoming something he could no longer stand. How special she was.

He *had* to say those things. Especially since her expression was so difficult to read right now.

"I mean . . ." He cleared the rasp from his throat. If only he didn't have all these dishes in his arms. He couldn't even take her hand and make this romantic. "What I meant to ask is if you would consider marrying me. I hadn't planned to ever marry. But then you came along, and you're so . . . special. So beautiful and wise and caring and . . ."

He still couldn't read her expression, and the weight

pressed harder in his chest. "But I understand if you'd rather not. It's a lot to ask, living in this mountain wilderness. The winters are hard and there's always some kind of danger around. I would spend my life protecting and loving you, but I couldn't promise . . ." Well, he couldn't promise much.

"Riley." Her voice came out so softly, yet it made his entire body freeze.

"Yes?"

She touched his arm. "Any woman would be honored by what you just asked. This country might be wild and a bit dangerous, but it's so beautiful, I can't imagine anyone not falling in love with this place. Not falling in love with you."

His chest tightened so hard he wanted to reach up and press a hand to the spot. Her words were right, but something in her tone told him exactly what he'd known all along.

He wasn't enough to hold her. She would be leaving him when she finished the mission she'd come for.

He had to fight to keep from moving away from her touch. Had to work to focus on her words as she continued speaking.

"It's just that my sisters and I have a plan. We'll be starting a horse farm again, and they need my help. Faith and Lorelei are still so young. I can't leave Rosie to raise them by herself. It's not fair to her. I can't abandon them when they need me."

She was right. Of course she was right. But it didn't make the weight crushing his chest seem any lighter. She was doing the right thing. Fulfilling her responsibilities. That was more than his own parents had done. This simply proved that she was everything he knew her to be—good and faithful and the woman he loved.

She was doing the right thing. If only his heart didn't have to be the casualty.

She was doing the right thing. If only his heart didn't have to be the casualty.

Juniper's chest ached as she walked back to the camp . . . alone. After she gave Riley her answer, pain had hung so thick in the air between them. She'd scrubbed only a few plates before he told her to take the clean dishes back to camp and he would finish the rest.

He'd been kind about it, of course. Riley couldn't be anything but a gentleman, giving and protecting no matter the cost to himself. That was one of the many reasons she loved him. One of the many reasons her heart was breaking now.

Why couldn't she simply say yes to his proposal? Why couldn't she be free to follow where her heart begged to go—to settle securely at his side on any adventure he wanted to take them?

But she wasn't. Her sisters needed her. She loved *them* too and had committed to them. The bond the four of them shared—especially she and Rosie—had been forged through a lifetime of togetherness. Through pain and happiness, dreams and heartbreak. She'd known it from the time Mama and Rosie went away for the treatments that she had a responsibility to her family.

And she couldn't turn away from them now, not when her sisters were all she had left.

Surely Riley understood. She'd seen in his eyes that he understood.

But she'd also seen the pain. The little boy who'd been scared and alone when he was kidnapped, then abandoned by his parents in all the ways that mattered after his return. She'd just done the same thing to him, told him by her actions that he wasn't important enough for her to stay.

Oh, God. Why is this so hard? Why can't both parts work together? Why did she have to say no to one love in order to accept the other?

Ahead of her, the figures around the campfire came clear. Lorelei and Faith bent low over something—the coyote, maybe. Faith was chattering, and it looked like they were feeding the animal its evening ration.

A swell of love for the girls washed through her. She'd helped raise them. During those dark days when Mama and Rosie were gone, she'd taken over the woman's role in the house. Prepared meals and coaxed them to eat. Read books to them and made up games to distract them when they missed Mama. Taught them how to cut biscuits and sew on buttons. Rosie had done the same for her and so much more, and she'd tried to be the older sister to them that Rosie had been for them all.

Her focus tracked to that older sister, who sat a little apart with something in her lap. Her rifle, it looked like, taken apart as she cleaned it.

Rosie's focus lifted, catching on her. With the firelight illuminating her face, it was easy to make out the lines of concern as she studied Juniper. How much could Rosie see? She'd not allowed herself to cry yet, so even if her sister's gaze could pierce the night shadows, she wouldn't see red, blotched skin. But it was impossible to hide the rending of her heart. The wound was too fresh.

Rosie dropped her attention back to the gun, gathered

the pieces together, then laid them aside. Without a word, she pushed to her feet, and her intention came clear.

Rosie did see. And she was coming to find out what had happened.

No. Juniper couldn't maintain the fingertip hold on her emotions if her sister started asking questions. But maybe that's what she needed—her big sister to talk to. Rosie's rational thinking would help set her straight and remind her of their plans. After all, they'd agreed at the outset of this journey that they would not form an attachment to any man. If only she'd held to that promise.

She paused for Rosie to reach her, and when they were near enough to touch, her sister gripped Juniper's elbow and turned her away from the fire.

"Let's go for a walk." Rosie kept her voice quiet enough that the others wouldn't hear.

She allowed her sister to steer her, and thankfully Rosie led them in the opposite direction from the creek. She marched them up the slope with a determination that made this walk more of a cavalry charge than a stroll. Even that thought reminded her of Riley. He didn't talk much about his cavalry days. Because they'd not impacted him as much as his life before that? Or had something happened that he wanted to forget about? Oh, how she longed to know everything about him.

When they were out of hearing range of the camp, Rosie stopped and spun her so they were facing each other. "What happened?"

She should be used to her sister's to-the-point directness but being asked the question made her throat squeeze too tight to answer. "I . . ."

Rosie's expression softened, but she didn't speak. Just waited.

Juniper swallowed, searching for where to start. "Riley asked if I would stay with him. Marry him." A new rush of heat attacked her eyes, and she fought to keep the tears back. She might not manage it this time.

"And?" Rosie's voice came gently now. "What did you say?"

Juniper stiffened. Did she really have to ask? "I told him I couldn't. I have a responsibility to you girls. We have plans. I can't just leave you all and become a trapper's wife, roaming the mountains with him for the rest of my days." Though the idea, now that she put it into words, sounded like the happiest life she could imagine. Adventures with Riley every single day. Endless views of these majestic mountains.

She wrenched away those thoughts. They would only make her miserable.

Rosemary was watching her. "June." She spoke that old familiar nickname in a quiet voice, one thick with something that felt like regret. Then she turned away, took two steps, and halted. She wrapped her arms around herself, staring out into the darkness. That outline wasn't the confident, protective woman she usually showed the world. This was the sister she used to be, back when they were girls and still trying to figure the world out. Before Mama passed and they'd had to grow up fully.

Rosie turned, and her hands dropped to her sides, her shoulders squaring. She'd made a decision. "You have to. Tell him yes, I mean."

Those weren't at all the words Juniper expected from her.

"What?" Rosie must have meant something different from what it sounded like.

She gave a firm nod. "You love him, don't you?"

The question brought a new stab of pain, but she nodded.

"I saw it back that first day we rode south to the Peigan camp and met all those women. There's something special between the two of you. It reminds me of the way Papa and Mama were together. As though you can sense what the other is thinking and feeling. Like you don't always need words to communicate." She took in an audible breath, then released it. "He's a good man, June. I wouldn't let you go to anyone who wasn't."

Confusion warred with hope inside her, clouding her mind. "But . . . our horse farm. We have plans. And Faith and Lorelei. I can't leave you all when you need me."

Rosie advanced the two steps between them, then reached out and took both of Juniper's hands. "June, you can't stop living your life because of us. Our horse farm was a wonderful plan, and I won't say I'm not going to miss you powerfully. But you can't turn away from the man you love—the man God made for you—to stay with your sisters. That's not the way God intends things." She squeezed Juniper's hands. "We'll always be there. We'll always be connected, both by blood and by heart. And we expect you to come visit any chance you can. But you have to choose Riley if he's the one you know in your heart God has for you."

Juniper had long ago lost the battle with her tears, and they flowed in steady streams down her face. A sob worked its way up her chest as all the realities of Rosemary's words sank in. Could she really leave her sisters? Rosie wouldn't hold her to their plans? She was free to choose Riley?

"Oh, honey." Rosie pulled her into a hug, and Juniper clung to her sister as their tears flowed.

TWENTY-EIGHT

Hope rose within Juniper as she strolled through the early morning light the next day. Fog still lingered low to the ground, but on the eastern horizon, what looked to be a brilliant sunrise had just begun.

She was going to talk with Riley this morning, as soon as she could get him away from camp. Hopefully, she hadn't hurt him so much that he would reject her change of mind.

For now, though, she needed these quiet early dawn moments to settle her heart. The coyote pup had begun whining early, and taking him for a walk had been a good excuse.

Boots frisked in front of her, charging ahead until he reached the end of the rope, then spinning around to gnaw at the tether. He'd grown so much that he would be old enough to release soon. He could eat meat with no problem now, but the main question was whether he could protect himself and bring down his own food in the wild. Perhaps not quite yet, but the day would come soon, probably long before Lorelei was ready.

She was walking around the side of the slope they'd camped on and had nearly reached a cropping of rocks where she would be able to see what lay on the other side of this small mountain.

The pup perked its ears, freezing as it stood at attention. "What is it, boy?" Her heart picked up speed as her thoughts slipped back to the last time she'd been walking this little fellow and he'd alerted to something. Just the memory of the snake's rattle sent shivers down her spine.

She kicked the grass and rocks around them in the early morning light. Riley had said rattlesnakes liked the sun and heat, so maybe it wasn't warm enough for them to be out for the day yet.

She took a step toward the pup, who still stood at attention. "What do you see?"

He glanced up at her, then turned forward again, hopping two steps so he strained at the end of the line once more. His tail wagged a little, though, and he wasn't whining like he had last time. Maybe this wasn't danger, just a rabbit nest or something similar.

She stepped toward him and leaned down to scoop him up. He needed to learn how to hunt his own food, but she wasn't ready to be his teacher this morning.

But as her hand closed around his body, the pup writhed, twisting out of her grasp. She scrambled for a better hold, capturing part of the rope tied around his chest, along with a clump of hair.

He squealed and fought harder, his teeth clamping down on her hand.

"Agh." She clutched tight to keep from losing him, even as she lost her footing and landed on her knees and forearms.

The pup slipped from her hands and darted away, his leash dragging behind him.

"No!" She scrambled to her feet, tripping on her dress before she righted herself.

The animal had run around the side of the mountain, and she sprinted after him. After one more stumble, she righted herself and rounded the cluster of boulders at the side of the mountain. The view on the other side brought her up short.

A valley spread before her, with at least a hundred animals grazing there.

Horses.

Where had this huge herd come from? She placed a hand on the rock beside her as she studied the animals. Such a variety of colors, but they were beautiful creatures. It felt like a lifetime since she'd seen this many horses together. Not since Papa began selling off his stock before they left the farm.

But whose animals were these? Was there a large native village in this area? Could this possibly be the same herd they'd seen the tracks of in that other valley after they left the Gros Ventre camp? Likely not. This was far away from that place. And many of the animals had the swayed backs of horses who'd worn saddles for many years. Did the Indians use saddles?

A flash of movement at the base of the slope caught her attention.

Boots.

The horses had distracted her from her chase, and now the pup had nearly reached the edge of the herd. His high-pitched yaps sounded over the distance, and the horses began to pin their ears and mill around restlessly. They didn't bolt away like wild horses. These must, indeed, be well-trained saddle horses.

She started down the slope, but as she moved, she glanced around the edge of the herd for any sign of people. No one in sight. The tall mountains on all four sides acted like a fence to help contain the horses. There must be water running through somewhere, or they wouldn't stay long.

Hopefully little Boots wouldn't frighten the animals enough to make them scatter. Even calm mounts could be startled by an unknown creature. Trying to scale those rocky inclines at a run might result in broken bones and trampled steeds.

Boots was still barking and snapping at horses by the time she'd nearly reached the bottom of the slope. Hopefully she could grab the rope still attached to him without having to wade too deeply into the animals. With the horses already restless, they might nail her with a stray hoof.

She approached the first animals cautiously, with her hand out and a welcoming set to her shoulders. The sorrel nearest her ducked away, sending the horses around it backward too. Boots was moving deeper into the herd. She had to reach him soon.

"Here, boy. Come, Boots. Here." She tried to use the same tone Lorelei spoke in when she was playing with the pup. He was so busy yapping, he might not even hear her.

She worked her way around a palomino and slid between a chestnut and buckskin. Just like walking into one of the pastures back on their ranch. A brown-and-white paint pinned its ears as she neared, but she took a stomping step toward it, and the animal shrank back. She'd handled more than one contrary animal before, and taking on a dominant posture usually calmed the situation.

The chestnut on her left was clearly older, from the angular lines on her head and the sway in her back. The horse regarded Juniper placidly, and she couldn't help pausing for a quick stroke on the animal's neck as she passed.

Something on its shoulder caught her attention, and she froze.

It couldn't be. Could it?

Had she found one of the horses her father sent to Steps Right? She stepped back and studied the animal. A glance underneath proved this was a mare. And though time had faded the lines, the marking on her shoulder was definitely one of the earlier versions of their farm's brand.

Her heart surged. *They'd found her.*

And the stallion . . . She lifted her gaze around the herd and searched for a bay with a patch of white covering its ears. The animals' rumps all seemed to blend together from this viewpoint, but the heads of those not grazing were easy to see. Some horses possessed white ears, but none that matched the rest of the description.

Except . . . there. Near the center of the herd. Could that be the horse?

She clutched her chest as her mind scrambled for what to do next. She had to get the others. But she didn't want to leave the horses. Now that they'd finally found them, she didn't dare take her eyes off the animals.

And who did this herd belong to? They had to find the owners. Riley would know how. And maybe Ol' Henry.

She stepped close to the mare again and stroked her glossy neck. "I'm so glad to find you, girl."

After a final pat, she turned to exit the herd. It wasn't until she reached the base of the mountain that the memory of why she'd come here in the first place surged back.

Boots.

She spun around and raised her hand to shield her eyes from the brightness of the morning sun peeking over the horizon. Where had that coyote gone? His yapping had quieted, and there was no longer restlessness among the horses.

A knot lodged in her chest. Had he been kicked senseless? Or killed? Lorelei would be devastated. *No, Lord.* She couldn't go back and tell her sister she'd lost the animal Lorelei had worked so hard to save.

She started back toward the herd, then paused. Should she go for help first? If her walking through the horses stirred them up, she might make them run and lose the two that belong to Steps Right. She couldn't risk it, not even for Boots.

She turned back to climb the slope . . . and froze.

A man stood not five steps away from her. A white man. Recognition swept over her.

Slim.

But what was he doing out here? This was several days' ride from the rendezvous, even if he took a more direct path than they had.

He watched her with a kind of curious half-smile in his expression, but no surprise in his eyes. Like he expected to see her here.

A tingle ran down her back. She needed Riley. Or at least her rifle. She only had the pistol tucked into her boot.

"Howdy." He spoke with a rasp in his voice, as though his throat hadn't yet cleared out all the sleep.

She had to answer him. Maybe he knew who these horses belonged to. "Hello." She cleared her throat to remove the shakiness from her voice. "Do you know who owns this herd?"

As far as she could tell, his focus didn't shift from her to the animals.

He didn't speak right away, so she asked a different version of the question. "Do they belong to an Indian village near here?"

Her words seemed to nudge him into action. He glanced at the horses, then back to her. "Yep. To the tribe camped just over that rise." He motioned toward the hill to the right of the herd. He tipped his head in curiosity. "Why? You lookin' for them?"

His manner seemed more normal now. Perhaps he'd been surprised to see her at first and simply showed it differently than most men would. After all, if a man spent long enough alone in this land, he might develop a few oddities.

She nodded. "Yes. We've been searching for them."

His bushy brows rose. "We?"

He couldn't think she was alone out here, could he? But best she make it clear she had the protection of a group.

"My companions and me." She motioned toward the slope behind him. "They're camped just over that rise, waiting for me."

He glanced over his shoulder where she pointed. Of course, no one could be seen. Would they wonder why she was gone so long and come after her?

She addressed Mr. Slim again. "Will you come to our camp with me? We have a few questions about that village. If you know the people, perhaps you can provide answers."

A wariness entered his expression. Was he a friend of the tribe and thought they meant harm? If Steps Right really was there, he might be trying to protect whatever secret the others had guarded.

She spoke quickly. "We came to pass along a greeting from a friend of theirs. Our questions are about whether that friend is still at the village or not."

The tightness in his face eased. Good.

He turned toward the village. "I'm going there now. You can come along and I'll introduce you."

A rush of hope spread through her. "That would be wonderful. Let me just call my sisters and the men traveling with us."

He shook his head. "I promised to be at the village at first light. Already late. Come now if you want."

She hesitated. "Our camp is just right up there. I can run up and tell them, then be back in five minutes." That timing might be a little optimistic, but she wouldn't take much longer than that.

He started walking. "Can't wait. Come with me if you like. Otherwise I'll tell the folks there that you're interested in their horses and are searching for one of their people. They're not a very trusting group, but I'll try to put in a good word for you."

Not trusting. If the natives in that village knew people were looking for Steps Right, would they hide the woman? She couldn't let this man speak of them before they arrived.

"No." She shook her head. "Don't tell them we're coming. We'll be there in an hour or so, and we'll introduce ourselves."

He paused and turned back to her, suspicion marking his brow. "You have something to hide?"

She frowned at him, doing her best not to show nervousness. "Of course not."

"Then come with me. I'll interpret for you, then bring you back here."

Did she dare? She eyed the man. He seemed normal enough now. And if he would introduce her and interpret ... This was the only way they could have the element of surprise upon entering the village. And maybe there would be less suspicion if it was only her coming to ask about Steps Right. Perhaps having their large group had raised caution among the camps they'd visited so far.

But no. She wasn't thinking clearly. Under no condition could she walk away with this man alone.

She took a step away from him. "I think it best I get the rest of my group. We'll be along shortly."

He frowned. "I don't think that's a good idea."

She glanced up the slope toward their camp. She could make a run for it. Would Slim chase her? If he did, she could scream and the others would come running.

But when she turned back to the man, her heart stopped. He held a rifle aimed at her.

Her mouth went dry as a sunbaked rock. She couldn't speak, even if she knew what to say. What to ask. Looking down the darkness of that barrel seemed to make all the colors around her far more vivid.

She could die. All he had to do was pull the trigger, and a bullet would slam into her body, destroying bone and organ. Would it hurt? Or would death be instant? *Let it be instant.*

But she couldn't succumb yet. Her sisters needed her. Riley needed her.

Forcing her focus to lift above the rifle's barrel, she locked her eyes with his. "What are you doing?"

The corners of his mouth curved. "Just protecting what

I worked so hard for. It's taken me a lot of years to find this many prime horses." He nodded toward the peak behind him. "And that's why I need you to walk calmly over that rise up there."

She started to shake her head, but he lifted the rifle a little, tucking it tighter into his shoulder. "You'll go quietly right now, or else I'll simply take care of you here. I'd rather do it over the ridge where the shot won't spook the horses, but one way or another, these are your last minutes on earth. Then, after you come your sisters, then your fella and his friends. I'll not be leaving any of you alive to spread the word about these horses."

A cold dread started in her throat and plunged downward. How had he acquired these horses? Especially the ones her father had sent to Steps Right?

So many questions she needed answers to, but for now the best thing might be to walk up the slope like he asked.

She started forward, one tentative step at a time. He motioned with the rifle for her to pass him, and she shifted a little to walk in an arc that would keep her out of arm's reach. The movement didn't seem to bother him. At least he didn't grab her, though the weapon could do damage enough. *God, show me what to do. Help me get out of this.*

Would Riley or Rosemary come looking for her soon? *Let them come.* Lorelei knew she was walking the pup, so she at least would be wondering about her by now.

Slim closed in behind her, but his step was so light, she barely heard how close he was. Not until the hard poke of the gun barrel jabbed the center of her back.

She nearly lurched forward but managed to stay upright and lengthen her stride. Now that they were close enough, she could smell the odor of sweat that proved the man was long overdue for a washing. Bile churned in her middle, but she focused on maneuvering the rocks and the steep incline.

After a moment of climbing, she glanced back at the horses, at the old bay mare that had to be the one her father sent to Steps Right all those years ago. She didn't dare look back for long, lest Slim's finger get impatient on the trigger.

But she managed one more glance back to find the stallion with the white markings on his ears. He was sniffing noses with another horse, his arched neck and long mane making him look regal, despite the age that showed in his angular lines.

That must be a mare he was sniffing, something she'd seen often while growing up on an active horse ranch.

Something about the mare . . .

Realization jerked through her, and she sucked in a breath. That couldn't be. But the markings were right. She was about the size of Bessie.

Could this man have snuck into their camp and stolen Dragoon's mare? Anger surged through her. After Dragoon had trusted him—even paid him—to race the horse. But maybe that had been this thief's method all along. He must be behind the rest of the horse thefts as well.

She steadied her voice to keep from breathing hard when she spoke. "I see you were the one who stole Dragoon's mare. Is that how you selected the others here? Got paid to race them, then took the ones you liked?"

"Of course it is." He barked the words as he jabbed the rifle in her back again. "Now shut up and walk. My men are waiting for my signal to come in and move the herd."

"Your men?" He wouldn't be able to manage such a large

group of horses by himself. He'd need at least a half-dozen helpers on horseback, maybe twice that many.

"Sure. There's plenty of fellas in these parts who'll do a day's work for good pay and keep their mouth shut." He poked the rifle in her back again, this time a little lower. "Faster."

The pain only increased her anger, but she held her tongue. She'd find a way to get free. Maybe one of his hired hands would help her. They wouldn't look the other way while a woman was murdered. Would they?

But saving her would also mean their crimes would come to light. Would they risk it?

She probably had a better chance of being saved by her sisters and Riley. Once she was over the rise, she would have to figure out a way to stall Slim. How long would it take Riley and the others to find her tracks? They would be distracted by the horses, as she had been. Would they even be able to pick out her prints in this rocky terrain? *God, give them wisdom.*

Or maybe she could slow him down now, give the others time to leave camp and come into view so they would see her and Slim before she crossed the peak.

But even though she tried to slow so gradually he didn't notice, the barrel jabbed her back before she'd taken three more steps.

"Move faster." He didn't even sound out of breath as he growled the words, though she was nearly panting from the ascent.

She surged forward into the same pace she'd kept up before. While she climbed, she slid a sideways glance to the mountain where the others should appear any minute.

Maybe they were already there, staring down at the massive herd below. If so, she needed to get their attention.

But no one stood in the spot where she'd come around the slope. Why hadn't they started looking yet? Was Riley still so hurt by her refusal last night he no longer wanted to even see her?

New pain washed through her. Riley would come after her, no matter how she'd hurt him. It was his nature to protect those he loved. And he loved her, he'd not been lying about that. Maybe even as much as she loved him.

She had to have the chance to tell him. But what if they didn't reach her before Slim put a bullet through her? Panic welled in her throat.

At least Rosie knew how she felt about Riley. If this man ended Juniper's life, her sister would tell Riley the truth. Juniper hadn't spoken to Rosie about her plans to seek Riley out this morning, but her sister knew she planned to accept his proposal if he was still willing.

At least Riley would have that knowledge.

But she would still be leaving him. Not by choice, not this time. Hopefully the grief of loss would be easier knowing that.

A new panic welled in her. Slim had said after he killed her, he would go after her sisters and then the men. *God, you have to stop him.*

Was there a way to take him out? Her own life would already be coming to an end, so if she could save those she loved in the process, she had to do it.

But how? Turn and wrestle the gun from him, then club him with it? She probably wouldn't be able to hit him hard enough to do real damage, for he'd fight back. Push him down the slope? Perhaps the incline would be steeper on the other side, but what they had just climbed wouldn't hurt him much unless he struck his head on a rock.

They finally reached the top of the slope, and she sucked in as much air as she could manage. Her side ached like a knife pierced it, but she didn't dare press her hand there. She couldn't do anything to make him suspicious.

"Keep moving." The barrel poked her back again, propelling her forward and over the rise.

This side was even less steep than the other, with a gentle boulder-strewn slope falling partway down before the ground leveled off into a flat grassy area.

Where was the native village? Clearly, that had been one more lie. He'd admitted to stealing horses from the rendezvous, but what of the two that belonged to Steps Right? If these were her last moments on earth, she wanted to hear the truth.

She swallowed to bring moisture into her mouth so she could speak, and she worked to keep up a steady pace. "It looks like you've stolen from more than just the trappers at the rendezvous. At least two of those horses belonged to a Peigan Blackfoot woman."

He snorted. "I suppose you're talking about those two your father sent with me. That old woman never saw them. Your father stole more than half my furs, so those horses were my due."

Shock nearly made her stumble, but she scrambled to keep her footing. She worked to keep herself moving at a quick pace so she didn't anger him. She desperately needed him to answer this next question. "How did you know my father?"

Another snort. "He never told you about me? Figures." Bitterness laced the man's tone.

He was silent a moment as she maneuvered down a steeper section. When he spoke, his voice came a little less gruff. "Folks 'round here known me as Slim, but my real name is Sampson."

Sampson. He couldn't be. She had to stop herself from turning to study him. "I know you. You were my father's partner. The one he went West and spent the entire winter with."

A humorless laugh bit the air. "I thought he was a decent fellow. It wasn't until we got back to Virginia that he swindled me."

Anger mixed with dread in her belly. Papa never would have cheated this man.

But that meant Sampson—Slim—had stolen the horses her father sent West with him. They never made it to Steps Right. She never received the gift of thanks for saving Papa's life.

The barrel dug into her back, and she locked her jaw as she forced herself to pick up her pace. "So you kept the horses all these years in retaliation?"

"They were prime horseflesh. Could tell that right off. Fast runners, can ride fifteen miles every single day without tiring. That stallion throws the same in his offspring too. Got me a contact with the cavalry that pays just fine. Half o' that herd's goin' to them come August."

"You sell the cavalry stolen horses."

"Well." He drawled the word. "Not all of 'em are stolen. Some I raise myself." They were nearly down the short slope, and he raised his voice. "That's far enough. Don't turn around."

Fury flashed into fear. Was this the moment he'd shoot her? She turned to see what he planned to do.

"Git back around!" he yelled.

But she'd seen enough. He'd positioned the rifle in the crook of his shoulder—firing position. This was the end. *Lord, be with my sisters. With Riley. Protect them and give them a wonderful life.*

"Now say your prayers, because you're about to meet the Almighty."

The boom of the rifle shook the ground beneath her as Juniper squeezed her eyes shut.

Lord!

❧

"What do you mean she's been gone nearly half an hour? Where did she go?" Riley spun to face Lorelei.

He'd needed a walk and a talk with the Lord to clear his mind after a night of such murky sleep. But he'd expected to return to the morning meal prepared and a long conversation about the group's next step. The food was ready, but it seemed everyone just now started to worry about Juniper's short stroll lasting far longer than she said she'd be gone.

"Rosie's gone after her. She's probably just out there sketching the sunrise. She has Boots with her for protection." Lorelei spoke that last bit as if she really believed a troublesome coyote pup would save Juniper from the kind of danger she might face out here.

He didn't have time to correct her. Juniper could be hurt. He turned and sprinted after Rosemary. Hopefully she was going the right direction.

She must've heard him coming, for she paused by a

cluster of rocks and turned to wait for him. Her expression looked curious, not worried, as though she wondered why he was in such a hurry. Did not even this protective sister sense that Juniper's delay meant something was very wrong?

He slowed when he reached her. "Juniper. Where is she?"

She pointed around the mountain. "Lorelei said she went this way."

He lengthened his stride as he maneuvered over the rocks, and when he stepped down from the last one, the valley on the other side stretched out before him.

He stilled as he took in the vast herd below, hearing Rosemary's stunned gasp behind him. Where had all these horses come from? He scanned the outer edges, searching for the smaller form of a person.

No one that he could see. Only a hundred horses at least.

"Look."

He glanced back to see what Rosie was pointing to. Probably the horses.

But she'd dropped down to her knees with her hand outstretched. Trotting toward her with its rope dragging behind was that coyote pup.

Without Juniper.

"What are you doing, fella?" Rosemary stroked a hand down its body when it came near enough, then scooped it into her arms and straightened.

Riley's gut clenched even tighter, and he refocused on the valley below. Where was Juniper? She wouldn't have let the pet go on purpose, leash and all. Something had happened to her, but he had no notion where to start looking.

He searched through the horse herd more thoroughly

this time. She must be among them somewhere. Had they trampled her? Kicked her unconscious?

He started down the slope at a run, shifting sideways on the deeper parts, his feet kicking loose rocks ahead of him. Rosemary's descent sounded just as loud behind him. Hopefully the others were coming too. They might need to split up for the search. Or if she was unconscious, it might be best to have all three men there to carry her to safety.

But when he reached the edge of the herd, he could still find no sign of Juniper among them. He turned to the outer edge of the group once more, then scanned the slope on all four sides.

"Where do you think she is?" Rosemary's voice finally held the correct amount of worry.

He inhaled a breath. *Lord, show us.* Then he exhaled to speak. "Maybe—"

His words were cut short as a rifle shot exploded through the air.

TWENTY-NINE

J uniper braced for the impact of the bullet. For the agony of the lead slamming into her body.

But it didn't come. Only the burning sulfur scent of gunpowder.

A groan sounded behind her, and she glanced back to see Slim on his knees, doubled over.

Her mind clogged at the unexpected sight. Had the rifle backfired?

Then another figure partway up the slope caught her gaze.

An Indian.

Recognition flooded through her, sending a tingle down her arms.

White Horse.

He stood with rifle in hand, a thin haze of smoke still clouding around him.

Relief nearly made her knees buckle. He'd shot Slim. White Horse had saved her life.

He began walking toward her, his stride sure and

measured. She did her best to remain standing, though her body longed to crumple to the ground.

But then White Horse spun toward the ridge behind him, raising his rifle to firing position. A second later, the pounding of footsteps sounded from that direction.

Her own heart thundered as she waited to see who it would be. Friend? Foe? If Slim's men had come to help him, they should be dealt with before they could cause trouble.

Her mouth felt as confused as her mind, and she only managed a silent *Lord, help* before a person appeared over the rise. A cry slipped from her throat.

Riley.

He slowed when he stepped over the ridge, moving with a wary step as he took in the violence that had happened here.

But then her body finally obeyed what her mind told it. She started toward him. Slim still lay facedown in a heap, but she gave him a wide berth.

Riley was walking toward her too, though his focus was on White Horse.

She swallowed so she could speak, then lifted her voice enough to reach Riley. "He saved me. Slim was about to kill me, but White Horse shot him instead."

Riley's gaze jerked to her, then shifted to the lifeless body, even as his step quickened into a half-run down the slope toward her.

When she reached him, she fell into his arms, and he wrapped her tight, holding her so close she couldn't breathe. She didn't need to breathe, only needed his arms around her. Protecting her.

"I've got you. You're safe. I'm sorry." With his cheek

pressed to the top of her head, he murmured the words over and over.

You're safe. She was. God had protected her from this evil man, one they'd not even known was a threat.

And White Horse. They needed to talk with him. They also needed to figure out where all those horses had come from. Bessie and Steps Right's horses had been stolen, so had most of them been?

Though her body begged to stay nestled in Riley's arms, she straightened and pulled back enough to look around. White Horse stood over Slim, using his foot to roll the body over. Slim looked lifeless, but she turned away before she glimpsed his face. The last thing she needed was that image bringing her nightmares.

Riley placed his hands on her cheeks. "Are you hurt? What'd he do to you?"

Tears filled her eyes again, but she shook her head and tried to blink them back.

Riley's hands moved down to her shoulders. "He didn't hurt you? What happened?"

She inhaled a long breath, then released it and began the story from when she'd first seen the herd. When she got to the part where she met Slim, Rosie appeared at the top of the mountain. Her sister released a cry, then sprinted down the slope toward her.

Juniper stepped away from Riley just in time to receive Rosie's full-body hug.

"Oh, June. You're safe. You're not hurt, are you?"

The tears were impossible to hold back as she held her sister. "Not hurt. I found the horses, though, the ones Papa sent to Steps Right. Slim was Papa's partner all those years ago—he went by Sampson then, I don't know if you remember him. He was the one Papa sent to deliver the horses. But he didn't." The emotion clogging her throat made it too hard to say more. Having her sister here, the familiar feel of her hug, soothed the last of the jagged edges of her fear.

At last, Rosie pulled back and held her elbows as she studied her. "When we heard that shot . . ." She looked over at Slim, and her eyes widened. "White Horse."

Juniper sniffed and wiped her sleeve across her eyes, then turned. White Horse was standing a few steps behind them, as though waiting to speak. She hadn't finished telling Riley everything that happened, and Rosie didn't even know that White Horse had saved her life.

She sniffed once more. "He saved me." She turned to White Horse. "How did you get here?"

"Came back to talk." He pointed to them. "Last night. I wait for sun. See horses." He motioned up the hill where the herd grazed just over the rise. "Sun come. See you." He nodded to Juniper. "See him. I wait. Watch. Hide." He motioned to one of the boulders she had walked past just ahead of Slim's rifle. White Horse must have been hiding behind it. Thank the Lord he'd realized she needed help.

While he spoke, she gripped Rosie's hand, and Riley slipped an arm around her waist. She leaned into him, absorbing his solid strength beside her.

Rosie was the first to answer White Horse. "I want to hear the whole story, but I'm so thankful you were here." She squeezed Juniper's hand. "We're all thankful."

Juniper sniffed again. "Slim's men are waiting for his signal to come move the horses. If we move quickly, maybe we can catch them."

Sounds of feminine voices rang from the other side of the slope. Her sisters. It was hard to believe only minutes before she'd been praying desperately for God to save them all.

And He had.

Her gaze found White Horse, and he met her look with strong, dark eyes. She never would have believed the Lord would use this man to answer her prayers.

Juniper sat in their camp with Riley on one side and Rosie on the other, and Faith and Lorelei tucked behind her. They'd stayed in a cluster since everyone had returned to camp, almost as if the girls formed a fence around her. Just now, having them close suited her fine.

They'd not found any of Slim's men. Maybe the rifle shot had scared them all off. Dragoon had posted himself as lookout, standing watch over the herd. If he ever found any of the men who'd helped Slim steal Bessie, she didn't want to be that fellow.

For now, she was content to sit with her sisters and friends. She'd just finished detailing the events of the morning and answering their many questions. If only she'd had time to ask Slim more about their father. But she'd barely managed to learn what she had.

Now it was White Horse's turn to speak.

He sat across camp from them, looking more comfortable than she would have expected. Silence settled over them as they waited for White Horse to begin.

"You search for Steps Right. She is my mother."

A gasp slipped out before Juniper could contain it.

"Your mother?" Rosie spoke the question bouncing through Juniper's mind.

He gave a single nod.

So many thoughts rose up inside her. "Where is she? Why didn't you tell us that before?"

He studied them, as though struggling over how much to tell. *Lord, please let him tell us everything. Let there be no more secrets.*

After a moment, White Horse seemed to make a decision within himself. "She has been sent away."

Once more, shock washed through her, but this time she held it inside. She should have expected something like this with the way people's demeanor changed when Steps Right's name was mentioned.

"My mother is great healer. She has helped many people in her life. Many who others left for dead, she would not leave. When our chief's son was sick, they called her to heal. She stayed by his side through night and day. He started to heal. Then his father, Son of Owl, began to grow . . ." His brow furrowed as he seemed to search for a word. He looked over at Ol' Henry and spoke something in a native language.

"Suspicious." Ol' Henry supplied the word with a nod.

White Horse turned back to them, his mouth tasting the sounds before he spoke them. "Suss–pi–cious." He straightened as he prepared to continue his story. "He has not ever trusted my mother, though neither will tell me why. When his son, the father of Flies Ahead, died, they both say my mother has done it. They will kill her if she does not leave our people. So she has gone away. And then you come, asking about her. I worry your mind has been poisoned by our chief. But when I reach village, he grumbles about you. Now I want to know why you come."

Juniper met Rosemary's gaze. So much of what they'd experienced in their search now made sense.

Rosie took the lead, turning back to White Horse. "Our father knew your mother many years ago when he came to this land. When he died, he asked us to return something to her." Rosie stood and moved to the pack where they kept the beads. She knelt to unwrap them from the fur-lined leather case Papa had kept them in.

Juniper glanced at White Horse to see his reaction as Rosemary lifted the strand and turned to walk to him. The moment recognition dawned, his eyes widened. Her sister wouldn't have seen his first expression, but she couldn't miss his rapt attention now.

"Do you recognize this?" She paused in front of him, then dropped to her knees so she held the necklace at eye level.

"My mother has arm necklace like this." He wrapped his fingers around his wrist like a bracelet. "She tells story of this necklace. When young squaw. She and her sister hunt during the cold moon. My father and other warriors had gone far to hunt, but women hungry, so they walk. Find food. She find man. White man hurt. Head hot like fire." He pressed a palm to his own forehead.

"Not live in night unless get help. My aunt walk to village, get help and healing plants. My mother stay with white man. Make shelter, stop wind. Make fire, keep warm in night. Keep white man live. Give white man blue beads. White man tell story for each bead, story about love." White Horse looked from Rosemary to Juniper. "White man tell story about woman and daughters' love."

A tingle spread over Juniper's arms, even as pain squeezed her heart. Oh, Papa. She'd known he loved them. He'd shown it every time he took them for horseback rides, or told stories in the evening, or taught them the inner workings of the ranch, of his life. But more than that, it was the way his eyes shone when he caught sight of one of them. That look of love sparkled in their depths. Even these past years, when he'd sank into melancholy in their Richmond home, he'd still worked hard for a smile for any of his daughters.

White Horse's expression softened. "All night, white man tell stories about daughters. Teach ride horses. Watch young horses born. Happy eyes. Sing with daughters. My mother say story keep white man live that night. Her sister come with sun, bring men from village, white man ride back on horse. My mother and father help white man until healed. When man leave, my mother give blue bead necklace." He made the motion of giving a gift. "From her mother, give white man. Know white man need beads to think of wife and daughters on far ride."

As his voice faded in the quiet of the camp, emotion burned Juniper's eyes. Why had Papa never told them the story?

But he kept these blue beads. Did he ever take them out and remember? Remember that night he almost died, and also remember the stories he told of his wife and daughters?

Rosie held out the beads. "Our father never told us any of that, but just before he died, he asked us to bring these back to your mother. He said the beads are special to her and she should have them back. We would like to meet your mother. Can you take us to her?"

White Horse's focus rested on the beads for a long moment. He didn't reach for them, though. Perhaps he believed they should be given directly to Steps Right.

Then he lifted his eyes to linger on Rosie first before moving to her and Faith and Lorelei. "I cannot."

Disappointment sank in her chest. Would he still try to hide her from them, even after he knew who they were?

His throat worked as he swallowed. "I take my mother to cave where safe, make home. I visit often. One time I visit, she not there. Blankets not there. All things not there. I search two moons." His jaw clenched. "You ask about Steps Right, I think . . . I come find you."

Words fled Juniper's mind as she took in this new twist. They'd finally found Steps Right only to lose her again?

Rosie's shoulders straightened. "We'll help you look. Together, we can find her."

Juniper nodded agreement. This woman who'd saved their father's life had been unjustly exiled from her home. They had to do everything they could to help her. Papa would have done the same.

White Horse's gaze met Rosie's, and his expression softened once more. "We look for her." He pressed a fist to his heart. "Here. I know safe. Not know why hide."

For a long moment, White Horse and Rosemary studied each other. It was hard to tell exactly what passed between them, for she couldn't see her sister's face.

Then Rosie nodded. "As you say."

THIRTY

Juniper stood at the edge of the horse herd with Riley and Ol' Henry on one side and Rosie and White Horse on her other. Faith and Lorelei had pulled the chestnut mare from the herd, the one their father had sent Steps Right. The old gal seemed to have been handled often, for she not only allowed the girls to stroke her, but she leaned into their touches as though she relished the affection.

For that matter, so did Dragoon's mare. He still kept the halter on her, and he now sat a few steps away from the rest of them, his rifle at the ready as the horse grazed.

The sea of animals before them was beautiful, though the horses had already grown restless as the supply of grass in this valley diminished. They needed to be taken to new grazing soon, in the next day or two.

But a bigger problem lay before them. What to do with all these animals?

Riley was the first to break their silence. "I suppose we need to find out if any of these are horses that were stolen during the rendezvous. I'm sure some of them were."

Ol' Henry nodded. "A couple of us can ride down and

tell the fellows to come retrieve their animals. Some of the boys may have already left the gathering, but we can leave word with the ones that are there. Any thoughts on where to have them come?"

Riley let out a long breath. "I guess that depends on who owns them." He looked over at Juniper and Rosie. "If Slim first started the herd with the pair of horses your father sent to Steps Right, some of these are likely descended from those." He turned his attention back to the herd. "Not all of them, of course. At least not from that mare. I wonder how many others are stolen and from whom. Both Indians and whites, most likely."

She moistened her lips. "How would we ever know?"

Rosie straightened and looked to White Horse. "The mare and stallion are definitely yours. You can hold them until we find your mother. And if we can determine any of their offspring, they're yours as well."

White Horse didn't answer, just kept looking forward. His expression looked uneasy. From worry over his mother?

Beside her, Riley shifted. "What of the others? My guess is that will leave at least seventy head."

Quiet fell among them again. It seemed impossible to know whom the animals belonged to, but much wrong had certainly been done here. To Steps Right and her son and to countless others. Maybe they could only make part of it right.

She glanced over at White Horse. "Perhaps you should take the rest of the herd too."

But he shook his head, his first clear response since they'd begun this conversation. "Not good. I leave camp of men not trust me. Cannot keep so many horses. Others steal."

Rosie's brows gathered, as though she was studying hard on the situation. Did she have an idea? But she didn't speak, not for a while.

At last, her expression shifted to something almost like a smile. She slid a glance at Juniper, one that was hard to decipher. Then she studied White Horse. "I have an idea. I haven't talked this over with my sisters yet, but I suspect they'll like it."

Faith and Lorelei both turned to face them, and Faith asked, "What is it?"

Rosie motioned toward the herd. "These horses need a home." Then she pointed to White Horse. "So do you. For that matter, so do we. My sisters and I have been planning to start our own horse ranch, similar to what our father owned when we were younger. I wouldn't have thought it possible out here, being so far away from the buyers. But if Slim had a contact in the cavalry and maintained a thriving business all these years, maybe we could do the same." She straightened. "An honest business."

A squeal erupted from Faith, and several nearby horses jerked their heads up. "Yes. Let's stay and start our ranch here."

Rosemary turned to White Horse. "We could split ownership of the herd with you. The horses descended from the ones my father sent your mother will be completely yours. The rest, we can either share ownership with you or share profits from the business. We can build houses on the farm, one for us and one for you. It would be a home, if you'd want it. And if we can find your mother, I hope she'll consider it her home too."

White Horse was silent for a long moment, his focus on

the horses ahead of them. Juniper's chest tightened as they waited for his response. How wonderful it would be to have her sisters here instead of all the way back in Richmond. Lord willing, when she had a chance to talk with Riley alone, her own future would not be tied to this potential horse farm. She wanted to be with him wherever he went.

She started to steal a glance at him, but then White Horse spoke.

"It is a good plan." He nodded to Rosemary. "You come far to honor my mother. It is good we work together."

Again, something seemed to pass between White Horse and her sister.

Beside her, Riley's hand touched the small of her back as it had so many times since she'd nearly been shot. She leaned into his side.

So much was changing. All their plans looked different. But she couldn't miss the hand of God clearly working all these things together for good.

Riley watched Juniper move around in the glow of the campfire.

Now. He had to talk with her now. So much had happened today, he hadn't had the chance to pull her aside. Now he could wait no longer.

She was wrapping up the food bundles. Rosemary and Faith had gone to wash the dishes in the creek, and Lorelei was feeding the coyote pup. He moved to Juniper's side and began fastening the tie around the meat pack. She glanced up at him questioningly. Wondering why he was stepping into her work, no doubt.

"Can we take a walk?" He kept his voice low enough that only she would hear.

Something flashed across her face just before she nodded. "I'd like that."

He didn't try to decipher what that momentary expression meant. Just stood and reached for her hand. When she placed her fingers in his and allowed him to pull her up, he kept her warm hand in his even after she'd risen and walked beside him.

He led her around the side of the mountain, toward the place where they could look out over the herd. Perhaps he should have put more thought into where he would take her for this conversation. But as they stood beside the cluster of boulders, this felt right.

The partial moon allowed them to see outlines of the animals below, especially those with lighter colors. All were at rest, taking comfort in the quiet and safety of the mountains around them.

He rubbed his thumb over the back of Juniper's hand. He should've thought about what to say. How to begin.

Perhaps it was better to just say what he was thinking. "Juniper, I—"

She turned to him and raised a hand, pulling her fingers from his and causing him to stop mid-sentence. The moonlight shimmering in her eyes made them hard to read. "I need to say something first, Riley. I'm sorry to interrupt, but this is important."

He nodded. "All right." How could he argue with a request like that? Yet her words made his insides bunch up. He'd planned to tell her he would go with her wherever she wanted to settle. That he would fight for her instead of watching her leave. Though the possibility of the sisters building their ranch here was exciting, he was willing to move all the way to Virginia. He would go to the ends of the earth if that's where Juniper wanted to live. As long as she would have him.

But maybe she'd thought through his request from last night and wanted the exact opposite—to cut all ties with him. Could that possibly be true?

Her lips pulled into her mouth before she spoke, as though she was nervous. "I was going to find you first thing this morning, as soon as I came back from walking Boots. But then . . . well, I couldn't." Her mouth lifted in a nervous half-smile.

Then she turned to him fully. "What I wanted to tell you is that I was wrong. My answer to you last night . . ." Her cheeks dimpled with either shyness or embarrassment. "Well, Rosie set me straight. She released me from my responsibility to the family. Told me I couldn't lose you simply to stay with them. She said if I really loved you, I wouldn't let you get away." She stood straighter. "So this is me praying I haven't messed things up between us."

He could barely breathe as he took in her words. Was she really saying she'd changed her mind? Had she said she loved him? He had to know for sure.

"I thought I was being honorable, allowing you to say no and walk away if that's what you chose. But after that man nearly killed you, I realized that I'm not willing to let you go. But I love you, Juniper Collins, and I'll fight for you if there's any way to win your heart."

She made a little squeaking noise, and he couldn't tell if it was happiness or a sob. And when she pressed her hands to her mouth, that made it even harder to determine. His heart thundered in his chest.

"Oh, Riley." She took a step closer, placed her palms tentatively on his chest, stealing all the breath from his lungs. "You already have my heart."

Every nerve and muscle within him vibrated from the desire to pull her close, so he gave in to the urge. Wrapping his arms around her and drawing her to him. Lowering his face and taking her mouth with his.

She kissed him back with hunger, with her entire body, her hands moving up his chest, around his neck, through his hair. It took everything within him to keep his own hands planted firmly on her back, but he savored the taste of her, telling her without words just how much she meant to him.

He had to end the kiss far sooner than he wanted to, but he couldn't let it go beyond what little control he had left.

As they both worked for breath, he rested his forehead on hers, sliding his hands up and down her arms, simply relishing the feel of her.

"Riley?" Her voice sounded breathy and far too alluring.

"Hmm?" He pressed one final kiss to her nose, then forced himself back before he found her mouth again.

"What I meant to say earlier is that I don't need to be part of my sisters' ranch. I want to be your wife. I want to join you in your adventures, ride up the spine of the mountains with you, and see as much of this beautiful country as God allows."

A new wave of joy washed through him, and he let loose his full smile. "I was thinking just the opposite. That we would build our own little house there on the ranch. Come back to it in between our adventures."

She fingered a lock of hair on his neck, nearly clearing all thought from his mind with her touch. "It doesn't matter to me what we do, as long as we do it together."

His grin pulled wider, if that were possible. "Always together."

EPILOGUE

Look at this place, June. Have you ever seen such thick grass?"

Juniper grinned at Rosie's exuberance as they rode across the wide valley toward the mountain range beyond. That much excitement hadn't rung in her older sister's voice since . . . well, she couldn't remember when. Maybe not since they were girls exploring the farthest pastures of their father's land.

"We should definitely build our ranch here." Faith gave a whoop as she kicked her mare into a lope and split off from their group, heading across the open land.

Juniper could almost feel Riley's chuckle vibrate through her. She glanced at him and caught his eye, just so she could feel the warmth of his affection settling over her. She would never get enough of the love shimmering in his eyes.

"That might be a good place for the barn."

Juniper tore her gaze away to see where Lorelei pointed. Her sister motioned to a flat area nearer the mountains.

"It's nice and level, and it has lots of room around it for small pens."

A grin tugged Juniper's cheeks. "How many animals are you planning to bring home?"

Lorelei didn't even look embarrassed as she flashed a cheeky smile. "All who need help."

Rosie rolled her eyes. "Can we at least build our house before we start constructing shelter for all your invalids?"

"I suppose so. I can always bring animals inside if they need shelter before the barn is built."

Rosie groaned. "Lor."

Juniper chuckled at her sisters, then turned to White Horse, who rode at the edge of their group. "Have you decided whether you'll build a cabin?"

When they'd first begun talking of places to build the ranch and how much room they would need, White Horse had said he would simply set up his lodge nearby. Rosemary hadn't liked the idea and had done her best to talk him into a sturdier structure. Did she think the man wouldn't stay with them long if he didn't plant his roots deeply enough?

And could that be true? Was White Horse only helping them get the ranch started before he moved on? He was impossible to read, though he'd been a welcome addition to their group these past two weeks since they'd discovered the horses. Now that the rendezvous had fully dispersed, Ol' Henry, Dragoon, and Jeremiah had left on a hunting trip, with the promise to return soon to help build the ranch house.

White Horse shook his head in answer to her question. "We build others first. If time, maybe house of logs for my mother."

The reminder of Steps Right sent Juniper's gaze toward the peaks rising up on the other side of the valley. They still had no idea where the woman was. White Horse had promised to take them to the place where he'd settled her in case there were clues about where she'd gone from there. But they'd not had a day to spare for the journey yet.

"If we agree this is the place for the ranch, maybe you can take us to the cave where you last saw your mother. Perhaps tomorrow?" She glanced around the group for confirmation.

Rosie nodded. "Tomorrow is good."

White Horse lifted an arm to point toward the mountains. "Beyond those two peaks. A cave hidden to most."

She followed the line of his finger and picked out the pass he must mean. It might take at least a half day to get there, depending on whether the slope was steeper than it seemed from this distance.

As she studied the spot, movement at its base caught her attention. A rider separated from the mountain, coming toward them at a lope. Nay, more than one person. As the strangers traveled the grassland that stretched between them, the single figure separated into three.

Tension thickened the air as they watched the newcomers approach. Rosie motioned for Faith to join them. Thankfully, their little sister had gone the opposite direction in her wanderings than these men now approached.

"White men." Riley murmured the words as details of the strangers became easier to see. The man in the lead wore a thick beard. The others too, from what she could see.

At last, the men halted in front of them, and the fellow in front raised a hand in greeting. "Howdy."

Riley had edged his horse to the front of their group, and now nodded to the men. "Hello."

The one in front pushed his hat brim up and swiped a sleeve across his brow. "Y'all must be the sisters I've heard tell so much of." Then, as though he finally realized he was in the presence of ladies, he jerked the hat from his head and slapped it on his chest. "Pardon me, ma'ams. Been a while since I've been in civilized comp'ny."

Juniper gave him a reassuring smile as Riley responded, "You fellows leaving the rendezvous?"

The man doing all the talking propped his arm on the front of his saddle and leaned in. "Yep. Been waitin' for Wally there to show up a'fore we left. Near gave up on 'im, but then he crawled into camp lookin' as puny as can be."

He pointed back at one of those behind him, a fellow who, now that she looked closer, did look a bit pale and willowy under his bushy beard and buckskins. She didn't have to ask why, for the spokesman kept talking.

"Turns out he'd been laid out nearly on his deathbed, burnin' with fever so's he started seein' visions." He turned back to the man. "Tell 'em, Wally. Tell 'em about the Indian woman who tended you."

But before Wally could speak, the front man turned back to her group. "You won't believe his story. I know I don't. He swears it's true, though."

Juniper wanted to tug the man's horse aside so they could hear the story from Wally himself, but thankfully, the fellow in front reined his mount over so they could see Wally better.

He looked like a strong wind could blow him over, and when he spoke, his voice came out soft and a little raspy, as though he didn't have enough strength to speak louder. "I took sick with the influenza, I think. Least that's what it felt like. It came over me in camp one night when I was on my way to the rendezvous. Last thing I remembered was huddlin' under my buffalo robe, tryin' to get warm. Next I woke up, I was laid out in a cave, a big fire roarin' not far from my pallet. An old Indian woman sat nearby it, mixin' up somethin' in a bowl. I had enough sense to wonder where I was an' how I got there, but not much more than that. The fever was eatin' me up somethin' awful."

Juniper could barely breathe. The woman. She had to be . . .

But before she could ask, Rosemary spoke up. "Do you know her name? Where is she now?" The desperate hope in her voice was as strong as that pressing in Juniper's chest.

But Wally shook his head. "I remember her sayin' a few things, like tellin' me to drink and pourin' a liquid in my mouth. But I wasn't clear-headed at all. When I did finally wake up with the fever gone, she'd taken off too." He shrugged. "I left the cave an' found my horse grazin' outside. Knew I'd be late for the rendezvous an' mighta missed it altogether, so I got myself to the Green River Valley quick as I could."

Frustration welled inside her. "You didn't look around for her?" She slid a glance to White Horse, who was watching Wally with an intensity she could almost feel.

When she turned back to Wally, he looked apologetic. "Sorry, ma'am. I needed supplies somethin' desperate, an' I knew the wagons had prob'ly already left, so the only way I could get trade was to catch Bert an' Marty here."

"But what did she look like?" Rosemary voiced the question.

He frowned slightly, like he was struggling to remember. "Old. Pure white hair in braids. A little on the heavy side." His expression cleared. "An' I remember she had this brace-let made o' blue beads. Real pretty things that glittered in the firelight."

Excitement lit in her chest. That had to be Steps Right. Surely.

Riley must be thinking the same, for his voice hummed with hope. "Can you take us to that cave? How far from here?"

The man frowned again, then turned and stared back at the mountains he and his friends had just ridden from. "I think it's not far as the crow flies. Prob'ly on the other side o' that tallest one." He pointed to the peak that rose above the others.

Then he turned and looked from one of his companions to the other. "I reckon I'm not opposed to leadin' you there, so long as Bert an' Marty don't mind takin' the time."

Bert, the fellow who'd been doing all the talking at the beginning, shook his head. "If it interests you that much, we can oblige you."

While Rosemary, Riley, and White Horse discussed lo-gistics with the men, Juniper nudged her horse up next to Riley's. Maybe they'd finally found a clue that would lead them to Steps Right.

Yet even then, this wouldn't be the end of their journey.

As soon as they finished building the ranch house, Riley planned to track down a preacher-turned-trapper he knew who could perform the marriage ceremony for the two of them.

Then they could spend the winter helping her sisters and

White Horse build the barn and other outbuildings and get the ranch in order. When spring came, they'd head to the southernmost tip of the Rockies—or whatever place Riley had been planning to start their expedition.

She glanced over at her beloved, and he turned to meet her gaze. Every other sound faded as she sank into the love in his eyes. Every moment with this man—whether on the mountaintops or in the deepest valleys—would be an adventure.

An adventure she couldn't wait to begin.

Would you like to receive a

BONUS EPILOGUE

about Riley and Juniper's
wedding day?

Get the free short story
and sign up for insider email updates at

https://mistymbeller.com/rmr-bonus-epilogue

USA Today bestselling author **Misty M. Beller** writes romantic mountain stories set on the 1800s frontier and woven with the truth of God's love. Raised on a farm and surrounded by family, Misty developed her love for horses, history, and adventure. These days, her husband and children provide fresh adventure every day, keeping her both grounded and crazy. Misty's passion is to create inspiring Christian fiction infused with the grandeur of the mountains, writing historical romance that displays God's abundant love through the twists and turns in the lives of her characters. Sharing her stories with readers is a dream come true. She writes from her country home in South Carolina and escapes to the mountains any chance she gets. Learn more and see Misty's other books at MistyMBeller.com.

Sign Up for
Misty's Newsletter

Keep up to date with
Misty's latest news on book releases
and events by signing up for her email
list at mistymbeller.com.

FOLLOW MISTY ON SOCIAL MEDIA!

Misty M. Beller, Author   @mistymbeller   @MistyMBeller